The MonsterGrrls

Book I:
Out From The Shadows

By
John Rose

A FRANKENGEEK PRESS BOOK

PUBLISHED BY FRANKENGEEK PRESS

This book is a work of fiction. Any resemblance to actual persons, places or monsters, living, dead or undead, is purely coincidental. No monsters were harmed in the making of this book, and the one currently standing behind you would probably like to read it when you're finished. *(Ha! Got you!!)*

Portions of this novel were originally published as *The MonsterGrrls*.

ISBN-10: 0-9771182-1-5
ISBN-13: 978-0-9771182-1-2

Cover art and design by Monster Shop Studios
The MonsterGrrls created by John Rose
FIRST PRINTING: October 2009
Visit the Grrls on the Internet at www.monstergrrls.com

Dedicated to the Maven and the Master, Claudia and Charlie White.

This book is also for the real MonsterGrrls, and one MonsterBoy: Anne-Marie Parker, Crystal Romney, Cheryl Gamez, Nikki Wade, Leah Tucker, Kay Abbey West, and Greg West.

Contents

One: Foreboding   7

Two: The Arrival   10

Three: Reflections   33

Four: New Crowd   75

Five: Strangeness   91

Six: Tryouts   103

Seven: Party Out Of Bounds   112

Eight: A History Of Monsters   135

Nine: This Is What We Are   163

Ten: Outsiders   188

Eleven: The Pritchett House   207

Twelve: Mayhem And Rescue   215

Thirteen: The Pact   224

"With my own eyes I saw them: myths and legends transformed from fable to flesh, brought to life, standing before me. And in those first moments of witness, I was reminded of the word 'monster' as being originally derived from the Latin 'monstrum,' which meant a showing forth or revealing. This proved to be an accurate description, for in those first days among them, I saw what was truly a revelation..."

--From the journals of Tobias Cochrane

ONE: FOREBODING

Dr. Richard Adams sat at his kitchen table and stared at the four file folders on the table in front of him. Beside the file folders were the remains of his dinner from a local burger joint, and beside that was a freshly acquired and badly needed six-pack of soda. One can was already open.

His eyes focused on the names written on each tab. *Franken, Francesca. Nightshade, Petronella. Ruthven, Bethany. Von Lupin, Harriet.* He sighed heavily.

Earlier that evening, he had presided over a school board meeting in his capacity as superintendent of Clearwater Public Schools. The meeting had mostly been about these four students: whether or not they should be admitted into the system, and if they were, what their best transition into the system was and how it could be done.

What they were.

He sighed again. That had been the crux of the meeting, once they had seen the photographs of them. He had met with all four individually and as a group, and despite the physical, social and cultural differences, he *liked* them. He really did. They were, most likely, the best hope for their species to come out of the shadows.

There was a tap on the window.

He looked up. A large black raven sat on the windowsill. Dr. Adams sighed.

He went to the window and opened it. The raven hopped in and perched itself on the corner of the table. Dr. Adams closed the window and returned to his seat. He picked up his burger and took another bite as the raven sat and watched him. The bird appeared to be waiting for something.

Dr. Adams chewed and swallowed. "They were voted in," he said. "It was hard going, but I finally won. Tell the Council that the girls will attend Clearwater High School as planned."

The raven put its head on one side and gave Dr. Adams an

appraising look. Then it lowered its head and looked directly at him. There was quiet reproach in its gaze.

"I'm aware that my brother is teaching there," said Dr. Adams. "Cochrane wouldn't have had it any other way. But it's not him you have to worry about. And besides, Daniel has been sympathetic to your cause for some time now."

The raven moved its head in a deliberate side-to-side motion: comme' si, comme' sa. Then it gazed at him again. The look contained a question.

"My brother," said Dr. Adams, calmly eating French fries, "will do what I tell him to do. His loyalty has been to his family, and to Cochrane, since that last mission with the Shadow League when he discovered they were trying to open the Barrier. He knew, and they knew, that it was off-limits. So he's since disassociated himself from the League. Your people know that, anyway."

The raven did not look convinced.

"I said I would handle it, and I did," said Dr. Adams wearily. "I got them in, didn't I?"

The raven appeared to think about this, and then nodded. It tapped the table with its beak. Dr. Adams went to the refrigerator and brought out a small plate. On the plate was a piece of raw steak that was extremely fresh; so fresh that it still oozed blood.

He placed the meat in front of the bird. The raven began to eat.

After it finished its meal, the raven politely bowed its head in thanks. Dr. Adams nodded, then got up and reopened the window. The raven turned and flew off the table, out the window and into the night. Dr. Adams closed the window, his face bearing a look of grave concentration. He sat down at the table and sighed, very heavily.

Whatever else happens, it's done. Now we wait and see.

The raven flew down the highway and turned off just past the billboard saying WELCOME TO CLEARWATER. It flew down a dirt path toward a hill in the distance, and began to ascend once it passed a dilapidated sign with peeling paint and faded letters: HARROW HILL.

It swooped up and into the thick, darkened forest at the top of the hill. If anyone had been there to see, they would have noticed a bright flash of green light coming over the tops of t he trees.

It faded as quickly as it had come.

Then there was nothing except shadows.

Two: The Arrival

It was two weeks later, in the death of the summer. It was also another evening in Clearwater, on a front porch at a house on Square Street.

The two girls sat side by side on the porch steps. The shorter of the two had her knees drawn up and was watching the sidewalk as though it was the most interesting thing she had ever seen. The taller one was watching the night sky.

"So what now?" asked the shorter one.

"I dunno," said the taller one, running her fingers through her hair. It was straight, lank and dirty-blonde. "School's starting next week."

The shorter one sighed. "Yeah, I know. Same old grind. School, home, school, home, school, home. Weekend. Nothing to do."

"Well, we've got each other."

"Yeah. That's all we've got, though."

There was no malice in this statement, it was simply fact. The tall one sighed, lifted her baseball cap, and scratched her head. "We could join some of the clubs at school. What about that, Emily? Maybe we could get on the yearbook staff."

"The yearbook staff gets picked on as much as we do, Theo. Maybe more. That's like asking for trouble." She took off her glasses and examined them.

Theo put her head on one side. She said, "Look, I'm trying to establish a little hope here, Emily."

Emily put her glasses back on. "There is no hope. It's school. How could it be hopeful? Everyone else has a group of friends. We don't." She sighed. "We're not interesting enough to anybody."

Theo sighed and waved her hands. "Well, I tried." She drew her own knees up and started watching the ground.

Emily looked at her friend for a minute, then sighed. "Oh, I'm sorry, Theo," she said. "It's just that--well, we're in high school now, and I thought that maybe we'd have a group or something, but we don't. We're just not popular."

"Well, that's not totally bad," said Theo. "That means we can do what we want. Some of those girls act like that whole Clique thing is their job or something."

"Yeah, but--" Emily sighed. "I mean, Jessica always has that party every year. And I thought maybe we would get invited when we became freshmen last year, but we didn't. We always try to be nice to people and stuff, but it never gets us anywhere. No one likes us."

Theo looked thoughtful. "Well, maybe this year things will be different. We gotta just be optimistic. We'll meet people. There's always new kids coming in. Things change."

"Yeah, eventually."

Theo thought about this, and sighed. "Eventually." She got up. "It's getting late. I gotta go home before my mom gets home. Thanks for supper and everything."

"Sure," said Emily. They walked together to the end of the sidewalk. "Are you coming over tomorrow?"

"Yeah. I'm going to see my dad, but I'll be back before dark. Hey, have you heard from your dad?"

Emily looked down at the ground. "No," she muttered.

The two friends looked at each other sadly. When one's family had fallen apart, the other had been there, and both knew what the other had been through. They hugged each other firmly, though somewhat clumsily.

Theo ran down the block toward her house. Emily watched her go, and then turned to go in herself.

She jumped, startled. A raven was sitting on the mailbox.

Emily had seen ravens before, but this one looked much bigger than normal. It was watching her very closely, with a strangely intelligent expression. She was suddenly afraid to move. Though the raven gave no indication of threat, there was something wrong about it. Its presence seemed to make the night become darker, more malevolent, as if there were hidden things in the world that she did not know about.

She swallowed. "Go away."

The raven eyed her. It bent toward her, and she backed away. "I s-said go away!" Emily shouted. "GO AWAY!"

The raven swooped into the night sky. Emily watched it go with some relief, and shuddered. She felt strangely chilly, but at the same time, she had an idea that maybe Theo was right. Things would be different this year.

She went inside. And for the most part, she forgot about the raven, until later.

The first day of school dawned crisp and clear at Clearwater High School. The buses rolled in, dispersing students who were ready, by various degrees, to assume usual school duties. In the few minutes before general assembly in the auditorium, many of them gathered and socialized in the courtyard.

Groups of old friends consorted, drifted here and there, caught up with each other on what had happened over the summer. Clumps of students gathered, gossiping, chattering and laughing at jokes and stories swapped back and forth. Girls smiled and made eyes at various boys wandering through the crowd, then turned away, giggling and comparing notes on the ones who had changed the most over the summer. Boys crowded around one table where a card game was going on, and the shouts and laughter drifted through the crowd as they played, making up new rules often on the spot. A group of older boys, dressed in imitation of performers on various rap videos, strolled up with a giant boom box, snapped it on, and poured out a hip-hop beat while they grooved and showed each other new dance steps. Teachers moved quietly among the students, saying hello to the ones they knew or remembered from last year, and quietly directing others when their behavior became too boisterous. Everyone was enjoying the clear morning.

On the sidewalk out front, a few students sat comparing class schedules and talking about new students, new music, favorite TV shows, and other things. One student, a red-haired boy in a T-shirt and jeans, noted something odd. He nudged his friends and pointed down the street.

A dark gray cloud was approaching, moving along the street,

very close to the ground. It appeared to be looking for something.

Some of the students commented about the need to fix a muffler. A few laughed, but as the cloud drew closer, they could see that it wasn't exhaust smoke, but more like a thick fogbank. The fog-cloud halted at the school gate, and hesitated for a moment, as if making sure of its location. Then it turned into the driveway and moved toward the school.

A low rumbling sounded, like distant thunder. The students stared as the fog-cloud approached, gaining speed. Those in the courtyard had seen it too, and word spread quickly.

The students moved back toward the courtyard as the fog-cloud turned a sharp curve and stopped directly at the sidewalk. The rumbling sound now had overtones of engine noises.

The fog-cloud began to dissolve. Curves and edges formed out of the mist, becoming clearer and gaining distinction, until the cloud disappeared completely, revealing a small school bus.

The chatter in the courtyard faded to a low mutter. School buses were not new to Clearwater students, but no one there had ever seen a *black* school bus before. The bus gleamed darkly in the sunlight, an ominous metallic black vehicle with gray-tinted windows. Along the side, in a sickly glowing green print, was written:

SPECIAL TRANSPORT.

The door opened with a rattling screech. Someone in a long dark coat and a tall black hat slouched in the driver's seat. The wide brim of the hat was pulled down and the collar of the coat was turned up, so that the face of the driver could not be seen. Both the coat and hat were covered in spiderwebs and dust. Because of the tinted windows, the bus interior was unusually darkened.

The driver regarded the students that gathered on the sidewalk. In the darkness underneath the brim of the hat, there was a soft red glow where the eyes should have been. The glow flared brightly for a moment, and one arm seemed to *unfold* from the shadowy mass of coat. It beckoned to the students, who were backing away in fear.

The red-haired boy, who was as terrified than the others, stepped forward. The glowing eyes burned into him. Then the driver spoke.

"Is this Clearwater High School?" The voice was dark, low and unpleasant, with a horrid undertone of rusted cemetery gates and rotted coffins being wrenched open. The unlucky student's flesh crawled. He shuddered at the sight of a fat, black spider crawling around the brim of the hat, and turned one knee into the other to keep them from knocking. He felt he might wet himself.

"Y–yes. Sir. *Sir!* Yes, sir."

"Thank you." The driver became aware of the spider, and plucked it off the brim of the hat. The wriggling arachnid was deposited into the darkness beneath the coat collar, and a soft crunch was heard. The student's eyes bulged with horror.

"Bloody spiders get into everything," the driver muttered. It raised its hand, giving a full view of gray, mottled skin, impossibly long fingers, hairy knuckles and black shiny claws as it beckoned toward the back of the bus. Seeing that the driver's attention was elsewhere, the red-haired boy fled to the safety of the crowd, which moved back quickly from the black bus. Through the dim windows, four figures were seen coming down the bus aisle.

The first to emerge was a sweet-faced teenage girl with shaggy platinum blond hair, carrying a backpack. She wore a pink ringer-style T-shirt with black cuffs and collar that accentuated her curvy figure. Embroidered on the shirt's front was a grinning jack-o-lantern. Her short black skirt was slightly ragged, and she wore bright red-and-white-striped stockings and two-toned Victorian-style boots with cap-toes. She blinked in the sun and adjusted the tall, wide-brimmed, pointed black hat on her head. She smiled shyly and waved to the students. A few waved back uncertainly.

The second figure stepped off the bus; a taller girl, with black frizzy hair in a strange corona around her head, shot through the sides and front with electrical streaks of white. She wore a new-looking black leather jacket over a black T-shirt and jeans. The students stared wonderingly at her; the girl's skin was *green,* and stitched scars ringed her neck and wrists. Small metal electrodes stood out on the sides of her neck, their polished surfaces twinkling like jewelry in the sun. Their gazes dropped to her feet, clad in black leather platform boots with soles that seemed much larger than normal. She also carried a backpack, and a small black case. She gave everyone a friendly smile, leading some students to wonder where she had found black lipstick.

A third girl joined them; an exotic-looking, gorgeous knockout dressed in an expensive-looking white silk blouse with billowy sleeves, black leather miniskirt and black velvet ankle boots. Over her head and shoulders was a short black hooded cape with a red lining. Sunlight glinted off a golden amulet on a blood-red satin choker necklace. She wore antique-looking dark glasses and a slightly nervous expression. Her skin was a pale chalk white, and her lips were bright red. She adjusted the chain strap of a patent-leather bag, then removed the hood of her cape and shook her head, revealing long black hair with a widow's-peak, save for a short white lock at her forehead. She regarded the students with some hauteur, and smiled, which made many of them uncomfortable; her eyeteeth seemed... *longer* than usual. It was like watching a shark smile.

The fourth figure emerged from the bus. There was a general murmur among the students, and a *lot* of staring. She was a girl like the others, but only in the sense of being girl-shaped. She had a trim, compact, slightly muscular build, and the movements of a natural athlete. Coarse reddish-brown hair was pulled back into a thick ponytail fastened with a yellow scrunchie-band, exposing sharp-pointed ears festooned with gold earrings. Her skin was unnaturally *leathery* and had a well-tanned look. The eyebrows above her golden-brown eyes were ungirlishly thick and bushy, uniting over her nose, which was... well, more *animal* than human. The nose was small, black, and strangely dainty. Nostrils flared, testing the air, as if she were *sniffing* everything around her.

The girl wore a bright yellow jersey top with frayed edges, a pair of blue-jean cut-offs, and red sneakers. Her shoulders and arms were covered in *fur*. Her fingernails were cut reasonably short, but still had a general *claw* look. She put down her backpack and rubbed her legs, which did not have fur. They were well-formed and looked recently *shaved*. Overall, she was handsomely pretty in one way and extremely disquieting in another.

She surveyed the students for a minute, and the strange *sniffing* continued. Satisfied, she smiled at everyone broadly, displaying large, shining, pointy teeth.

The bus door slammed shut, causing the entire mass of spectators to jump. Its engine growled to life, the fog-cloud instantly enveloping the bus. It pulled away from the curb and headed back the way it had come.

The four new girls and the spectators surveyed each other. The smiles on the new girls' faces slowly dissolved when they realized that no one was going to smile back, or even speak. The girl in the pointed hat drooped a little. The students could only react by staring; no one had ever entered Clearwater High in this manner before.

The bell rang, and the spell of awkwardness was broken. Everyone fled into the building as fast as possible, leaving the new girls standing on the sidewalk alone.

A general sad sigh came from the group. The girl in the hat stared down at her boots, big tears rolling down her cheeks. The girl in the leather jacket and the girl in the silk blouse looked at each other, frowning. The starnge wolfish-looking girl crossed her furry arms, staring grimly at the empty courtyard.

Then the girl in the leather jacket said resignedly, "Well, that went well, I thought." She put an arm around the girl in the hat, who sniffled and wiped her eyes, and gave her a rough, big-sisterly hug.

The girl in the silk blouse sniffed disdainfully. "*Hmmph.* No manners at all, I'm sure. So what now, Frankie?"

"General student assembly, I guess," responded the girl in the leather jacket. "Just like back at our old school. C'mon, Punkin. It'll be okay." She gave the girl in the hat a comforting pat, then hoisted her belongings and headed toward the door.

The girl in the hat said tearfully, "I wish I was back at our old school." She sniffled, then followed glumly, slinging her backpack over her shoulder. The girl in the silk blouse shrugged, smoothed back the white lock of hair, and nudged the wolfish girl, who was thoughtfully picking her teeth with her little fingernail. "Come on,

Harriet," she said. Harriet sighed, grabbed her backpack and trudged toward the door.

"You shouldn't have smiled, Bethany," she grumbled. "You know that people freak out when you do that."

"I don't know why you say that," sneered Bethany. *"You* smiled, and your teeth are an inch longer than mine."

"Are not."

"Are so."

"Are not."

"Are so..."

Ron Herschel, principal of Clearwater High School, peered out from a corner of the stage at the full auditorium of students. He wondered if the *new* students were among them.

He'd received a call about a week ago from Dr. Adams, who had informed him at length about the four new girls. He had been instructed, *very* specifically, to take care of them and their *special* needs. The list he had been given had been quite odd, but reasonable. The Franken girl was taking some kind of energy supplement, so that meant going out of class once in a while to the water fountain for something to swallow the pill with... and, let's see, Ruthven had to wear sunglasses due to an eye problem, and was bulimic or something; she couldn't eat regular school lunch but instead was on a completely *liquid* diet, poor girl... and Nightshade was from an odd religious sect that required her to wear a hat all the time. All it would take was some minimal bending of the rules here and there.

The lunch business for Von Lupin, though, now *that* would take some doing. He would have to speak with the school dietician, and possibly the food services manager too. No less than *four* extra portions per meal, Dr. Adams had said. And Mrs. Jenkins, the board vice-president, had called no more than an hour after Dr. Adams' phone call, raving on about having to cut back the sports program because of unforeseen budget problems, so no girls' basketball team this year. That meant that getting four extra portions would be problematic, because the food budget was already spent. Well, at least *one* extra portion could be provided since Ruthven wasn't participating. He wondered what was wrong with Von Lupin, since she had to eat so much. Maybe she was anorexic. Was it bulimia or anorexia where you kept throwing up and thinking you were fat? He could never remember.

It would be easier if he had a picture of what he was getting. For some reason he didn't quite understand, he had not been provided with standard ID photos of his new students. He had called the Central Office and been told that the photos had somehow been lost, and no one in the office could find them. He'd had a hard time with that one; he didn't know how he was going to find them in a school of 400 students without some form of physical ID. Well, he would have to improvise.

He remembered that before the general assembly, he had heard some commotion in the courtyard. He'd rushed over to see what was going on, but just as he got to the main hall, the bell had rung and *all* the students had come into the building, automatically. *That* had certainly been odd. Usually there were a few stragglers that had to be coaxed in, but this time they'd all gone to the auditorium as fast as they could. It was almost as if they'd been *scared* of something…

He'd heard snatches of conversation among the students as he had entered the auditorium and made his way to the stage. Most of it seemed to involve red eyes, green skin, pale skin, and fur. He'd heard several references to teeth, and caught a couple of bits about a black pointed hat. It had all sounded like some sort of Halloween thing, and that was odd, because Halloween was at least two months off. He sighed. Kids were in such a hurry these days.

Time to give them the speech.

He walked out to polite, somewhat forced applause, took his position at center stage, and treated his students to a bright smile. Show them that though he was tough, there was a *friendly* guy under there, a guy who would be their *pal* if they would let him.

"Good morning, everyone. Welcome to a brand new year at Clearwater High School. We all hope you had a nice summer, and we are delighted to welcome you back to Clearwater High and hope you are ready to resume your studies here." This brought a sarcastic cheer from a few students; he noted their positions. Apparently some students were not ready and would have to be helped along.

He coughed. "As you know, our goal this year is to be a more diversified institution of learning. We will share and celebrate the things about each of us that make us different, yet be united as a whole–a group of individuals, banded together as a single unit, having different points of view, with a single goal in mind–to be… diverse."

He had the vague feeling that he was making no sense at all. The blank looks from some of the students seated in front reinforced this. He continued anyway.

"A whole is nothing without the sum of its parts. Each and every student here is a part of this school, a continuation of a great unity. Each of you has something to contribute to our small but useful village, and as such, I expect great things will happen this year, and I expect great things from each of you." That, he felt, was very good; throw the ball back in their court, and parents *loved* the village thing. "I especially expect great things from our *new* students, who grace us this year with their own special and diversified interests--the new stars in our realm." *That* should let the new girls know they were welcome.

He paused, his eyes scanning the crowd for anyone who looked out of place. Where *were* they? This was going to be impossible…

Ah.

The idea arrived as neatly and quickly as a freshly stapled triplicate report across his desk. He gave his fidgeting audience a bright smile.

"Each of your homeroom teachers has your class schedules and other pertinent information. We will now adjourn to homerooms, where you will receive them. In the meantime, I would like to see–" he fumbled for the slip of paper with their quickly scribbled names-- "Francesca Franken, Petronella Nightshade, Bethany Ruthven, and Harriet Von Lupin in my office at this time. Thank you all. You are dismissed."

He left the stage. The students began to file out of the auditorium. There was a slowly widening circle around four strange figures heading for the door. Those students close enough to them were able to hear someone muttering, "Dunno why we got called to the principal's office, it's not our fault, all we did was ride our regular bus in, shoulda told us if they wanted us to ride one of their buses, it's not like I've even *done* anything yet..." followed by another voice hissing, "Oh, *shut up,* Harriet, and come on!"

The four girls sat waiting in the outer office, next to the door marked *RON HERSCHEL--PRINCIPAL.* All were irritated by the secretary, who kept staring at them and shuddering. All of them had given her friendly smiles, and by mutual agreement no one had shown teeth, but she still shuddered anyway. Harriet fidgeted in her seat.

"Stop that, Harriet," said Bethany.

"I'm nervous," growled Harriet, literally. "I don't like going to see the principal. It's too much like going to the vet."

There was a squeal and a thump from the secretary's desk, as if someone had dropped a coffee cup.

"See?" whispered Harriet, as the shaking woman knelt to clean up the mess. "She knows what I'm talking about. She doesn't like going to the vet either. I dunno what we're doing here. We didn't do nothing."

"Anything," corrected Bethany.

"We didn't do that either," said Harriet.

Frankie sighed. "Cool it, you two. The principal probably just wants to meet us, since we're new students."

"Yeah!" said Punkin, seizing on this opportunity for optimism. Her voice twanged softly. "He probly calls in all the new students like this. Besides," she grumbled, dropping her voice to a whisper, "y'all are makin' *me* nervous, so *quit."*

Harriet scrunched down in the chair, a deep frown on her face. The outer door opened and Herschel bustled in, reading a memo. He was not looking at the girls.

"Good morning, girls, I'm Mr. Herschel, your new principal, and I wanted to–"

He looked up. He stared. He was suddenly and terribly aware of why he had not been provided with ID photos.

Frankie stood and offered her hand, giving Herschel her best smile. "Hi, Mr. Herschel. I'm Frankie Franken, and these girls are

Punkin Nightshade, Bethany Ruthven, and Harriet Von Lupin. We're the new students, and we're all so pleased to meet you. We've heard so much about what a great principal you are."

This disarmed Herschel. He looked at the others standing beside Frankie. Punkin smiled and gave a little wave. Bethany's smile was pleasant but tight-lipped. Harriet managed a sort of nervous grimace.

His professional demeanor overcame the gnawing fear that his new students were different in the extreme. He took Frankie's black-nailed hand, with its prominent row of stitches around the wrist, and clasped it, smiling politely. There was a tiny tingle of electricity.

"Well, thank you," he said, rubbing his hand discreetly. "I had wanted to speak with each of you individually, but I thought it might be better to see all of you at once. There's been a lot of discussion among school officials about you." He tried to keep his voice light.

"Can't imagine why," said Bethany dryly.

Mr. Herschel glanced at her. His eye caught a glimpse of Harriet and very quickly snapped back to Frankie. He noted with some discomfort that the four white streaks in her hair lined up with four metal clamps that appeared to be *attached* to her head. "Um, if you'll all come into my office?" He motioned toward the door.

The girls began to enter. He took note of each student's individual diversities: Punkin's hat, tattered skirt and striped stockings, Bethany's chalk-pale skin, widow's-peak hair and stormy violet eyes, Frankie's shock-corona hair, neck stitches and pastel green skin, and Harriet's... Harriet's...

He shook himself. He remembered, vaguely, an argument from his own adolescence over a pair of paisley bell-bottoms. He was not usually judgmental of students' fashion tastes, or lack of. He liked to think of himself as a *progressive* administrator. Why should he be upset if these girls wanted to dress like Halloween characters?

Still, they *did* seem extreme. But they'd all done an excellent makeup job. Well, he would discuss it with them during the interview.

He turned to the door and got a full view of Harriet, standing in the doorway. He took in the shaggy ponytail, the bushy, ungirlish eyebrows, hairy arms, and the inhuman nose, and had to fight an urge to shudder. She was regarding him quizzically.

"Um. Sit anywhere?"

"What? Oh. Oh, yes, anywhere." He glanced at his secretary, who was staring at Harriet, eyes wide with terror, her hand to her mouth as if to suppress a scream. The image was not encouraging.

Harriet saw the look. She leaned forward and whispered, "She might need to go to the vet. Could be distemper." Then she turned and walked into the office.

Mr. Herschel blinked. *Extremely* good makeup.

Then duty overcame confusion, and he entered his office.

He found Harriet sitting in his desk chair and staring straight ahead with an alert expression, much like a hunting dog on point. He observed the others, who were seated in front of his desk. Punkin was trying to hide under her hat. Frankie was staring at the ceiling, with an expression of quiet amusement. Bethany, horrified, was trying to catch Harriet's attention.

Harriet finally noticed the others. She caught Mr. Herschel's gaze, said "Oh!" and raced around the desk to an empty chair beside Bethany. Furious whispering surfaced.

Mr. Herschel relaxed. Obviously the girl was nervous. He went to his desk and sat down, smiling to himself.

"Sorry," muttered Harriet. Frankie's mouth was twisted; she was fighting not to smile and losing. There was more heated whispering from Bethany, and Harriet muttered, "Well, he *said*–"

Mr. Herschel smiled at them. "Well, girls," he said, "let's–"

Harriet broke in. "I didn't do it."

Herschel was nonplussed. "Didn't do what?"

"It. Whatever it was, I didn't do it. I don't know why I'm here, and I'm sure there's probably a reason, but I didn't do it." She looked uncertain. "Whatever it is."

The others stared at her. Punkin looked confused, while Frankie had a resigned expression. Bethany's face was a mixture of amazement and outrage.

Mr. Herschel, who could not remember any incidents of discipline problems listed on Harriet's records but was desperately trying to, coughed into his fist. "I think we have a misunderstanding, Miss–"

"Harriet. Harriet Von Lupin."

"Harriet. I have called you all here to meet you and have an informal chat. Our superintendent has taken a personal interest in each of you, and wants to insure a smooth transition for you into our school system, so I thought perhaps we should get to know each other." Harriet looked blank. He decided on a more direct approach. "No one's in trouble for anything."

"Oh," said Harriet, relaxing instantly. "Well, that's all for that, then." She leaned back contentedly in her seat.

Mr. Herschel regarded her for a moment, then picked up a sheaf of papers on his desk. "I have reviewed your records from your old school. I believe it was called…"

"Graf Orlok High School," said Bethany helpfully. "Old family member of mine. Or supposed to be, anyway."

"Oh, really." He frowned. Something about the name was odd. He dismissed the thought and continued. "I see that Frankie, here, was valedictorian of her eighth-grade class. Very good."

"Yes, sir," said Frankie, smiling proudly. Herschel returned the smile. He was beginning to like Frankie, even if she did wear black lipstick and green makeup.

"I also see that–Bethany, is it?" She nodded. "I see that Bethany was elected Most Beautiful that same year." Bethany gave an elegant smile. "Your parents must be very proud of you."

"Yes, sir."

"There's a photo here; you must have had your growth spurt that year." He smiled affectionately. "You look as mature now as you did then. Very striking."

Bethany's smile tightened only a bit. "Yes, sir."

"You may have some tough competition here, though, if you decide to run again. Our Most Beautiful last year was Jessica Hardin-St. James." He could not help grimacing at this; Bethany took note of it. "She'll be in your homeroom, I believe. And I also see that Harriet is quite the athlete. *Extremely* high scores in competition games." He sighed. "Unfortunately, I'm afraid I have to tell you that Clearwater High will not have a girls' basketball team this year. Our assistant superintendent has had to move funding from our sports program to another area of study in our system. I'm very sorry."

"Oh," said Harriet, disappointed. She wondered what basketball was.

"I do encourage you, though, to try out for our *current* basketball team. Due to the funding problems we're trying an experimental co-ed team, and I'm sure that when Coach Edmund sees how talented you are, he'll find a place for you there. So chin up."

"Yes, *sir*," said Harriet. She saluted.

Even hair under *the arms.* He rubbed his chin. He was having dark suspicions about Harriet and pushing them away hurriedly.

"What does it say about Punkin?" asked Frankie. Punkin, who had been examining her shoes for most of the interview, looked up nervously.

"Punkin? Oh, yes, the one with the cute nickname." He smiled at her; she returned it. He shuffled through the papers. "I see here that, for a time, you were home-schooled."

"Yes, sir," said Punkin shyly. Her voice had a soft, slightly countrified accent that Herschel could tell she was trying to control. "My Mama and my Aunty Grimadene wanted me to have a good background in the Craft afore I went off to a school."

"Ah. Making things," smiled Mr. Herschel. "They wanted you to have a good education in the arts, then. It says here you're quite talented."

"Yes, sir, you could say that," said Punkin carefully. "Aunty Grimadene says I'm a natural." She swallowed. "B-But it warn't all the Craft. Mama taught me a lot of my basics, like reading and writing." This last came out *readin' and writin'*, in spite of her intentions.

"Well, she did a good job. Your records indicate that you currently read a few grades above your normal level, and that you retain what you read. You also appear to know some Latin. Did you learn that at home?"

"Aunty taught me a few things. B-But I learnt most of it in Remedial Spells at Graf Orlok." She winced. "Um, I mean Remedial *Spelling.* Spelling class." She looked sheepish. "Um, I had trouble sometimes with spelling… so I took a class."

"She's a great speller," said Harriet, the voice of support.

Mr. Herschel looked from one girl to the other. All their expressions were neutral. He had a vague feeling that Harriet was trying to be funny, but he wasn't sure.

"Ye-es," he said. "Well, I'm certain that none of you will have any trouble fitting in here at Clearwater High." He paused to think about what he'd said, and decided to change the subject. "I have a paper…" he fumbled through the sheaf, "that says your bus has been arranged. You will ride it every morning, and your bus driver is–"

"Mr. Sabbat," said Frankie.

"Er, yes." An unpleasant image rose in Herschel's mind. He shoved the thought away and decided to wind up his talk. "There is one more thing… one that I feel I must touch on personally. Dr. Adams and the school board have insisted on a diversified school populace. I am in full agreement with this, and I certainly believe that students should be allowed to express themselves in different ways."

The girls nodded. *Good, then.* This was going well.

"However, I still have a school to run, and so I must say that if any methods of self-expression produce negative reflections upon the school, I will have to demand that the student… or students involved," he said carefully, "shall curb these methods and find some other more *acceptable* method."

"Yes, sir," said Frankie.

"We can understand that," said Punkin.

"Good." He smiled. "So you can understand, then, why I would ask you to come to school dressed in… well, something more conservative."

The four looked blank. Harriet said, "What's wrong with our clothes?"

"Oh, nothing. Nothing wrong with dress per se. Both Frankie and Bethany here look quite fashionable." Bethany preened a bit. "I think what I'm speaking of, mainly, are the costume elements."

"Costume?" said Frankie.

"Elements?" said Bethany. She was regarding Herschel with the beginnings of a slow burn.

Mr. Herschel decided directness was in order. "The makeup."

"Makeup, sir?" said Frankie.

"Yes." He waved his hand at her lamely. "The, uh, green skin, and the black lipstick and nails, and the, uh–"

"I don't wear makeup, sir," said Frankie flatly.

Mr. Herschel blinked. "I–well, Harriet, here… sort of has the best makeup job of all of you, and…"

"Now wait a minute," said Harriet. "I shaved my legs. That's OK. I used that depilit–depilit–whatsis–"

"Depilatory," sighed Bethany.

"Thank you," said Harriet, ignoring the condescension. "Yeah, that stuff. I used that on my face and I think this looks cool, but I'm not, repeat, *not* shaving my arms. You gotta draw a line somewhere, you know."

"But–"

"Werewolves don't shave ordinarily, see." She leaned forward. "My Mom, she was the hairiest one in her litter, and that was part of the reason Pop married her and stuff." She smiled fondly. "He always said Mom was a beautiful purebred bitch."

"*Harriet!*" Bethany yelped.

Mr. Herschel saw something he could grab onto, and jumped. "Now, see *here,* young lady. We don't talk like that at school."

Harriet looked puzzled. "Why not?" she said. "It's true. I mean, in my family all the females are bitches, and I'm a bitch too, so…" Her voice died out under Herschel's and Bethany's identical expressions of shock. "Oh, wait a minute, you think I'm talking about something else…" She put both her hands over her mouth and sat back.

Mr. Herschel stood up. Things were rapidly spinning out of control, and he didn't know how to stop it. "What *I* am talking about," he said in a forceful manner, for him, "is the somewhat outre form of dress. You, uh, you all look very… *different* from your peers."

"That's because we *are* different," said Frankie, attempting to smooth things over. "I'm sorry, sir, but we don't really understand *what* it is you're speaking of. This is how we really *look*."

"Look!" said Mr. Herschel, snapping his fingers. *That* was the word he'd wanted. "That *is* what I'm talking about. Your...look. I mean, Punkin, here..." he waved a hand at Punkin, who couldn't help recoiling, "I should certainly think that such an attractive young lady wouldn't come to school dressed like a witch."

Punkin stood up and stamped her foot. "B-but I *am* a witch!" There was a mysterious rumble of thunder. "Sir," she said uncertainly.

Mr. Herschel, who had seen Punkin as the Quiet One of the group, was not expecting such outright if somewhat mild-mannered rebellion. He lost control. He shook his finger at Punkin, and put on what he liked to think of as his expression of Authoritative Anger. "Now, *see here!* I–"

A low growling sound interrupted him.

Harriet was out of her seat. Her lips were drawn back in a gruesome snarl, and the hair on her shoulders and arms seemed to raise itself. Her eyes glowed bright yellow. Mr. Herschel saw a full view of her long, pointed fangs for the first time, and his eyes widened. A terrible realization dawned.

He fell back in his chair. His eyes raced from one girl to the other. Frankie and Bethany were standing as well, with their hands raised in a conciliatory manner... or it might have been something else. The stitches... the skin... the hat... eyes... hair... teeth... *oh, God, the teeth...*

"Dear God," he whispered. "You're--you're all..."

There was silence. Harriet had stopped growling, but seemed frozen in a watchful position, and was regarding Herschel with a trancelike expression. Punkin was fingering her skirt like an embarrassed child, big tears rolling down her cheeks. Frankie looked shamefaced.

Bethany, however, was glaring at Herschel with grim resignation. Then she smacked Harriet on the shoulder, bringing her out of her trance, and gave an angry huff. "Yes, sir," she said. "We are." She drew her lips back in a rude grimace, displaying her own fangs. Mr. Herschel shuddered.

"Monsters. In my school." He tried to get his head around the idea. Bethany rolled her eyes.

"Yes, sir," said Frankie. "We thought Dr. Adams had... well, explained to you about us." She sighed. "I guess he didn't."

"We're sorry," whimpered Punkin.

Harriet looked at the floor, ashamed. "Sorry, Mr. Herschel," she mumbled.

Herschel stared at the four girls. Then he swallowed. "Yes, yes, well--here are your schedules, you'll find everything you need..." His shaking hands scrabbled at the papers on his desk; he thrust them at the girls. Frankie gently took them from him; he shuddered at her touch. "Locker--locker numbers are on the schedule form," he quavered.

"Yes, sir," said Frankie, looking sadly at the schedules. She took hers and passed the rest to the others, who took them without a word.

"Good, good--you're dismissed... go... *please...*"

The girls filed out of the office. Harriet, who was the last to leave, turned to Herschel with a regretful expression. "I really am sorry, sir," she said.

Mr. Herschel stared after her as she left. He slowly sat down at his desk, then covered his face with his hands. He stayed like that for a long time.

The row began as soon as they were out on the sidewalk.

"*God*, Harriet!!"

"I didn't do *anything*. I just growled at him, don't you start in on me..."

"Please (sniffle) don't fight... I hate it when y'all fight (whimper)..."

"But he's the *principal!!!* You don't *growl* at the *principal*, you... you *lycanthrope!!!*"

"Well, he looked like he was gonna hurt Punkin! You *know* we gotta look out for Punkin! Her mom *asked* us to! ...What's a lycanthrope?"

"Ohhhoooo..."

"But… but *anyway!!!*"

"But anyway *what!?!* Whadya expect me to do?? Lookit, now you've got her crying!!"

"I have *not!!!*"

"And *what'd you call me a lycanthrope for, anyway??*"

"OHHOOOOO…"

"*GIRLS!!!*" Frankie shouted. Her voice had taken on a hollow, bloodcurdling quality.

Everyone fell silent. Punkin sniffled and wiped her eyes roughly with the heel of her hand. Bethany started to retort, then thought better of it; when Frankie talked like *that* she meant business.

"Well, there's no need for you doing the Voice at *us*," she finally muttered.

Frankie closed her eyes tiredly. "Look, this is just a small setback. It's all going to be okay. We'll be the best students we can be here. We just have to remember that they're not used to people like us."

"You mean monsters," said Bethany flatly.

Frankie sighed. "Yes, monsters. *Please* don't make me do the Voice again. Dad always has to tighten my vocal chords if I do it too much."

Bethany huffed. "I *knew* this wasn't going to work. I tried to tell my father, but he has all these high ideals. He thinks that somehow I can fit in. But I'm a *vampire!* Hello? I'm not *built* to fit in!"

"You're not *built*, either," said Frankie, frowning. She shouldered her backpack and moved down the sidewalk. "I am. *Was*, anyway. I've still got copies of the blueprints."

The group morosely followed her toward the main building. Harriet put a consoling arm around Punkin, who gave a sad little smile. After a moment she said, "You know, Bethany, you ain't ever took a human victim, and neither has Harriet. Frankie's never chased down a bunch of villagers, and I ain't turned anyone into a toad. We've never done nothin' *horrible* at all. How come we can't fit in?"

"Because we're monsters," snapped Bethany, who was in no mood to discuss the finer points of culture clash.

"Yeah, but what does that mean?" asked Harriet. "Punkin's right. We don't act like these people say we do. What's the big deal?"

29

"Look, it's just what you are," grumbled Bethany. "You either are or you aren't. We *are,* and they *aren't.* We look different from them, and because of that we're going to be weird and scary to them no matter what."

"Punkin doesn't look all that differen t."

"It's the hat. Believe me, they're *not* going to like us. Or want us to be here."

"Because of the way we look?"

"Yes!"

"That's *dumb,*" said Harriet. Her tone said that she didn't want to argue the point. "We're all good students, and *we* all know we're good students. Herschel was *telling* us all that good stuff we did, from those records and stuff, so it's there. Anybody wants to see it, they can."

"But *still...*" began Bethany, who sensed that she was losing the argument.

"But still *what?*" said Harriet. "Why don't you just admit it, Bethany? You're mad because your dad's making you go to this school and you don't wanna go, and you were *scared* because you didn't think that Eye thing you're wearing was really gonna work against sunlight. You think *everybody's* gonna auto--auto-whatcha--"

"Auto-*matically...*"

"Thank you. *Automatically* turn on us because we look *different* and we're monsters. Well, I don't care." She crossed her arms and glared at Bethany with a defensive look. "I want to try. And besides, I wanna play that basketball thing he was talking about, for my new school."

The others stared at her. Punkin sniffled and said, "I want to try too. I'm with Harriet." She wiped her eyes. "I'm sorry if I get scairt sometimes, but I can't help it." She looked miserable. There was another distant rumble of thunder, even though the sky was clear.

Frankie and Bethany traded a look. Then Frankie smiled and said, "Okay, I'm in too. I don't really want to leave either. I like the newness of everything, and I never could resist a challenge." The smile became a grin. "I'm like my dad in that way. Besides, it'll be an adventure." She put an arm around Punkin, who had a truly happy smile for the first time that day.

That left Bethany. She shrugged and said, "All right, you've all made your point. Especially Harriet."

"Sorry," said Harriet. "But it's true."

Bethany sighed. "I know," she said. "I'm sorry too, Harriet. Sometimes my father's *political aspirations*," she spat, "get on my nerves. But I'll stay, too. Punkin's right about one thing, I *am* a bag-and-bottle vampire. I don't take victims, don't hunt humans--"

"For which some of us are thankful," replied Punkin.

"Well, you don't count. My great-great-great-great-grandsire *still* remembers that run-in with the last natural Adept in your family."

Punkin shrugged. "News to me."

"Well, *anyway*. I don't do the hunting thing, and that makes me a child of convenience like all the other little mallrats here, so at least I can fit in on that level." She smiled, and the smile was genuine and quite charming. "And of course, *who* would look after Harriet?"

Harriet stuck out her tongue and blew a raspberry. Bethany laughed, and Harriet grinned.

"So we're all in, then," said Frankie. "But one thing. We all watch out for each other. Agreed?"

The others nodded.

"Just one thing," said Harriet, reading her schedule and frowning. "That's gonna be hard to do, because I don't have any classes with any of you." She waved the schedule form. "Didn't we all sign up together for the same stuff?"

The group examined their forms. "She's right," said Bethany, "and I don't either." She grimaced. "I'll bet that stupid Herschel person rearranged our schedules."

"Oh," said Punkin in a small voice. She looked downcast.

Frankie patted her on the back. "It'll be okay, Punkin, I promise. We'll see each other in the halls and at lunch, and after school and stuff. Come on. You said you wanted to try."

"Buck up, sweetie," said Harriet. "We'll look after each other. Right, Bethany?"

"Absolutely," said Bethany. "After all, you know vampires don't think as a species, so I can use the practice."

Everyone laughed at this, and Punkin smiled. The group entered the main door together, and clasped hands one final time before going their separate ways to their homerooms.

Frankie set off to find her classroom, scanning the numbers on the lockers as she went; she wanted to put away her generator. She finally found her locker at the end of the hall. Someone had put a large and very heavy-looking padlock on it.

Well, this was supposed to be hers.

She tried to peer into the slots on the door, to see if someone's textbooks were in there. No luck. She sighed, looked around the hall to make sure there was no one there, and took hold of the lock and *squeezed.*

The lock burst apart. She opened the locker and found, thankfully, that it was empty; otherwise she'd have had to get someone a new lock. She hefted the small black case that held the generator into the locker, and tossed the pieces of the broken lock in; she'd throw them away later. She closed the locker and put her own lock on it--an ancient and slightly rusty antique that Igor had modified with a new hasp--and headed for her classroom.

She was nervous. For one thing, she was late to class, and that bothered her; Frankie strived to be punctual. But there was a deeper undercurrent that felt new to her; she was in a new school, and she found herself very aware that she was different from the other kids.

Technically speaking, Frankie was a Creature. *Creature,* as she had learned from her father, was the traditional name given by the Mad Scientist to what got off the slab after the storm had passed and the generators were charging down. There'd been some Creatures among the population of Graf Orlok High, where the students had been mostly vampires. Now there was one--her--at Clearwater High, where the students were mostly human. She had said as much to her father, who had with ome iritation told her to stop worrying, to look at the thing as a new frontier and herself as a trailblazer.

But then, she thought, Dad was always sort of forward-thinking.

Frankie's father was Doctor Eliot Franken, and he was a large part of what made Frankie the kind of Creature she was. Most Mad Scientists made Creatures in their laboratories because they had advanced far enough in their research to attempt the original Experiment, which had created the first Creature.[1] After a certain point in study, making your own Creature was simply the next logical step.

In Doctor Franken's case, it had been a means to an end. His reason for creating Frankie was that he wanted a daughter.

This had not gone over well with the Mad Scientists' Guild. Mad Science was supposed to be a quest for what could be viewed as a highly specialized establishment of reason in a world gone arguably mad. Mad Scientists craved things like power and notoriety and attaining Knowledge Of Things Man Was Not Meant To Know. Creating something so mundane and practical-sounding as a *daughter* was a bit flustering to the Guild. But Dr. Franken was not your average Mad Scientist.

For one thing, he never laughed during Experiments.

This should be explained. Mad Science is a cottage industry, or at least a castle tower industry, and mad laughter was part of the stock in trade. It didn't particularly matter whether it was a lunatic giggle, a psychopathic guffaw or a demonic howl of triumph; Mad Scientists were expected to do it. It was a sort of personality-based calling card that made nosy villagers keep away from the castle and cower in terror at night, and more importantly, it let the lab assistants know who was boss. It was *traditional*.

But when the thunder was rumbling in the sky, when the generators were crackling with thousands of watts of amassed power, when the slab maneuvered into position by weathered chains on the gurney and ascended into the loft to catch the lightning, Dr. Franken would simply stand on the observation ledge and watch the slab ascend, never laughing, never even smiling; only glaring ominously, as if daring anyone or anything to interfere with the Work.

This behavior had led the Mad Scientists' Guild to believe that

---

[1] It was common knowledge among all Mad Scientists that a certain rather snotty woman named Shelley had attempted to document this, and had gotten it dead wrong.

Dr. Franken had gone through madness and *out the other side,* which was potentially dangerous. You might challenge the gods themselves, but you weren't supposed to *dare* them, and besides no one can work around a room full of generators and lightning without getting *some* ideas about the more irreparable conditions of mortality, no matter *how* mad they are.

But despite this, Frankie had been created. And he'd taught her everything he'd thought she needed to know. Instead of being dissatisfied with what he had created and chaining it up in a dungeon, as if its rough points were *its'* fault, he'd begun almost from the moment she'd sat up on the slab. There had been lessons in grammar, vocabulary, etiquette, poise, vocal articulation, and for some reason tap dancing, although she'd never needed to do that. Not yet, anyway.

There had been tutoring in most academic disciplines. She'd learned to read and write, and still considered those the two most valuable things she had learned. Soon after she'd gotten fluent at both she'd asked for a notebook like he had, and started to keep a diary. Once that notebook was filled, she'd asked for another, and then another. These now filled a shelf on a wall in her room.

There had been visits to art museums, which she had enjoyed, and she had been unable to understand the sulky looks on the faces of other children who had been dragged there by their parents. There had been almost two years' worth of constant refinements of her physical structure, and *that* had been a chore. She'd looked up the word *puberty* in the dictionary one day and was surprised to find it *didn't* mean riding the slab to the loft three times a week.

The Guild had paid a visit, and though they were still puzzled by Dr. Franken's approach, they were charmed by the well-mannered and pleasant demeanor of Frankie. She'd learned how to talk in the Voice for those older Guild members who just couldn't get their heads around it at all, and it was finally decided that young Franken was simply working in his own field of study. And *that,* from a certain point of view, was what Mad Science *was.*

And then Igor had come, and *that,* Frankie thought, was when the trouble started.

Mad Science and Igors went together, and every M.S. had

35

some kind of hunchbacked servant around the lab called Igor; it was almost a brand name. There was even a Guild of Igors, which served as a combination employment agency and, well, *production factory* for Igors. Dr. Franken, because of his rather exacting principles, tended to go through Igors by the month, and most of them left in a huff or very hurriedly in the dead of night, shaking their heads as they went. He was not an unkind man, but he was a tyrant in the lab; hence the succession of Igors.

And so finally the Guild of Igors had sent him *the* Igor, perhaps the best or worst model the, ahem, *production factory* branch of the Guild had been able to come up with. Igor had been a thing of magnificent ugliness: a hump so enormous that his walk was like a broken tin-toy monkey, knuckles thick with hair that had been matted with dust and mud from where they dragged the ground, a spectacularly swollen forehead under which the eyes bulged from deep-sunken sockets within the hideously scarred face. Dr. Franken had noted, with a surgeon's eye, the natural musculature and broad yet deformed back of Igor. Negotiations were made and a position was filled, and Franken had taken Igor down to the lab to show him his duties. They had entered the operating theater and before Igor knew what was happening, Dr. Franken had slapped a chloroform-soaked rag over Igor's nose and dragged him onto the gurney slab, and there he had *fixed* him.

The results had been quite advanced from a surgical point of view, and quite breathtaking, cosmetically speaking. To start with, there was no longer a hump.

She'd heard Igor sobbing miserably in his room the first night, and then she had spent the better part of a week in either her room or the courtyard garden, doing a lot of reading and trying to ignore the row that raged around the castle. When she found herself beginning the same book for the third time, she'd decided enough was enough, and had a long talk with both of them. And then there had been a week of sullen and pouting silence.

And one night over supper in the Great Hall, Igor grudgingly admitted that it was much easier to perform heavy lifting with a straightened back, and that he'd been enjoying the appreciative looks of the local village girls. *And* that he had a date on Saturday with

Mary Mahoney, who was a serving maid at the Brewhaus Of Doom in Town, and would the Doctor lend him a tie.

And Doctor Franken admitted, equally grudgingly, that he could be a bit too non-traditional at times, and that perhaps he should have asked first. And yes, the ties were in the armoire in the bedroom, and for heaven's sake do be careful. *Mary* Mahoney, was it?

Yes, sir, Igor said. And Dr. Franken had a funny little smile and a faraway look in his eyes for the rest of the evening, and that had been that. Igor had returned to work that next week with a somewhat loopy smile on his face, and once or twice Frankie had heard him *giggling* to himself. She'd made a mental note to herself to do some private research into the matter later.

They'd decided to tell others that he was the gardener, since Igors were often not seen anywhere except the lab, and he was supposed to tend the roses anyway. It had worked for awhile.

And then the truth had come out, which is to say that it was passed around and injected with lies until it was no longer recognizable as the truth, and Dr. Franken had been brought before the Guild, and there'd been a row. They'd called it the worst plague upon Mad Science since that horrid Shelley woman's book, which Frankie had secretly read and found quite entertaining. And Dr. Franken had been blackballed.

The Guild had expected the usual reactions; glowering, threats, mad raging, exaggerated promise of revenge. There had been none of this. Dr. Franken had simply stood before the Guild Council, glaring at them in the same way he glared at the slab when it was rattling up to the loft during a thunderstorm, and then he had turned to Frankie, taken her by the hand and led her out, without a word to anyone.

Oh, well, they said. He'll let it out at home. There'll be attacks on the Guild Hall, and a rash of robberies from the graveyards and the morgues, and after the next few thunderstorms there'll be attacks on local villagers and we'll be called in, and we'll sort him out. Nothing to it.

Nothing happened.

And when nothing continued to happen, the puzzled Guild

members realized that instead of retaliating in the traditional manner of making bigger, hastily stitched Creatures with the finest quality abnormal brains that could be stolen in the dead of night from local medical colleges and facilities, and then sending them lurching out to wreak havoc and destruction upon villages that were somewhat resigned to such matters, Dr. Franken was simply *not talking to them.*

Despite the bluster they'd shown in the Guild Hall, most of the Guild was quite relieved, because Dr. Franken was the first M.S. they'd ever blackballed, and they hadn't really known what to do. But none of them had expected this course of action. As a result, many of them were very surprised, and even somewhat hurt.

So in the end, the Guild left Dr. Franken, Frankie, and Igor alone.

Frankie passed a mirror in the hallway, and gave herself a critical look. She wondered if she'd end up scaring her homeroom class without meaning to.

Her father had seriously advanced the Creature-making process. The green skin, stitches, clamps and neck electrodes were there mainly for traditional reasons; if Dr. Franken had not left some things to tradition she'd have stood out among monsterkind more than was necessary. But Frankie had no facial stitches at all. He'd been adamant about that.

She raised her head and stroked her face thoughtfully. Her skin had the usual toughness and resiliency that was a hallmark of Creaturedom; it healed fast and tended to bend anything smaller than a kitchen knife blade. But the green was more tint than color. She was quite attractive, really, if you were willing to be open-minded about it.

I can see why Mr. Herschel thought it was makeup, she thought. *Compared to some other Creatures I've seen... I look almost human.*

Her father had told her, repeatedly, that the whole point of the original Experiment was not to *create* life, but to learn how to save it, preserve it. Life was precious, beautiful. Often very painful at times, but still beautiful. Why should we not respect it? How could we not?

She'd realized then that *that* was what set her father apart from the rest of the Guild: he looked a little deeper, researched more thoroughly, worked a little harder. She'd learned that, and it had set her apart from other monster children; she, a Creature, had been top student at Graf Orlok, which had been unheard of then. When they'd been selected to enter the human world and walk among them, there'd been an unspoken declaration that she was leader of the group. They looked to her for support, followed her path. Even Bethany, who was naturally willful and combative due to being a vampire, had accepted Frankie's leadership without dissent.

That's what should set me apart here, too.

She put on a determined look, turned on her heel, and headed for her classroom.

Science with Mrs. Parkinson was currently abuzz with activity, but Frankie was puzzled at first. No one was doing Science, unless having desks pushed together and chatting quietly was a new form of Mad Science. Obviously, classes here were quite different from Graf Orlok; her old Mad Science teacher, Dr. Corinthian, would have had a demonstration lesson the first day. This might be more interesting.

She entered the classroom.

Silence fell over the class. Everyone stared at her. Whispers flooded the room; the hair, the skin, the lips, the nails, the boots, the *stitches*, the *electrodes*. She faltered for a moment, but put on her best smile and walked up to the teacher's desk. On the way she caught a comment from someone that sounded like "nice leather," and this gave her a little lift.

Mrs. Parkinson was a tall, motherly-looking woman with glasses and long, slightly graying blond hair in a braid that draped down her back. She was writing student's names in textbooks, and did not look up when Frankie approached the desk.

"Good morning, ma'am," said Frankie. "Are you Mrs. Parkinson?" She prepared herself for the inevitable start that would occur when the teacher looked up.

Mrs. Parkinson looked up. There was not a trace of reaction in her face. Her eyes did not widen in horror. The most that happened was the raising of one eyebrow, in what seemed to be an often-used expression.

"Yes, I am," she said. "I did wonder why it got so quiet in here. You must be Frankie Franken."

"Yes," answered Frankie, a little shyly. "I must be."

Mrs. Parkinson looked at her more closely. She said, "Dear, I have to ask this. Where in the world did you find black lipstick?" There were a few snickers from the class.

The smile on Frankie's face vanished. She sighed. "Ma'am, it's not lipstick. I don't wear makeup of any kind at all. I've already discussed that with Mr. Herschel today, sort of, and that's the only answer that I can give you. It's not lipstick." She looked defeated. "This is how I *look.*"

Titters were heard in the back of the room. Mrs. Parkinson shot a look in that direction, which immediately went silent. She looked at Frankie and said, not unkindly, "You were with Mr. Herschel in his office this morning?"

"Yes, ma'am," said Frankie. *Here we go again,* she thought.

"How was he when you left?"

Frankie drooped. She looked at the floor and said in a small voice, "He was horrified."

She expected the class to burst into laughter. There was none. She looked up and saw that Mrs. Parkinson had a very friendly, slightly mischievous smile.

"Good," she said. "Welcome to my classroom, dear."

Frankie sat in a desk at the front of the classroom, one of the few students not in a group. Mrs. Parkinson had explained to her, with some irritation, that today would be a free day because most of the lab equipment needed for class had not arrived yet, and wouldn't be there until tomorrow. ("I teach a very lab-intensive class," she had said, which had cheered Frankie to no end.)

She'd been issued a textbook, and was the only student in the class reading it. She had been surprised to find that most of the lessons were things she knew already. Interaction among students might take some doing, but if *all* of the classwork was like this, then the education part of high school with humans would be a snap.

She felt eyes on her. Sitting in the desk next to her was a

small, plain-looking girl with brown hair and glasses. The girl seemed to be observing curiously as opposed to staring, but there was an intensity in the gaze that refused to be ignored.

Frankie allowed her to go on observing for awhile. Then she gave her a sidelong glance and stage-whispered, "See anything *green?*"

The girl started at this, and Frankie grinned at her. After a moment, the girl smiled back. She said, "You're real."

Frankie hadn't heard that one yet. "Yes."

"Were you in an accident?" There was an uncertain tone to this; the girl seemed afraid of being offensive. Frankie relaxed.

"No. You mean the stitches?"

"Well, yeah. I mean, you know, you don't have them *out,* or anything... it's kind of like they're... holding you together," she finished lamely.

Frankie thought a moment, and decided she couldn't be delicate about it. "I'm not exactly like you. Human, I mean. But I suppose that I was at one time." She paused, and added, "Dad always does a good job of matching parts."

"*Parts?*" The girl's eyes widened.

"Um, yeah." She looked embarrassed. "The reason that I look this way is because I'm a Creature, and my dad is a Mad Scientist. I was created in his laboratory."

The girl stared at Frankie with horrified fascination, and said, "You mean you *need* the stitches." It was not a question.

"Yes."

She seemed to consider this, then gave Frankie an admiring smile. "*Cool.*" She offered her hand. "I'm Emily," she said. "Emily Peters."

"Frankie Franken," said Frankie. They shook hands, and Emily jumped at the tiny shock that passed between them. She looked at her hand, mystified. "You *tingle.*"

"Yeah. Dad's tried to get rid of that, but he can't for some reason. I'm sorry about that."

"No, no. It's cool. It's like you have your own joybuzzer."

"What's a joybuzzer?"

"It's... you know, it's..." Emily faltered. "It's like a prank that you play on people. A joke." She considered this, and added, "Except that it's probably not all that funny. When you say Franken, do you mean like Frankenstein?"

Frankie's eyes narrowed. She whispered, "If you ever meet my dad, don't you *dare* say that. All Mad Scientists have read that book and they all *hate* it. They say it's a biased and inaccurate description of what really happened. He'd probably think it was like your unfunny joke."

"Oh. Well, I won't, I promise. Um... who were those girls you were with this morning? Are they like you?"

"Well, yes and no. We're monsters."

"Monsters?"

"Yeah. I'm a Creature, and Punkin's a witch, and Bethany's a vampire, and Harriet's a werewolf. We were all sent here to school. Our people have a ruling court, see, called the Council Of Monsterkind, and they've decided that monsters have to learn to live among humans, so... well, my dad would say we're trailblazers. They've sent us here to see if it will really work."

Emily gave Frankie a long look. She said, "Um... the werewolf's name is *Harriet?"*

Frankie laughed. "Well, gee, Emily, what did you expect?"

"Gosh, I don't know. I mean, you know, *monsters.* Wow." She looked excited. "I never imagined I'd meet someone like you in Clearwater. It's like there's this whole world out there I don't know about, all different from boring old Clearwater."

Frankie smiled. "Clearwater's not all *that* boring. It's new to me, you know. I'll bet you could tell me things about it, and then you'd see it wasn't as boring as you think. Do you think you could show me the ropes around here?"

"Me??" Emily's face lit up. "Oh, wow, yeah! But you have to tell me everything about...about... um, where is it?"

"Morlock Heights," said Frankie, amused. After the disastrous interview with Mr. Herschel, she was pleased with Emily's joyful interest over meeting an actual monster. "It's the place where we all live. I'll tell you anything you want. Fire away."

"Are the others as nice as you?"

Frankie was surprised. "Well, *yeah.* You mean that's your first question?"

"Well... yeah." Emily had a downcast look. "I mean, it's always good to know if someone's nice or not. You might become popular or something, and then you wouldn't be nice anymore." She stared at her desktop. "I mean... I don't know a lot of nice people here. I don't have that many friends. I've got Theo MacKenzie, and she's my best friend. But she's not popular either."

Frankie studied Emily. *This is someone who feels a lot like me,* she thought. Then she gave Emily a big smile and said, "Well, now you've got a new one, and pretty soon you'll have three more. We need all the friends we can get, really."

Emily's smile was grateful. "I do too. Thanks, Frankie."

"Do I get to meet Theo?"

"Sure!" answered Emily happily. "That would be *cool.*"

Frankie pulled out her schedule form. "What's your class schedule like? Do you know any of these teachers?"

Emily studied the form. "Hmmm. Well, Mr. Glass is okay, but Mrs. Woolcott... I don't know. People say she's hard." She fumbled through her own notebook, and pulled out a crumpled paper. "Let me see, here's mine..."

They compared schedules, and began talking in earnest, discussing classes and teachers. At one point Frankie looked up and saw Mrs. Parkinson gazing in their direction. Their eyes met, and Mrs. Parkinson's face broke into a pleased smile. Frankie smiled back.

Bethany wandered along the rows of lockers on the north hall, trying to find hers. *Why did they put us on separate halls, at the end of each hall? It's as if they're keeping us as far away from each other as possible. They must be really scared of us.*

Here was the last one, and... Oh. There was a padlock already on it.

She read the schedule sheet again. Number A13. Yep, this was it, so what was going on?

Well, she'd have to break it off. She wasn't as strong as Frankie, not in the daytime, but people often underestimated the strength of a vampire. She grasped the lock.

The world went white.

Bethany came to a few seconds later, shakily getting up from the floor. The disorientation was replaced by a hot flash of anger.

Uninvited! Here!? At my own locker!?!

That was one of the many things Bethany really *hated* about being a vampire: they absolutely could not enter certain places unless they were Invited. There were many more public places now than there had been, say, two hundred years ago, and that made things easier, but you still had to be careful. She leaned against the wall and shut her eyes tightly. Nausea pulsed in her stomach.

But why here? A school's about as public as you can get, isn't it? I should be able to get into my own... my own locker.

She glared at the lock while she waited for the sick feeling to pass, then dusted herself off and picked up her bag. She felt inside and was relieved to find that her bottle of blood had not burst open, otherwise there would have been an awful mess and she'd be going hungry. She could have faked it and eaten the school lunch, but it wouldn't satisfy her, and it would be several days before her body could absorb the food. And she would have had unhealthy thoughts about her classmates all day.

I guess I should think about getting a thermos. Maybe a bloody bookbag, too.

She dejectedly walked down the hall, heading toward her classroom. This whole business of sending her and the others to school with humans was ridiculous. It had all been her father's idea, and he'd convinced the Council Of Monsterkind *and* the High Court Of Vampyr to go along with it, and *that* was doing something. Some of the High Court were so old they had been brought in as ashes in jars and *rebirthed* right there with a bit of blood. She'd never thought that those vampires would like the idea, but they had.

But her father had masterfully sold them on it. She remembered the High Court meeting, with him sweeping about in his best evening dress, wearing the medals that displayed his ambassadorial status among the humans. The High Court had been amused, because Count Andreas Leonidas Ruthven had a reputation for being an eccentric among vampires, a race of monsters for which eccentric behavior was practically genetic code. He was the first older vampire to live among humans for awhile, and in the eyes of some High Court members he was almost a traitor to the breed.

He'd presented the argument, and when the initial reaction had been *no,* he'd gone to *work.* It had taken two hours.

Then there'd been the meeting between the High Court and the Council, and she'd seen him present almost the same spiel: discussing all the possibilities, answering every argument with the same cleverness as any human politician, and displaying the grace of a master showman. The Council hadn't been nearly as hard to sway. They were aware of the changes in the world, and they were ready to come out of the shadows, as it were, and take part.

She'd watched with grudging admiration, and remembered that she'd seen him dispatch many of his victims in this same manner. Her father was not a savage killer as some vampires were; instead, he wore his victims down gently, using grace and charm.

In fact, that was how he'd been when he'd sired her, long ago, and...

No. We don't think about that. We don't ever think about that.

She stopped, and drew herself up to her full height. She closed her eyes and let the anger she felt at being Uninvited, at her father, at that stupid ridiculous *damp* little *fool* Herschel, at *everything,* wash over her. Her mind descended into a dark, evil, *pleasant* red haze.

Her lips drew back and she felt her fangs extend. Her eyes opened; the irises were a bright, glowing red. They narrowed to slits. She snarled like a cougar.

Kill. Kill them all. Make them pay.

She hissed angrily. She was very, *very* glad she was alone in the hall, because she was in killing mode, and God help *anyone* who crossed her because if they gave her an inch of space, just an *inch...*

Then she blinked, and sighed to herself. She bowed her head and stood still. Her eyes cleared, and her fangs withdrew to their normal slightly disturbing length. She took a deep breath. She was aware that technically she didn't have to breathe, but she found it helpful at times like this.

Of course, it wouldn't do to murder the entire school on the first day. There'd be all kinds of questions, and a horrible mess, and the others would be so mad *at me.*

She continued walking. Her mind settled back from uncontrolled savagery into its usual state of mild irritation. She was not particularly horrified at her transformation; sometimes you just needed a *release.*

Why they all thought they could get along with humans was beyond her. Humans were too scared of things they didn't understand. They always wanted everything to be someone else's idea of *normal*, despite the fact that nature and circumstances and life in general often contrived to keep that from ever happening. No matter what she did, or how she behaved, humans would always see her as an enemy and themselves as potential victims.

She turned at the corner and was brought up short by a mirror in the hallway. She cast no reflection; this made her even angrier than before. She thought about smashing it, and decided it wasn't worth it. She nastily mimed primping her hair, and turned to continue down the hallway.

Oh, no.

The wall on her right extended into a grid of large windows that looked out onto the courtyard. Sunlight was pouring through them. To get to her classroom, she'd have to walk straight through the sunlight.

The look on her face was a mixture of outrage and defeat, with a smattering of naked terror. She removed the choker around her neck with trembling fingers, and stared at the amulet on it: a golden stylized sun, with a smooth dark red crystal, the color of fresh blood, at its center. As she stared into it she saw an eye open within its liquid depths, then flicker away like a primordial fish swimming through black water.

The Eye Of Azrael had been given to her to use. There had been horrible uproar among vampires because of that; some Houses of vampires she'd known for years had stopped speaking to her father because of it. They had been certain that Count Ruthven was sending his only sire-daughter to her doom.

Vampires had known about the Eye for centuries. The Eye was supposed to enable a vampire to walk in direct sunlight. Though vampires *could* move around during the daytime, but it wasn't done very often. There was that definite less-than-fresh feeling due to being undead, and of course they didn't dare get out in the sun because exploding into flame was apt to ruin anyone's day.

No one had ever wanted to use the Eye, though, because no one was actually sure if it worked. After you'd unlived a few decades you saw fake magic talismans as often as real ones, and no vampire was confident enough of any magic talisman to risk becoming deadmeat flambé. *Especially* the older ones.

So the Eye had become a relic of curiosity. Those vampires with a more entrepreneurial frame of mind had done a tidy business selling big red glass beads in gold settings as a novelty item, saying they were from the same crystal that the Eye had come from. Those vampires who bought them carried them as a good-luck charm, like a rabbit's foot. But even so, none dared to guarantee their protection, or walk in the daytime.

She stared at the rays of sunlight. Dust motes twinkled in the air like razor-sharp glitter. She had never been so completely terrified in her whole unlife.

Well, it worked okay this morning... but still...

She gathered herself and swallowed hard. She snapped the choker around her neck and began to walk briskly past the windows, with a tightened expression on her face. If she had had a heartbeat, it would have been roaring in her ears at this moment.

There was a notable lack of bursting into flame. She slowed her walk, and stopped. Her expression slowly changed from fear to surprise. She looked at her hands, wide-eyed. No smoke rose from them; no flames raced along her body. Her skin did not blacken.

She looked through the windows at the courtyard outside, a distinct, un-Bethany-like expression of wonder on her face.

I've never seen what the world looks like in the daytime. I've never seen the sky. That's possibly the most beautiful blue I've ever seen. Does it always look like that? Do the clouds always look that white? They look like you could swirl them on your fingers, like cotton candy at a fair, or like you could curl up on them and go to sleep.

As she stared at the scene outside, her peripheral vision caught a movement. There was someone standing in front of her.

What the...

She had a *reflection* in the window glass.

How... how is that happening? *Is it some kind of trick of the sunlight? Is it the Eye?*

She looked at herself for the first time in two hundred-plus years: her pale skin, blood-red lips, violet eyes, raven's-wing hair with its single white lock, and she realized that this whatever-it-was, this *day*, this weird mission she was about to embark on, was a *gift*.

She'd been given a chance to change things for herself and everyone she knew in Morlock Heights, and it wouldn't be easy, but it would be worth it. In the end, it would be worth it.

Maybe I c an actually do this.

Maybe I could get a tan.

She thought hard about that. *Well, then again, maybe not.*

She smiled to herself, and the reflection smiled back. Then it was gone, because she had turned away and was heading to her classroom.

At the classroom door, Bethany faltered for a moment. What if she was not only Uninvited from her locker, but from everywhere in the school? How would she get into her classes?

The door was open. Students were seated in groups at desks, talking quietly among themselves. She deliberated. *An open door is sometimes the same as an Invitation, but not always, so maybe if I...*

Oh, bugger it.

She lowered her head and charged through the open door.

There was no barrier, so her momentum carried her into the room, where she promptly ran into a desk because she wasn't looking where she was going. She managed to keep from falling, but only just.

"Hey! Watch where you're going, doofus!"

She looked up. An oval-faced blonde occupying the desk she had run into stared at her indignantly. Beside her were two other girls who were attempting to copy her in style and dress, and not doing as well as she was. The fourth person in the group was a sweet-faced brunette who looked concerned.

Bethany recovered her manners first. "I'm sorry, I--"

The blonde gave her an appraising look. "Hmm. Goth

much?"

There were sniggers from the other girls, almost on cue. Bethany's eyebrows furrowed. She was about to respond with a barb of her own when she felt a hand on her shoulder.

"Are you all right?"

She turned and found a young man dressed in a knit shirt and what appeared to be *pressed* blue-jeans, wearing wire-rimmed glasses. She steadied herself and gave him a direct look.

"I... do I *know* you?"

He smiled. "No, but I expect you will soon. I'm Mr. Harrington, and I'm your teacher here in our Literature class." He noticed her general appearance for the first time but did not react; instead he looked curious. "I... think you are one of our *special* students." There was snide whispering from the group of desks.

"Uh, yes." *Special?* "I've been in the office with Mr. Herschel and the other *special* students," she added, putting a mild edge on it. She assumed her usual aristocratic air. "I'm sorry, but I don't have a note or anything. They didn't give us one."

He smiled. "That's all right, Miss..." He walked quickly to his desk to check his roll book, which gave Bethany a good view of him from the rear. She raised an eyebrow. A tiny smile appeared at the corner or her mouth. *Kind of cute, actually.*

There was barely controlled giggling from the desks beside her. Bethany turned a cold glare on the group of girls. The two flunkies saw the look in her eye and went silent immediately, but the blonde was giving her a knowing smirk, as one equal to another. *Except that she isn't,* thought Bethany. The brunette, however, was waiting to see how it would all play out, which aroused her curiosity.

This one is apparently their crony, but she's odd one out if I ever saw it. What's she doing with them?

"Ruthven, is it?" said Mr. Harrington. He had found her name.

"Yes," she said, and caught herself, remembering that she was a student. Sometimes being two hundred and change was irritating. "Yes, sir."

"Yes. Here is your textbook." He returned to her with a thick book. "We start each day in class with reading, and then discussion.

You may find a group and begin in the first chapter. The selection today is Mr. E. A. Poe."

"Poetry or short story?" asked Bethany. "Because he's not bad with most of the tales--I rather liked *Hop-Frog*--but I think his poetry tells so much more about him and how much he missed his sister."

Mr. Harrington's eyebrows went up. "You're... familiar with Poe."

Matched the old sot drink for drink one night in Kentucky. Charming when he wasn't acting depressed and melodramatic, which was almost never. "Yes, sir. He's actually something of a favorite." Beside her, the blonde was regarding Bethany with a mocking expression. Both of them caught it.

"I think I'll assign you to Miss Hardin-St. James's group here," he said. There was a nasty glint in his eye. "After all," he continued, regarding the blonde student, "they could use a bit of motivation, I think." The two flunkies winced visibly. The brunette was smiling to herself; Bethany decided she rather liked her. The blonde was fuming.

Harrington smiled warmly at Bethany and said, "Find a desk, and join this group. We will start discussion in ten minutes. I will be interested to hear your thoughts on Poe."

She returned his smile, being careful not to show her teeth. "Thank you," she said. He left them and returned to his desk.

Bethany pulled up an empty desk and sat across from the blonde, who was giving her that sizing-up look again. She returned it. The blonde was quite good-looking, with full lips and a strong jawline, but the nose was a bit big, and her eyes had a coldness to them, as though everything was either supposed to amuse her in some way or disappear. Bethany automatically disliked her, but at the same time she felt it must be a terrible strain on the girl to maintain such affected boredom.

"Hello," she said. "I'm Bethany Ruthven. Sorry about running into you there."

"Hi," responded the blonde. "It's OK. I'm Jessica Hardin-St. James, as you heard from *Mister* Harrington. You sure work fast, babe." She languidly offered a hand, and Bethany shook it. Jessica shivered, and rubbed her hands. "Wow. Your hand's *cold.*"

Bethany's response was a quiet smile. She was aware of the other three watching her. "Thank you," she said.

Jessica blinked. She said, "That blouse you're wearing--is that satin?" There was a tone of mild condescension.

"Silk," responded Bethany coolly.

"Mmm. Who's the designer?"

"I don't really know," said Bethany. "Father got it for me when we were in Paris." Jessica's eyebrows went up; the others looked interested. "It's an original, and handmade, so there were only a few." *Also, the poor woman's shop was burned flat when the Revolution started up because she took in sewing from the Royal Palace from time to time,* she thought.

Jessica smiled. It was not a particularly nice or warm smile, and Bethany realized that she had passed some sort of test, which irked her. "It's cool."

"Thank you." She returned the smile, but without teeth.

"You smile funny," said the girl sitting next to Jessica. She was a bottle redhead with a pair of half-moon spectacles, and seemed to Bethany to be... well, not *stupid,* but as if she never thought much about anything. "I mean, like, you don't show your teeth." Her voice had a stoned, drawling quality.

Bethany regarded them all, and sighed to herself. She felt a tiny twinge of sorrow for the brunette. *All right, you sods,* she thought. Her lips spread across her teeth, revealing her fangs.

The reaction was immediate. Everyone drew back slightly. There were whispers of "Wow, I *never...*" and "*That* is..."

"Who do you go to to get *that* kind of thing done?" said Jessica.

Bethany stared at her. "Done?"

"Yeah," said the bottle redhead. "Dentist. You know." She peered through her spectacles at Bethany's fangs. "*Wow.* How much did that set your parents back?"

"*Back?*"

"Y...Yeah. Money," said the third girl, a short, somewhat snippy-voiced blonde who seemed to have *henchman* written all over her. "How much does that kind of cosmetic dentistry cost?" She asked pertly.

Realization hit Bethany immediately. "Um…it's a bit more than you might want to pay," she said. Inside her head, a mental version of herself was doubled over, giggling. "It was something all the kids back home were getting, so I got it too." Her mouth quirked as she struggled to keep from laughing at them.

"Hey!" the hench-blonde said. "I bet you've read all those Anne Rice books!" She appeared pleased to have worked this out all by herself. The mental Bethany pounded the desktop, shrieking laughter.

"It's… different," said the bottle redhead, in general tones of *whatever*. Hearing this noncommittal attitude helped Bethany to calm herself internally. She took a deep breath, mostly out of reflex.

"I think it looks cool," said the brunette.

Bethany scrutinized her. She had a general appearance of girl-next-door beauty, in sharp contrast to the high-fashion-groupies she was with. Bethany gave her a genuinely warm smile. "Thank you. Thank you very much." She noticed that Jessica seemed displeased; the general expression was one of *I saw the new girlfriend/flunky first.*

"I'm Stephanie Leland," said the brunette, offering a hand. Bethany shook it with genuine warmth, for a vampire.

"I'm Heather Langley," said the bottle redhead. "Look, we weren't trying to give you a hard time and stuff. We're all really nice."

And I know spin doctoring when I hear it. "So what was your deal, then?" she asked.

"We're the ruling class around here, you know," said Jessica airily. "Got to be careful about who you're seen with socially. But you're OK." She smiled the hard smile again. "You're *definitely* not afraid to be different."

Ah. Now I know everything I need to know about you. "No, I'm not."

"I think we should invite her to your party, Jessica," said Stephanie. There was almost, but not quite, a tone in her voice that said she was plainly tired of such an immature approach to making friends and influencing people. "Then she could get to know everybody."

"Maybe," said Jessica. "It's still two or three weeks away, anyway."

"What party?" said Bethany.

"Oh, yeah, you don't know!" said the hench-blonde. "Jessica's parents always go off on vacation just around the time school starts, right, and so Jessica always throws a big final party for us, but you wouldn't have known that because you're *new* and everything, and by the way I'm Tiffany Stewart and I'm *so* pleased to meet you, Bethany!" This was very nearly said in one breath.

"Well, that sounds nice. Maybe I'll come," said Bethany, whose brain had shut down in self-defense somewhere around *vacation.* Vampires did not view boundless enthusiasm as being very good for people in general. She turned to Stephanie. "Are you going to be there?"

"Yeah, I always do," said Stephanie. She smiled, and it was slightly haggard.

"Stephanie's cool," said Heather, in tones of one who was attempting to be diplomatic but couldn't quite maintain the commitment. "And she's smart."

"Yeah, that's why we keep her around," said Jessica. She laughed, but it didn't seem funny to Bethany; in fact, it made her quite angry. "By the way, you're invited to the party, if you can come."

Thanks ever so for the bone, darling. "I might have some friends who might want to come with me. *If* that's all right," she said tartly. "After all, I would *certainly* want them to meet the *best* people of our new school." She looked directly at Stephanie when she said this, and smiled. Stephanie smiled, and Bethany noticed that it was grateful. Heather and Tiffany, who hadn't caught the sarcasm inherent in Bethany's voice, smiled, pleased with themselves.

Jessica had. She regarded Bethany with a curious look. Bethany gave her a warm smile, but her eyes presented a tiny vision of the vampire beneath. "Don't you think so, Jessica?" she said.

Jessica held Bethany's gaze for a minute, and the tension level rose slightly. She knew that something was very, very *weird* about the newcomer, but she couldn't figure out what it was. "Oh, all right, I don't care," she said finally. "I guess if they're with you it's cool."

"Thank you," said Bethany. Heather and Tiffany were looking at Jessica with a slightly puzzled air; something seemed to be wrong with the dialogue. Stephanie looked impressed.

"Okay, class," called Mr. Harrington from his desk. "Reading is over. We will begin discussion of the poem 'Annabel Lee' by Edgar Allan Poe."

The group reluctantly turned to join the discussion as Mr. Harrington slid into his lecture. Stephanie smiled brightly at Bethany, and it seemed that it was the first true smile she'd had in a long time. She felt that this girl *needed* her friendship somehow.

Well, I've got one new friend. It's these other three I'm not so sure about.

She looked at Mr. Harrington, and was sure that he was observing her. His eyes had a different expression from the smiling man she'd seen at the beginning; they were intense. *Watchful.* She was definitely sure, now, that she'd seen him somewhere before. Where was it?

Then he smiled at her, and she could not help smiling back. *Charismatic,* she thought. *Guess I'm just being paranoid. Need to stop that if I'm going to be a proper high school student.*

Mr. Harrington continued with his lesson, and the students listened in the usual manner of captive audiences everywhere. Bethany eyed Jessica, who was regarding Mr. Harrington with a mulish, unpleasant expression.

Then again, thought Bethany, *maybe I should be paranoid a little. But this girl's not going to rule over me.*

She settled into her class.

Punkin walked despondently down the hall to her locker, cradling her backpack in front of her. She looked around and, seeing no one, unzipped the backpack. She rummaged in it and pulled out a rather beat-up teddy bear. One eye was gone, replaced with a stitch, and the fur was worn in several places. She took it out of the bag and stroked it, feeling the tears she'd been struggling to hold back all morning well up.

She'd hid the bear in her backpack that morning, feeling stupid, but unable to stop herself. She'd been scared the others would find out, even though she knew they would understand. But she'd been more scared of being in an unfamiliar place without something she loved, so the bear had gone in the backpack.

She felt the tears trickling down her cheeks, and wiped them away roughly. She told herself firmly that she was not going to cry, and that she should pull herself together. It was only *school*, for Goddess' sake.

She swallowed hard and wished that she could be like the others. Frankie was just so strong and... well, *grown-up*. She could handle anything you threw at her. Bethany was, right now, probably shutting some old meanie's mouth with one of her patented barbs. And Harriet... well, Harriet never worried about *anything*, because she was part wolf. She just let life wash over her. Punkin wished *she* could do that.

She zipped the bear back into her backpack and went to find her locker. She was crestfallen to discover a lock already on it. Punkin sighed, and the sound was not really a sigh; more like a whimper of defeat.

Well, I don't have no key, and there ain't no other way to get the lock off, so here goes.

She concentrated and felt the Power well up within her. The pupils of her eyes *swelled*, enveloping the whites, becoming a glowing deep blue. Sweat popped out on her brow as she felt the Power twist within her, struggling to escape.

No. I don't need all of it.

She stretched out her arm, clenched her hand into a fist, and made a twisting motion. The lock clanged to the floor, glowing red-hot. The hasp, separated from the body of the lock, melted quickly into a puddle that hardened as it cooled, shining dully.

The Power roiled within her. She gritted her teeth and closed her eyes, forcing it back down within her, feeling it struggle to burst forth as she did. Her stomach knotted. The muscles in her body clenched.

Down... down... down...

She bent at the waist and leaned forward on the locker, pushing against the door with both hands. She could feel it twisting inside her skull, trying to break loose. She gathered her strength and forced it back.

GET DOWN! BACK! GO BACK!

She felt it go down within her, dissipating. She wiped the sweat off her forehead, panting, and opened her locker. She put the backpack inside, closed the door and leaned back against it, sighing.

The door felt odd against her back. She turned and saw the dents made by her hands in the door. Part of the vents in the locker were wedged flat.

Punkin sighed. It could have been worse.

Punkin's real name was Petronella Nightshade; *Punkin* was a family nickname. Her family were witches of the Coven of The Nine Stones, which was named because the founder of the Coven had felt that a group of unmarried women who practiced midwifery, herbal medicine, and the last remaining vestiges of an ancient and highly suspect religion (as far as Puritans were concerned) needed something ominous-sounding enough to keep away the curious, who would come to find out what evil forbidden rituals the witches were up to and then be disappointed at finding nothing but an extended tea-and-muffin klatch.

The Coven had been very upset when Punkin had been selected to walk among humans. Some of them were old-fashioned witches opposed to the idea of school in general, and thought it was bad enough that Punkin went to Graf Orlok, because they felt that a school that had selected a Vampyre (who spelled it that way because he was one of *those* vampires[2]) for a headmaster was a horrible place where no one could learn anything. Certainly not *proper* witchcraft.

But the major reason for their concern was that Punkin was an Adept. It was said that she'd done levitation spells in her mother's *womb*, which, apart from being mildly uncomfortable at times, had tickled slightly. She'd amused herself one day at age four by doing a complicated Transmogrification spell on the apple orchard, making the apples grow to the size of her head and become rainbow-colored. She'd *figured out* the recipe for her great granny's double nut chocolate fudge and strawberry cream trifle cake, *on her own*, which

---

[2] The ones with bald heads and the distasteful rat look. They are obsessive about a great many things, and one of them is a certain manner of spelling.

was nearly grounds for being of an occult persuasion in itself. *No one had known how to make that recipe like Great-Granny Rasputina had; it had gone with her to the grave.* This had, rather unfairly, put the idea in the Coven's heads that Punkin was a potential necromancer, possessing an ability to communicate with the dead.

This bothered Punkin immensely, and not just for the obvious reasons. Necromancy was a branch of magic that most witches (except for certain ones in Louisiana that her Coven made a point of not seeing) did not as a rule venture into; it was the point where magic started crossing over into an exact science.[3] At any rate, she'd never spoken to any dead people she could think of, unless you counted Frankie, who had been assembled from dead folk but was now technically living, and Bethany, who was only technically dead and got snippy when it was brought up.

There'd been a special emergency Coven meeting called about Punkin's *new* school. The only Coven witches not opposed to it were Punkin's mother, Eleanor, who was open-minded to the idea of humans in general due to having had three human husbands and many consorts in-between; and her Aunty Grimadene, the Coven's current Elder Witch, who had reached the age where "do what thou wilt" was not so much an occult-tinged catchphrase as an attractive philosophical outlook. They had tried to calm the Coven witches, who would have none of it.

They'll see her Powers! they cried. *It'll be terrible! You know what humans do to witches! They'll burn her at the stake!*

And Eleanor and Grimadene had stood beside their terrified shaking child and declared firmly that there would *not* be any stake burning, and Punkin was going to human school in Clearwater because it was *necessary*. The world was moving on, and it was time they all went on with it.

And Cousin Bevadelia, who was a distant family relation and had never liked Eleanor or Grimadene because they baked *cookies* with Punkin instead of teaching her certain spells and curses, had said, *We all know the child's a natural necromancer. What's going to*

---

[3]   This is also why there are more *male* necromancers, because it's more complicated and *macho*. A female necromancer is usually a witch with a serious necrophilic kink.

happen when she starts raising the dead? What happens when things start crawling out of the ground and eating *everybody? What are you going to do then,* you foolish witches?

And Punkin, who had worked for years to control her powers and had been schooled by the best of the best in the Craft (namely her mother and aunt), had become so horrified that she had done something she'd never done before in front of the Coven. She'd burst into tears and run out of the room.

And Eleanor and Grimadene, who loved Punkin more than anything else in the world and could be very hard-minded about her well-being, had stared after her, then turned and favored Bevadelia with a grim look. Then they rolled up their sleeves and begun to *discuss the matter* with her, because sometimes witch-coven business is not always settled by verbal debate, or even magical means. Grimadene had very kindly treated her bruises afterward with her special ointment, and sent her home. But she'd been mad for awhile because she'd hit Bevadelia with the teapot and had broken it.

Eleanor had come to Punkin as she lay crying on her bed, sat and held her, stroked her gently and wiped away her tears. *You don't worry about nothing, baby,* she'd said. *You just go on to that school and do how you know you're supposed to, and you'll be fine.*

Mama, Mama, I'm so scared! she'd sobbed. *It's like my Power is getting stronger, and I don't know what to do! I don't want to make nothing come out of the ground! I don't want to hurt nobody... oh, Mama, I'm so* scared!

Eleanor had hugged her hard and said, *I don't know nothing about necromancy. I don't know if you're able to do that or not. But I do know that you're my Punkin, and I love you, and I'll always love you no matter what you do. And your Power is getting stronger because you're growing up. You're becoming a woman, and Adepts always have a rough time when they come of age, because they be more powerful than most of us. But I'll be here, and so will your Aunty. Just like she is now.*

And Punkin had seen, through her tears, her Aunty Grimadene standing in the doorway, with a few tears of her own in her eyes. She had come to the bed and taken Punkin's hand firmly in her own.

You listen to me, child. Power is not everything. Power is not the be-all-end-all of our existence. *That's what that fool Bevadelia thinks it is, but no. The thing that matters is what you do with your Power and how you use it. And you remember this; love is more powerful than any magic. Love is the most powerful thing in the world, and with it you can do anything you want. And your mama and I would love you if you were the most powerful witch in the world, or if you couldn't even do a simple scrying. That kind of thing is what real magic is, what real power is.*

Punkin was quiet for a minute. Then she asked, *Am I really a natural necromancer?*

Eleanor and Grimadene had looked at each other, and Grimadene had said, *Child, we don't know. No one can tell about that sort of thing. But if you are, you're the first to turn up in our line in many a year.* She'd smiled then. *And certainly the prettiest. Most of them are old haggy things. But you not gonna be raising up nothing 'less you want to. So you ain't gonna make nothing come out of the ground, and especially not on your first day of school.*

So you go on to that school, and remember who you are, said Eleanor. *We are both so proud of you.*

And everything had seemed all right after that. But Punkin still worried, because her Powers *were* growing. She didn't want to make anyone *afraid* of her just because she was a witch. So she'd started trying to *rein it in*.

Which was *hard*.

Punkin read her schedule. Her first class was something called Career Arts, which she didn't remember signing up for. She wondered what a career was. If it was some *new* form of magical ability, she didn't want it. She had enough magic-related problems to worry about.

There was a mirror in the hallway. She walked over to it, straightened her hat and took a good look at herself; she didn't want to walk into class looking like she'd just done magic.

She had a beautiful, heart-shaped face, and bright crystalline blue eyes, and hair that was an almost unnatural shade of platinum-blond, and it stuck out and frazzled and ratted just like her mother's did. She had her mother's figure, too. She'd *developed* early. Some of the boys they'd passed in the assembly had stared at her,

59

and she knew at first that it had been about the hat and the general witchy dress, but then she'd caught their eyes doing this little bounce. And she knew then that they were staring at something else.

This bothered her for two reasons. One, she did *not* want to be like her mother. She loved her mother dearly, but her mother was a bit wild when it came to men, and had been married a *lot*. And if *she* was going to get married, then she only wanted to be married *once*, to a boy she really loved. She also suspected that her mother had other reasons for being married so much, because she'd found a little book at home entitled *Tantrica Sexualis Folio*, and had decided very quickly that she wasn't ready to read that book.

The second reason was, basically, that she felt that Bethany was so much *prettier* than she was. She wondered why the boys hadn't stared at *her* in the same way. Well, a *couple* of them had, but she hadn't liked the look of them. Neither had Bethany.

She remembered meeting the others, soon after she was told she'd been selected. She'd been very scared, because she had thought that they wouldn't like her. There'd been a lot of monsterkind who were mad about a witch being selected, because the Council Of Monsterkind had been quite frank with their reasoning: *there should be at least* one *child that the humans can relate to.* In the eyes of certain Creatures, werewolves, vampires and others, this meant "one who looks human," meaning a witch. Hence the furor.

But after talking with Frankie, Bethany, and Harriet, Punkin had realized that *they* didn't care about that. They were united in the space of a few minutes, and when she'd told the others how worried she was about being Adept and letting it get out of hand, they'd all promised to help her. Even *Bethany* had said she would help, and Bethany was a vampire and supposedly had an uncaring attitude about everything, which Punkin had suspected to not really be true.

And she'd realized that they were not only different from humans, but different from other monsters, too. *They* would be the first to walk among humans in a long time.

She straightened herself. She faltered a little when she saw how tight her shirt looked, but she decided that was okay. *People are always gonna talk about you,* her mama had said, *so sometimes you might as well give 'em something to talk about.* She smiled, a big, bright smile, and gave herself a little wave. The image in the mirror waved back.

She headed for her classroom.

The Career Arts classroom was an overbright, somewhat desperately decorated room. There was a general theme of pink. The classroom was overcrowded with students, who all sat at tables writing in notebooks or talking among themselves. There was quite a bit of chatter, and the noise level unnerved Punkin a bit.

She swallowed hard, and quietly stepped into the classroom. No one seemed to notice her; everybody was busy with something. The teacher was a short blonde woman dressed in an ensemble that was nearly the same color pink as the room decorations, moving around the room and marking on a clipboard. Punkin decided to wait until she was finished to announce her presence.

She examined the classroom. Various posters were on the walls, decorated around the outer edges with borders. The posters were mostly pictures of working people who all seemed to enjoy their jobs just a little too much. Punkin stared at one in particular: a picture of a grinning woman dressed in an uncomfortable-looking uniform, standing in front of a cash register at a fast-food restaurant. The woman looked as manning a cash register was the most exciting and satisfying vocation on the planet, and that everyone would want to do it once they tried it. Punkin couldn't explain why, but that picture *seethed* with wrongness. She hoped that Career Arts wouldn't turn her into someone like that.

She felt a hand on her shoulder, and found the teacher behind her. The woman was smiling, but the smile had a terrible clenched quality. "You like that?" she said.

Punkin looked into the woman's eyes, and couldn't find the heart to say no. She slowly nodded.

"*Good!*" the teacher said. "*Many* of my students have started *very* rewarding careers working cash registers at the Mac King Burger Land restaurants. You know," she said, leaning forward conspiratorally, "the Mac King offers *scholarships* to kids who work there while going to school. Free money for college, you know." She sounded as though she were imparting a great secret.

Punkin decided that a change of subject was necessary at this point. "Um... are you Mrs. Carson?"

"Yes!"

"Well, I'm your new student then." She handed Mrs. Carson the schedule form. "I'm Petronella Nightshade."

"Oh, what a *beautiful name!* And so *unusual!!*" Mrs. Carson looked at her, and seemed to see Punkin fully for the first time. There was a distinct sensation of changing oars in midstream. "And you seem to be a most... *unusual* student." Her voice had dropped a notch in volume.

It's the hat, Punkin thought. *Guess Bethany was right about that.* "Yes, ma'am," she said politely. "I am. I'm one of the new students that came on the special bus this morning."

"Oh!" said Mrs. Carson. She took a step back, and Punkin felt that she was being thoroughly examined, which made her uncomfortable. She wondered if maybe the Coven had been right about stake burnings after all.

Mrs. Carson seemed to make up her mind about something. "Well, dear, I'm sure you'll do very well here." The carefree quality had all but vanished from her voice, and she seemed to have become serious. She handed Punkin a folder. "This will be your folder for worksheets in the class, and I'll be issuing textbooks in a few minutes." She made a note on her clipboard. "There we are, Petronella."

"You don't have to call me that," said Punkin. "Everbody calls me Punkin."

This seemed to light Mrs. Carson up again. "Oh, that's so *cute!!!*" she said. "Find an empty seat, dear. I'll be with you in a few minutes." She bustled away.

Punkin did not know what a dual personality was, but it seemed to her that Mrs. Carson was two people. She stared after her and wondered if she was crowded in there.

She looked around the classroom. All the tables seemed very occupied, except for one in the back of the room. A boy was slouched in a chair beside it, typing on a laptop computer. No one else was at the table.

Punkin decided to sit there, since he was the only one in the room being quiet. Besides, she thought it might be best to start slow at making friends, considering her experience with Mrs. Carson. She walked over to him.

"Do you mind if I sit here?"

The boy seemed not to hear. He was absorbed in the laptop. Punkin looked at the machine with some fascination; she had never seen one. It looked like a slim little book, with a window in one side and a lot of buttons in the other, like a typewriter. She knew what typewriters were, but this seemed to be something more.

He was tapping furiously on the keyboard, and text flew across the screen. She watched for a minute, then repeated her question.

"May I sit here, please?"

"Sure." He did not look up. Punkin raised an eyebrow.

Well, he *ain't two people. He's all one person, and all in his own* head *for sure.*

Mrs. Carson came up to the table. "Got that assignment done, Stuart? I'd hate to interrupt your valuable *hacking* time." She was smiling, but Punkin recognized the tone of voice immediately. It was the same one that Bevadelia had used at the Coven meeting, and it was like venom crystallized in sugar.

"Yes, ma'am, got it right here," said Stuart in a bored voice, and Punkin recognized *that* tone, too; sometimes Bethany used it. He held up a sheet of paper. "Also, I'm not *hacking,* because I'd need an Internet connection to do that, and you don't have one here." His tone was a bad imitation of hers.

Mrs. Carson smiled. "Punkin, this is Stuart Nelson, our resident computer expert. He's kind of a legend around here. After all, he's the one who made extra money by breaking into the school's computer system and changing grade averages for students last year. That's why he's *repeating* this year." She sighed. "He's a very bright child, but he doesn't use his *full potential.* Are you sure you wouldn't rather sit somewhere else?"

Stuart had finally noticed Punkin. His eyes kept returning to the hat. "That's... really *witchy,*" he finished.

"Mrs. Carson, it's okay with me, sittin' here. And besides, everbody makes mistakes," said Punkin. She was beginning to think she might have made a mistake by not protesting the change of her class schedule.

Mrs. Carson sighed, and Punkin knew she had disappointed her by wanting to sit with Stuart. "Very well, dear," she said. Then she brightened again. "You know, dear, you're really a very *positive* person. Perhaps you'll be a *good* influence on Stuart," she purred. A wide, rather plastic smile was forming on her face. "That would be *wonderful*, wouldn't it?"

"Yes, ma'am," said Punkin wearily. Mrs. Carson's double personality was beginning to tire her.

"*Good*," she smiled. "Here's your worksheet, dear. Have it completed by the end of class." She shot a final glare at Stuart and then bustled off, smiling.

Punkin stared after her, feeling dazed. She picked up the worksheet and examined it. It contained thirty questions, all of which seemed to be multiple choice. She had no idea how to begin answering it.

She looked at Stuart, who was examining her with studious concentration, as though she were some new creature. She noticed that he wore glasses and that he was a bit thin, as though he didn't eat enough. *Aunty and Mama would say he needed a good meal*, she thought. He said, "Are there any more at home like you?"

It was a standard question, but he had a way of speaking that made everything he said seem like a challenge or a sarcastic remark. She decided to be truthful. "Yes, there are," she said. "Lots."

He stared at her, and she realized that he hadn't expected that answer. "So...what, you all live in the Blair Witch woods or something?"

"Well, we live in a swamp, actually. But we don't have no witches named Blair in our coven." She thought for a moment, and said, "I've got a cousin named Lucy, though."

"You're a witch." This was not a question.

"Yes."

He continued staring for a long time, and Punkin realized that he didn't know anything about what had happened in the courtyard that morning. Probably he'd been in here, typing on that computer thing, and no one had told him... because he didn't have any friends.

She felt bad for him.

He snorted. "Well, are all our brooms safe?"

Well, there's *why he has no friends,* she sighed to herself. She said, in the most Bethany-like tone she could muster, "We all got our own brooms, thank you. We don't need to steal nobody's." She met his steady gaze, and lost her nerve. "And besides... I can't fly a broom yet, anyway. I haven't learned." She looked at the table, embarrassed.

Stuart thought about this, and said quietly, "That's okay. My parents won't let me get my driver's license yet." He sounded very unhappy when he said this, and Punkin suddenly understood why he acted the way he did. "It's like, every *other* kid's parents let them get theirs and drive, but not me. I think they're scared I'll be in a wreck or something."

There was a moment of silence, and a bit of staring at the table. In it, they both became aware of how very out of place the other felt.

Stuart finally broke it. "So... are you *really* a witch?"

She nodded. "Yup. You know, you already asked me that. Don't you see the hat?"

He stared at her. "You're serious."

"Yes!" She threw up her hands. "I mean, I don't *know* what you're expectin'. I don't even know what I'm doin' in this class." She stared at the horrid worksheet. "I don't even know how I'm goin' to answer this."

Stuart passed her his worksheet. "Here. I can *guarantee* every answer is correct."

Punkin looked uncertain. "You... you ain't supposed to copy."

"It's not as if you've got much choice," replied Stuart blandly. "*You* don't know what's going on, and besides, you already heard Carson. I'm a *criminal.*" He waved the worksheet at her. "Go on, take it. Make a few answers wrong if you like and throw her off the scent."

"Maybe Mrs. Carson was right about sittin' with you."

"So what are you going to do, turn me into a toad?"

Punkin eyed him. "I *could,* you know."

Stuart saw something in her gaze that said she meant it. He swallowed and said, "Whatever. I'm just trying to help you out." His voice had lost some of its sarcastic edge.

Punkin gave him her warmest smile, and saw his face soften. "That's very nice of you. I bet you're really a nice person, even if you don't always act like it. Thank you." She took the sheet and began to copy his answers.

Stuart watched her. He eyed the hat, watching the point bob as she wrote, then looked at her legs and feet, clad in the striped stockings and the little granny-boots from another era. He had the unnerving feeling that he had met someone who was very, very different from other kids he knew, and he wasn't sure what to do.

She finished, and returned his sheet to him. She tapped his computer. "What's this here?"

He stared at her. "You've never seen a laptop before?"

She tried the word. "*Laptop.* That's a funny name for it. It looks like a book."

Stuart realized, dumbly, that she did not know about computers. "Well, people also call them notebooks. It's a computer. People use them for... for..." He stopped, having no idea how to proceed. He settled for, "It's a machine that people use." His brow furrowed. "Here on our planet," he said, unable to help himself.

She glared at him. "That was unkind, Stuart. I know I ain't from around here, but I ain't from another planet."

"Sorry."

"It's okay. So what's it do?"

"Well, I do homework on it, and I store stuff in it. Papers and notes and stuff." He pursed his lips, thinking. "Um, some people make artwork with them, and do spreadsheets, like, accounting, and... well, there's a whole lot of things you can do with them." He found himself smiling for no reason that he could name. "I also use the Internet a lot."

"What's Internet?"

He fumbled for an explanation. "The Internet is like... what you use to hook different computers together. You can send information back and forth to other people."

"And you hack."

"Yeah." He felt guilty. He couldn't explain why, but she seemed to have that effect on him for some reason. "Hacking means that I sometimes break into other computers and look around at stuff on them. But I don't change anything."

"But you changed all them grades."

"That was different. People were paying me to do that." He winced at the defensiveness in his voice. "Look, it wasn't like I broke into the Pentagon or something. There are some hackers who really screw up very important systems, and steal all kinds of information and money and stuff. But I don't do stuff like that." He straightened up. "I *could*, you know."

Punkin grinned. This boy reminded her, in some ways, of Bethany, but he had none of her self-confidence. *Except*, she thought, *when he's talkin about this computer stuff. He really needs a friend.* She began to relax.

"Could you show me how to work your computer? I'd like to learn." She shrugged. "After all, I'd like to feel like I was learnin' *somethin* in this class."

Stuart looked at her uncertainly. Then he pushed his laptop over so that they could both see the screen, and tapped some keys. "Okay, this is your desktop."

She tapped the table. "I thought this was the desktop."

"No, no, different thing. Okay, now these are icons..."

Punkin watched Stuart while he worked. He wasn't exactly what she had expected in a first friend, but he was a start. *This school*, she thought, *may turn out to be okay after all.*

S   he watched. And learned.

Of course, there was a lock on Harriet's locker too. But werewolves are nearly as strong as Creatures, so there was no chance of its survival. And Harriet was also in a hurry. She yanked open the locker and threw in her backpack and the broken lock, slammed the door, and set off at a hard jog for the gym.

The thing that was really different about this new school, thought Harriet, was the *smells*. She remembered the dark halls of Graf Orlok High School, whose walls smelled of old limestone and ancient moss; the sharp chemical odors and clean electrical smells from the laboratory where the Mad Science classes met, and the herbs and potions and the fire underneath the cauldrons in the Witches' hall, all pine kindling and well-used iron. Her other classmates: the witches, who went in the swamp to collect herbs and plants, the Creatures and the young Igors who always smelled slightly dried and *old,* a smell that was a distant cousin to the rich earthy smell of the vampires, and her favorite smell of all; the woodsy-mountainy smell of the other werewolves, most of who were kindred to Harriet in one way or another. The Von Lupins were a large Clan, and there had been a lot of cross-breeding with other Clans.

There weren't as many different smells at this new school. The building itself was only about sixty years old, give or take a few. They'd painted everything about two years ago, and someone kept it really clean, which meant that there was a lot of bleach and cleaning fluids. There were faint smells of some of the students: makeup and different perfumes, which smelled to her like plants and flowers murdered in alcohol; weird fruity chewing-gum smells that smelled nothing like real fruit, and old textbooks, and pencil shavings, and from the direction of the gym the sharp smells of sweat and canvas and rubber.

She frowned as she jogged along. Her head was full of thoughts about the others and where they were. Frankie was probably okay; Frankie was tough. Punkin had been scared, but she'd been hiding it well, and that meant that she was pulling herself together and was also okay. Bethany, now... when Bethany got mad at someone she was hard to get along with, and she was really mad at her dad right now, and she'd been really *afraid.* Or at least that was how it had been when she'd left the others.

Harriet sighed. She didn't really like thinking much, but she loved her friends, and sometimes that meant you wondered about them and hoped they were okay. But this thing of Bethany being afraid bugged her a bit. Bethany didn't ever get afraid much, because her attitude was that nothing in the world was scarier than her. But she'd been really worried about the sunlight-protection thing. That meant being *adventurous,* and vampires had *no* sense of adventure when their self-preservation streak started up.

She stopped and sniffed. The canvas-rubber smell was

getting stronger, so up this way, and *stop*. She sniffed again. The canvas-rubber smell was stronger on her left, so *turn* here and stop *here*.

She was in a room with lockers and benches on each side. Harriet heard the shouts and bouncing of balls on a wood floor, and smiled. She'd found her way in through the locker room, so if she kept straight ahead, she'd be in the gym. Then she could *play*. *Play* was a good thought, to Harriet; werewolves tended to see most things as some form or another of *play*.

There was a mirror on the wall. She stopped for a minute and looked at herself. She made a face, and the Harriet in the mirror made a face back. She smiled.

She headed toward the door at the other end. Harriet's sense of smell was very strong, even for a werewolf, and she could smell the clothes of the other students, even though the locker doors were closed.

Ugh, there was that perfume thing again. Why did humans cover up their natural scents by drenching themselves in scents of dead plants mixed in alcohol? That was *dumb*. A scent was how others knew who you were, how *you* knew who you were.

But then, maybe humans don't tell each other by their scents. Maybe humans don't like the way they smell. That's sad. She supposed it had to do with that cleanliness thing that Dr. Adams had told her about. *High-gene.* He'd said she'd have to take a bath or a shower daily, if she wanted to come to school.

She hadn't minded doing the whole bath and shower thing, really. It was like swimming in the river at home, but a lot warmer, and the waterspraying thing was really relaxing. It was using soap that bothered her. She hadn't liked that until they went to that bath store where they sold all that *natural* soap made out of *glih-cer-een*, and she'd found a soap called melon cucumber. She'd liked that a lot; it didn't smell as strong as the other kind of soap, and it didn't hide her scent. The family had all liked it so much that *they* had started bathing, and Pop had had bathroom stuff built in some older chambers of the Stronghold.

She saw a big opening on one side of the room. She heard water dripping. Soap. That was the shower room, where they took showers after they played games. Dr. Adams had toured the school one day with them, and…

She stopped. Her ears twitched.

Somebody's here.

She listened. Harriet's ears were just as good as her nose, and she could hear, over the amplified sounds of the dripping shower faucets, the sound of someone trying to be quiet.

Her face split into a huge and somewhat terrifying grin. Hide-and-seek was one of her favorite games. Wonder if there's a hide-and-seek team here.

She moved quietly to a position just by the door. The someone was moving in what they thought was a quiet manner toward the door, on the right. Harriet crouched and sniffed with just the tiniest intake of air.

Girl. Right by the door. Okay…

She leapt into the shower room, and pounced. *"Gotcha!"*

"AAAAAAAAAAAAHHHHHH!!!!"

The scream, which was amplified by the shower room, belonged to a tall, somewhat gangly girl with dirty-blonde hair. Her eyes were wide with terror. The resulting noise made Harriet's ears ring, and she was so surprised that she staggered and fell back through the door, dragging the girl along with her. They ended up in a heap on the floor.

"Wow, that's *loud,*" said Harriet, shaking her head.

The girl screeched and huddled in the doorway, goggle-eyed. "W-who are you? *What* are you?"

"I'm Harriet," said Harriet. "Who are you? How come you were hiding in the shower thingy room?" She got up and brushed herself off. "If you're gonna be on the hide-and-seek team, you need to learn how to be quieter."

She looked at the girl, and stopped in surprise. The girl's lips were quivering, and her eyes filled with tears.

"Hey, what's wrong?" said Harriet. "I'm sorry, I didn't mean to hurt your feelings by what I said. Hey, maybe you were practicing--"

"I'm not on any team!" shouted the girl defensively. She hugged her knees fiercely. "I was hiding so I wouldn't have to go to

P.E.! *I hate P.E.!"*

Harriet stared at her. "You *hate* P.E.?"

"Y-Yes!" She was sobbing.

Harriet put her head on one side. "Who's P.E.?"

"What?"

"Who's P.E.?" She sat down beside the girl. "If you hate him so much, maybe we should beat him up or something. I used to have to beat up the other pups because they were always picking on Mordecai when he was a pup."

The girl stared at her in confusion. Finally she said, "Who's Mordecai?"

"Oh, he's my little brother," said Harriet. "One of them, anyway. I was first of my litter, but some of the pups in the other litters were younger than me, so I have a lot of little brothers. Mordecai's a new-moon pup."

"A what?"

"A new-moon pup. See, we're werewolves, and we--"

"Werewolves?"

"Yeah. Anyway, Mordecai was a new-moon pup. See, sometimes werewolves have a pup that's either all-the-way wolf or all-the-way human. Can't shift between wolf and human, or change form at all, so we call 'em a new-moon pup. So the other pups would pick on Mordecai and try to fight with him because they thought he was funny-looking, and because he couldn't shift. So I'd have to beat them up."

The girl blinked. She had seen werewolf movies on TV, and what was now sitting next to her was nothing like any of them. Harriet's physical appearance was right, but her friendly behavior seemed the complete opposite of *werewolf*. "Well... didn't *you* think he was funny-looking?"

Harriet stared at her. She was a little shocked by the question. "Of course not," she said. "I thought he looked like *Mordecai*. And anyway, he' s my little brother and I love him. Wouldn't *you* beat up someone who said your brother was funny-looking?"

"I suppose I would," said the girl. "I don't have a brother, though. But I see what you mean."

"Oh. Well, that's all for that then. So what do we do about

this P.E.?"

"We?" said the girl. "Oh, wait a minute... P.E. isn't a person. It's the name of the class. The class I was hiding from," she said. "Physical Education. P.E."

"The class right now?"

"Yeah."

Harriet was puzzled. "How come you hate *that*? You get to play games and run around and stuff! That's the coolest thing in the world!"

"It is not!" cried the girl. "I hate P.E.! I always get picked last for teams, and everyone yells at me because I'm so clumsy and I fall down and everything. I'm no good at it." She sniffled and rubbed her eyes.

Harriet stared at her thoughtfully. She was reminded of Punkin. "What's your name?"

"Theo MacKenzie," she moaned. "It's short for Theodora."

"Theo," said Harriet, trying the word. "That's nice. I never knew anyone named Theo before. I bet the others haven't ever either." She paused. "Well, maybe Bethany has."

Theo eyed her curiously. Harriet seemed to have accepted her as a friend almost completely, and she found herself warming to it. "Is Bethany another werewolf?"

"Oh, no. Bethany's a vampire."

Theo's eyes widened. "A *vampire?*"

"Yeah. But don't worry, she doesn't bite humans. You have to ask nice."

"*What?*"

"I dunno. It's something she always says. 'I don't bite unless you ask nicely.' I guess it's an okay thing to say. People always laugh at it." She shrugged. "She's not liking it right now that she has to go to this new school. She's worried about all the sunlight, even though she's got a protection thingy. And she doesn't..." Harriet looked uncomfortable. "She doesn't trust humans very much."

Theo raised an eyebrow. That was something new. "Why not?"

"Well, humans always worry about things they don't understand, and she's scared that everyone won't like us, because we're monsters." She noticed Theo's surprised stare, and added, "But we don't do all the bad stuff that humans say monsters do, you know. By the way, I guess I should say that even though I'm a werewolf, I don't eat humans. In fact, none of us eat humans any more."

Theo was glad to hear this, but could not help entertaining a morbid curiosity. "Why not?"

"Well, you all taste bad now."

"Huh?"

"Yeah. See, Grandpop told me once that humans used to not have junk food and fast food restaurants and pre... pre..." Her brow furrowed as she struggled with the word.

"Preservatives?" said Theo uncertainly.

"Yeah! Thank you. You're *smart*. Anyway, Grandpop said that all that stuff *stays* in humans, and it's been around so long that it's made them not taste good now, so we don't eat humans anymore. At least, not civilized werewolves." She frowned. "I've got some cousins in Bulgaria that'll eat just about *anything*. But I don't ever see them much, so you don't have to worry," she added quickly.

Theo stared at her in wonder. Whatever else Harriet was, she was one of a kind. "I suddenly think I have a lot to learn about you, Harriet," she said.

Harriet grinned at her. Theo could not help shuddering at first, but after a moment she smiled in return. She could see that Harriet's grin, though ringed with a mouthful of *very* strong and definitely canine teeth, held no malice. In fact, Harriet was anything but unfriendly.

"I bet I'll learn a lot about you, too," she said. "So, are we friends?"

"Friends?" Theo had never had *anyone* ask to be *her* friend before, and she suddenly felt special. She felt *selected*.

"Yeah." Harriet hopped up and pulled Theo up from the floor. She took her to the mirror and positioned her so that they stood side by side. "See?" she said, pointing at the reflection. "Friends."

Theo looked at their reflections, and her face split into a big smile. She nodded. "Yeah, friends. Definitely."

The bell rang. "Aw, *man!*" said Harriet. "Class is over. We didn't get to play any games!"

"But we'll have class tomorrow," said Theo.

Harriet smiled. "Yeah, we will," she said. She gave Theo a serious look. "You won't hide anymore, will you?" she said.

Theo smiled. She felt bad that Harriet had missed the first day of her favorite class, and swore to herself to make it up to her. "No, I won't."

Harriet's grin was huge. "Great. C'mon, let's go see what the next class is like!"

She ran back the way she had come, with Theo beside her.

The day wore on, and Clearwater slowly became aware of its new additions. Some remembered them from the courtyard that morning, while others came into contact with them through classes, and were either horrified, confused, or curious. But before the day was half over, the student body was abuzz with the news that there were monsters at Clearwater.

And some of them were actual *students*.

FOUR: NEW CROWD

It was noon period, and classes were moving for lunch. The hall was crowded with students at lockers. Emily worked her way through the crowd, and ran up to Theo at her locker.

"Hi! I've been trying all morning to find you!" The two girls hugged. "I thought we were supposed to have all our classes together."

"So did I," said Theo, tossing her books in her locker. "In fact, I thought we were both in the office this summer at the same time, and that we had worked out schedules so we had all the same classes."

Emily gave Theo a look. "Mr. Herschel?"

Theo nodded. "Mr. Herschel."

The two sighed. It was a long-standing and unfortunate tradition at Clearwater that Mr. Herschel would often regroup the schedules in accordance with some plan of his for each student to receive a more efficient education. No one seemed to know what this plan entailed, and some were not sure Herschel himself knew.

"I don't know," Emily said as they left for the cafeteria. "I thought that Herschel only used the Plan on the problem students. We had classes together last year, and I had straight A's."

"Maybe we shouldn't have talked so much in Woolcott's class," muttered Theo.

"Oh, hey!" said Emily, suddenly remembering. "I've got to tell you. I've got Science with Mrs. Parkinson, and I met one of those new kids. All of them are *real monsters,* just like everybody was saying. And she's really *cool.* We were sitting in class, and--"

A large grin filled with sharp teeth appeared in front of her without warning. *"Hi!* Are you Theo's friend Emily?"

Emily goggled. "Y-yes," she quavered.

"Well, I am so pleased to meet you!" said the grin, bouncing up and down happily. Emily's field of vision seemed full of pointy teeth. "I'm Harriet. I met Theo in P.E. and she told me all about you.

You sound really cool. Are you coming with us to lunch?"

"Y-yes. Yes, I am," said Emily nervously.

"Oh, that's great! Hey, there's Punkin! I gotta go tell her to come with us. *Hey, Punkin!*" Harriet loped off through the crowd of students, who parted quickly around her.

Emily stared after Harriet as she bounded down the hall. She turned to face Theo, unable to speak.

"I know," said Theo. "I met one, too."

"Hi," said Frankie, who had come up behind Emily. "You're Theo, right?"

Theo was not used to girls who were *that* tall or had skin *that* shade of green. "Uh, yeah. Yeah, I am. Are you the girl Emily met in Science?"

"Yes. I'm Frankie Franken. Emily told me about you." She extended a hand, and Theo saw the ring of stitches. She nervously took the hand and shook it gently, for fear it might come off. "Ooh, that's…" She flapped her hand to stop the tingling.

"I'm sorry," said Frankie. "It's a little electrical pulse. It always seems to get stronger around time for a recharge. Dad thinks it might be reverse polarity."

"Isn't she cool?" said Emily.

"Recharge?" said Theo.

"Yeah," said Frankie, holding up the little black case. "I always have to recharge when I eat or I get sluggish. Dad and I made this generator together."

Theo wondered what kind of father Frankie had. *"Wow,"* was all she could say.

"Oh, it's just a little thing," said Frankie, smiling shyly. "Are we all going to eat lunch together?"

"Yeah!" said a voice. Harriet had appeared with Punkin in tow. The witch smiled bashfully at Emily and Theo. "This is Punkin," said Harriet proudly. "She's a witch, and she's real smart and pretty and stuff." Punkin blushed.

Theo, who had already experienced Harriet's pride in her friends, smiled and shook hands with Punkin. "Hi," she said. "Welcome to Clearwater."

"Hi, Punkin," said Emily.

Punkin smiled back, partially in relief. "Hey, y'all," she said. "It's been some kind of morning. This school is so much bigger than Graf Orlok."

"Graf Orlok?" said Theo.

"Our old school," Frankie said. "We only had about 250 kids in our student body. Most of them were vampires."

Theo tried to imagine this, and found the idea of a predominantly vampire student body very discomforting. It seemed too much like reality. "That must have been interesting," she finally said.

"Where's Bethany? I thought she was going to be with you guys," said Emily. She'd been very curious about Bethany, mostly because she couldn't figure out how Bethany was walking around in the daytime. Vampires, as far as she knew, only went out at night.

"I guess she's at her locker," said Frankie. "They seem to have spaced us pretty far apart. Let's go find her."

They moved off down the hall, with Emily and Theo behind them. Something was preying on Theo's mind. She nudged Emily and whispered, "What do you think of them?"

"Well, I was kind of scared at first, but I like them. They're cool."

"Monster girls," said Theo thoughtfully. "Maybe it should be *Grrls* instead of girls. You know, like *grrr*."

"That sounds cool, Theo. Monster Grrls. So what do you think of them?"

"I don't know," said Theo. "They're... well, they're monsters. How do we know we're not hanging with the wrong crowd?"

"We've never *had* a crowd before," said Emily. "How am I supposed to know?"

They found Bethany, in near-hysterical rage and despair, standing in front of her locker, with a pile of textbooks on the floor and her white forelock hanging in her face.

"What happened?" asked Frankie.

Bethany's voice trembled with near-psychotic anger. "I can't get into my damned *locker*," she hissed.

Frankie reached out and snapped off the lock, which caused a few stares from the students moving around them. Emily and Theo, not used to being so conspicuous, smiled nervously as they passed on.

"Try it now," said Frankie.

"It's no good," said Bethany hoarsely. She seemed mere moments from bursting into vengeful tears. "I'm... I'm Uninvited."

There was general shocked reaction from the other girls. Emily observed that being Uninvited was obviously quite serious. "What's Uninvited?" she asked.

"Vampires have to be Invited into a new place," said Frankie. She took Bethany gently by the shoulders. "Did you try already?"

"*Yes*," muttered Bethany. Punkin came up and patted her gently.

Emily was nudged by Harriet. "Go on, do it."

"What?"

"Invite her in." Harriet pushed her forward. "If you do it it should work. You've been going here awhile, and somebody needs to do something. Bethany's bad when she's like this ."

Emily hesitated, then stepped forward and opened the empty locker. "Welcome to Clearwater," she said uncertainly. "I--I invite you in."

"We invite you in," said Theo. She felt that something was required of her, and had moved to stand next to Emily.

Bethany stared hard at them, and neither could help swallowing. The anger on her face was terrible. Emily said, "Do--do you want some help with these books?"

Bethany blinked, her rage dissolving. She said, "Yes, I would. Thank you." Her voice sounded very cultured and polite, but there was still a slight quaver.

The two girls began to pick up the books, and Bethany knelt and helped them. Together they all shoved the books into the locker, and Bethany viciously slammed the door with a bang. Emily and Theo jumped.

"Sorry," said Bethany. She had calmed considerably, and smoothed back her white lock of hair. "I'm sorry, I didn't get your names...?"

"I'm Emily Peters," said Emily. "I met Frankie in Science

class."

"And I'm Theo MacKenzie," said Theo. "I met Harriet."

"And you survived the experience?" smiled Bethany. Harriet made a face at her, and grinned. Bethany returned the grin. "I used to know someone named Theo," she said. Behind her, Theo saw Harriet rolling her eyes, and smiled.

"So," said Emily, unable to control herself, "are you really a vampire?"

Bethany eyed her, then turned to Frankie. "Does *everybody* around here not get it?" Not unkindly, she bared her teeth at Emily. "Hello? Fangs? Pale skin? General ghoulish look?"

Frankie smiled at Emily's embarrassed expression. "Emily is just *really* excited at meeting you, Bethany," she said.

"Yeah," said Harriet. "Be nice."

"I'm sorry," said Emily. "I didn't mean--I mean, I just wondered, and everything…"

"It's okay," said Bethany, patting Emily's shoulder. "I don't mean to snap. It's--it's just been a bad morning." She looked a bit embarrassed. "Thank you both for Inviting me."

There was a moment or two of everyone looking at anything but each other, and in it they drew together in that hesitant, slightly awkward way that teenagers do when they are beginning the first stage of friendship. Then Punkin broke the silence. "Y'all hungry?"

"Starving," said Emily.

"Uh, yeah," said Theo.

"Well, then," said Bethany. She regarded Emily with a large, very toothy smile. "Let's take our new friends to *lunch.*"

"Yeah!" said Harriet, grinning hugely. Then they both became aware of the slightly unnerved looks from the human girls. "Hey, wait a minute," said Harriet, "we didn't mean--"

Frankie took charge of the situation, and began herding everyone toward the cafeteria. "We know, guys. Come on, everybody. I've got to recharge soon, or else you're going to be carrying me back to class."

Heads turned as Emily, Theo and their new crowd trooped out of the lunchline.

There'd been a small problem getting lunch. The servers had reacted vocally to Harriet's requests for extra portions of food. Harriet, who until she was refused food had been rather happy-go-lucky, had begun growling, which had caused an even louder vocal reaction from the servers. Then Mr. Herschel had appeared with the cafeteria manager *and* the school dietician, and taken the workers aside. There had been some conversation in low tones with the occasional worried glance at Harriet from Mr. Herschel, while the line was temporarily held up. At one point in the conversation, *every* server turned and stared at Harriet, who responded with a friendly smile. Then the servers had returned and silently done up *four* additional trays. There had been grumbling from the students behind them about this until they caught a look from Mr. Herschel, and then they went quiet. Harriet had smiled at Mr. Herschel and given him a friendly wave as they moved through, and Mr. Herschel had nervously waved back.

Apart from the strangeness of everything, Emily observed that Mr. Herschel seemed a bit *different* from the usual befuddled figure she saw in the halls. He had *handled* the situation, and he'd done it without one of his usual Plans For Efficiency. He'd also behaved like he was *frightened,* which gave her pause. She had thought Mr. Herschel was too oblivious to be truly frightened of anything. But at any rate, Harriet had gotten more food.

Each of the MonsterGrrls (which was how they'd come to think of them) carried two trays of food. Emily and Theo came behind them, with their own trays. They found an empty table in the middle of the cafeteria and sat down. Frankie and Punkin handed one tray each to Harriet, who transferred the food in them to her own. Bethany handed over both her trays and took a bottle of dark red liquid and a plastic cup out of her bag.

"Is that all you're having?" asked Theo. "Just juice?"

"It's not juice," said Bethany, shaking the bottle.

"But--"

"*It's not juice,*" said Bethany firmly. She unscrewed the cap and poured. The liquid was unusually viscous, and had a somewhat meaty odor. Theo realized what it was, and gulped. "Oh," she said. "I'm sorry."

"It's all right," said Bethany, sipping delicately from the cup. Theo watched this for a moment, then shrugged and began eating.

Frankie unlatched her little black case. She removed a metal box that looked a bit like a cannibalized vacuum-tube radio, with an angled control panel of dials, small switches and a large red contact switch on one side. She flicked one of the smaller switches, and the machine produced a loud electrical hum. The lights in the cafeteria flickered for a moment.

Emily and Theo stared as Frankie connected the main plug of a Y-cable to the machine, inserted a detachable crank into its side, and cranked it vigorously. The hum grew louder, and everyone began shifting their chairs toward the other end of the table, where Harriet was eating calmly and taking no notice of anything.

"Are you sure you should do that here?" said Bethany, glancing nervously at the machine.

"Safe as houses," said Frankie, connecting two alligator clips at the ends of the Y-cable to the electrodes on her neck. "We tested it in the lab and it worked fine. Of course, there may be a little difference in the electrostatic charge here..." She began muttering to herself, and turned a couple of dials. The hum decreased, but there was a dangerous-sounding crackle that replaced it. Other students had begun to notice and were watching curiously.

"Transistors okay... now... *contact!*" Frankie threw the red switch. The crackling sound grew louder, and Frankie shuddered as the electrical charge surged into her. Her neck electrodes sparked. There were shouts from the watching students. Several of them got up and moved away quickly.

The scary thing about all this wasn't that everyone could *see* the electricity surging into Frankie, or that sparks were snapping and frizzling in her hair, or that her skin was glowing a bright eldritch green, but that she was *grinning.* After a minute or so of this she threw the red switch, and the glow faded. There was a decreasing electrical whine.

"*Mmmm,*" said Frankie, her Voice a sandpapery purr. She unplugged the contacts. "That was a good one."

"Are... are you all right?" quavered Emily.

"*Wonderful,*" growled Frankie. She tapped one of the clamps on her forehead, and there was a soft crackle. She patted the generator and began disassembling it. "My dad is the *best*," she said proudly.

Mr. Herschel suddenly appeared at the table, his face ashen. "That--that--what *was* that?"

"Energy supplement," said Frankie, as she latched the case. She looked up and noticed Mr. Herschel's expression. "I have to have a fresh charge every day," she said. "Didn't Dr. Adams tell you?"

Mr. Herschel's mouth opened and closed for a moment. He looked at the others. Emily, Theo, and Punkin were all frozen in place. Bethany was watching Herschel with mild interest, as if waiting to see what would happen. Harriet was deep into her food and seemed completely unaware of much else.

Herschel gathered himself. "He told me," he said finally, "that you required an energy supplement. He did *not* tell me that it was that *complicated*."

"Oh," said Frankie, embarrassed. "I'm sorry."

"Quite all right," said Mr. Herschel, from the edge of a nervous breakdown. "However, it might be best if you did that *before* you came to the cafeteria," he said, biting his lip. "I don't want to--well, is that--is that dangerous?" he said, pointing at the generator.

"Oh, no, sir," said Frankie. "It's designed to generate a maximum charge of 2000 volts for my central nervous system. But I wouldn't want someone to touch me while I was charging. It's probably better if I charge in the bathroom before lunch."

"Ah. Yes. Central nervous system." Mr. Herschel had very clearly heard *2000 volts*, and his throat was working. "Well, that would be fine."

"I'm very sorry, sir."

"No, no. It--it was quite a show, really." Mr. Herschel formed a somewhat pained smile, and left the table jerkily. Frankie sighed, and began to eat. Emily and Theo followed suit, doing their best to ignore the dark stares of students around them.

"What a sad, strange, *damp* little man," said Bethany, watching Mr. Herschel work his way across the cafeteria.

"Don't worry about it, Frankie," said Emily. "Herschel's always like that. He worries a lot."

Frankie shrugged. "It's okay, Emily. I guess there's going to be a period of adjustment for everybody." She took a bite of her food. "So what was everyone's classes like?"

"I met a boy," said Punkin. "He's showin' me how to work a computer."

Theo and Emily looked up. "Stuart?" said Theo.

"Yes! Well, Mrs. Carson said that was his name. Do you know him?"

"Yeah, we do," grumbled Theo. "*Everybody* knows Stuart."

"Stuart got held back for changing grades in the school computer system last year," said Emily. "Mr. Herschel was really mad about that. He tried to have Stuart prosecuted, but there wasn't much he could do because Stuart's still a minor."

"He still owes me back for what he charged me," said Theo. "He got caught before he got to *my* records, and I ended up with a C-in history. Stuart's okay, but he's a weird guy."

"Like us?" said Bethany.

"Er, no. Not like you." Theo sighed. "I'm sorry, I didn't mean that. It's just that he's real abrasive and everything."

"I can understand why," said Punkin. "Mrs. Carson's strange. It's like she's two people. One's really nice and the other's really mean." She looked thoughtful. "I wonder if it's some kind of illness."

Emily's mouth quirked at this. "Well, Mrs. Carson does take antidepressants."

Bethany's eyes widened over her cup of blood. *"Mmm. That says a lot."*

"What's an antidepressant?" said Punkin, looking fearful.

"It's a type of drug," answered Bethany. "Don't worry about it, darling. We'll watch out for you. Right, Harriet?"

"Urmf," said Harriet, still eating. Theo looked at her strangely.

"Never mind her," said Frankie. "She's always like that when she's eating. Not a care in the world. Right, Harriet?"

"Oovfl glup."

"Well, I have some good news," said Bethany. "I was invited

to a party that's supposed to happen in two weeks or so. Some sort of annual thing."

Emily looked up. "Not Jessica Hardin-St. James's party?"

"The one she throws every year?" said Theo. "The one that *college boys* get invited to?"

"I don't know about any college boys, but I think that's the one. Do you know her?"

The other two stared at her, impressed. Finally Bethany said, *"What?"*

"You got invited to one of the *biggest* parties at Clearwater," said Emily breathlessly. "Jessica's parties are the stuff of *legend. Everyone* talks about them."

"That sounds nice," said Punkin. "Did you ever go?"

There was silence. "Well... no," said Theo. "We weren't ever invited."

"Well, then they're not all that great, then," said Bethany. "Anyway, we're all going. I was told that I could invite friends, and I'm asking all of you to go with me."

Emily looked shocked. "Wow! Really?"

"Really," said Bethany, smiling.

"I don't know if we should go, Emily," said Theo. "I mean, we're not exactly their sort of people." She looked downcast. "We're not really high in the social chain."

The monsters at the table all digested this (except for Harriet, who was busy digesting food). Then Frankie said, "Why not?"

"Well, Jessica's like one of the most popular girls in the school."

There was a derisive snort from Bethany. *"How?"*

"What do you mean, how?"

"Because if we're talking about the same person, the Jessica I met was a rude, smart-mouthed, despicable little brat who thinks she rules the roost."

"Mmm," said Frankie, grinning. "Wonder if *we* know someone who acts like that."

"*I* don't think I rule the roost, darling," retorted Bethany. "I *know* I do. But there was this nice girl named Stephanie in that group, and she treats her like *dirt.* She treats her other friends like dirt, too, but they seem too stupid to know better. How does someone who behaves like that become popular?"

Theo's response was a despondent one-armed shrug. "Jessica... well, Jessica's real rich and gets whatever she wants and her parents let her do whatever she wants, and that's why everyone wants to be friends with her," she said. "She was the first girl in our class to get a car. Her parents have a lot of money."

"So do I," said Bethany. "Vampires always have money."

"Really?" said Emily.

"Of course. You hang about a few centuries and it tends to accumulate, mainly because you get bored with spending it," said Bethany.

"Hey, I have a question," said Theo. "If you're a vampire, how are you walking around in the daytime?"

"Yeah, how?" echoed Emily.

Bethany set down her cup, and touched the gemstone at her neck. "This," she said. "It's the Eye of Azrael, an old relic among vampires. Any vampire who wears it can walk around in the sunlight." She leaned forward so that they could see the stone.

Emily started. "I--I think I saw an eye open in there."

"That's cool," said Theo. "Why don't all vampires have them?"

"Because we've never known if it works, or if it will *keep* working." Bethany leaned back and sipped her blood. "Also, it could be said that not *all* vampires need to have one."

Theo considered this, and shuddered. "No, probably not."

Emily had a thoughtful look. "That's pretty brave of you."

Bethany shrugged. "So far, so good. Anyway, I think we should all go to this party of Jessica's when it happens. I don't see why you shouldn't come with us."

"But we're--we're--" Theo stammered.

"We're nerds," said Emily. She sighed. "They don't like us because we're not like them. We don't have money and expensive clothes and boys following us around all the time."

This argument withered underneath Bethany's glare. "You're not like *us*, either," she said. "But *we* like you all right." The glare softened a bit. "After all, you Invited me in when nobody else could

85

or would. And you both seem like smart young girls, despite a rather low self-esteem."

"Young?" queried Theo. "Oh, I get it. Vampire." She looked curiously at Bethany. "Um, how old *are* you exactly?"

Bethany raised an eyebrow at Theo, and said with just a hint of acid in her voice, "Two hundred and thirty."

There were soft snickers from Frankie and Punkin. Harriet was oblivious to everything but her food.

"Two hundred and thirty-five," said Bethany. The acidic tone increased a notch.

Snicker, snicker.

"Oh, all *right*, you two," snarled Bethany sourly. "I am *officially* two hundred and fifty-five years dead. And if you ask me to buy you some beer I'll *brain* you." She took a long swig of her blood, ignoring the smiles of the others.

Theo thought about this, and blurted out, "You don't look a day over a hundred."

This brought a surprised and somewhat amused stare from every monster at the table except Harriet. Bethany smiled admiringly at Theo. "You know, for someone with no self-confidence, you do have a bit of cheek about you. But like I said, there's nothing wrong with either of you."

"You're friendly," said Frankie.

"You seem real nice," said Punkin, shrugging. "You been nicer to us than any of the other kids so far."

"Mmph fggl gllg," said a voice at the other end of the table. There was a soft burp.

"I think that translates to what they said," said Bethany. She downed the rest of her blood. "Anyway, we have no problem being friends with you, even if they do. So we're all going. I'll find out more details and fill you in."

"But--" protested Theo.

"But *nothing*," said Frankie. "Bethany's right. We should all go. And you can go with us."

Emily was touched. She had a grateful smile. "Wow. Thanks."

Theo looked thoughtful. Then she appeared to reach a

decision, and nodded, grinning. "Okay," she said. *"Okay. Sure."*

"All right!" said Harriet, who had finally finished eating. "Um, what are we doing?"

"Going to a party in two weeks," said Punkin brightly.

"Cool," said Harriet. "That's all for that, then."

She gathered up her trays. Theo stared at Harriet as she headed toward the lunchline to deposit her stack of trays. "Life must be very *simple* for werewolves," she said thoughtfully.

"Only when it's not full moon," said Frankie, picking up her tray. The others followed suit as the bell rang, dismissing the students to afternoon classes.

Emily turned to Theo, grinning. "See? I *told* you they were cool. See you later." She picked up her tray and left the cafeteria with the others.

Theo wondered about the discussion as she went back to the lunchline to drop off her tray. She saw that the MonsterGrrls didn't seem to understand or care about the accepted order of things at Clearwater, and it bothered her. But at the same time, she had the unnerving feeling that Bethany was right. She and Emily *were* better than Jessica and her friends. *Maybe this year people will see that,* she thought.

"Hey! Hey you!"

She turned around, and was stunned to find Heather Langley standing there, talking to her. She was on a different lunch schedule from Theo, and had just come into the cafeteria. "Is it true?"

Theo stared at her. "What's true?"

"Oh, wow, it's *terrible!*" said Heather. "Like, we just heard that some girl tried to *electrocute* herself in the cafeteria, right in front of Mr. Herschel and everybody! Can you believe it?" She noticed Theo's expression. "Do you know anything about it? I mean, people like that are *sick* and should get some help or something."

Theo started to say, that's not true, Frankie's not a sick person. Unfortunately, she couldn't make her lips form those words. "Nope," she said. "I don't know anything about that." She felt terrible for saying it. "I just got here myself," she muttered.

"Oh," said Heather. There was distinct disinterest in her voice, and Theo felt small. "Well, whatever, then. See you around."

She wandered off.

Theo stared after her as she walked away to rejoin her friends. She saw Jessica and Tiffany chattering with her as they went into the lunch line. She felt, as usual, a bit stupid, and very sad that she wasn't *popular* like they were.

But then, if I were popular like they were...well, I wouldn't be all those things the MonsterGrrls said I was. I mean, Heather didn't even care if someone got hurt or not. All she cared about was the latest gossip.

Then her face settled into an expression of grim determination. The Grrls *were* right. She *was* better than that, and she was going to start acting like it. Or at least a lot better than she'd just acted.

She left for class.

The first few weeks progressed without incident. The black bus arrived daily and on time, depositing the MonsterGrrls at the school, and though it was still frightening, the faculty and students eventually got used to it. However, no one dared to approach Mr. Sabbat, the Grrls' bus driver. News like Mr. Sabbat's general appearance and the incident of the spider travels fast, and many students still remembered the fearsome sight of the gaunt, shadowy figure from the first day of school. Mr. Sabbat himself paid little attention to anyone at Clearwater. He was a boogeyman (as Frankie explained to Emily one day) and did not like the sunlight, and his main concerns were dropping off the Grrls and getting the bus door, with its darkened windows, shut as fast as possible so that the thick cloud of fog would envelop the bus again.

The Grrls met Emily and Theo for lunch daily, with Frankie sometimes being a little late from performing her recharging duties in the bathroom, as per Herschel's request, and they met together in the courtyard during daily break time. There were still occasional stares when they trooped out of the lunchline doing Food Detail (as Emily and Theo came to call it) for Harriet, but neither of them minded. Theo had told Emily about the incident with Heather, and they had subsequently committed themselves to being friends with the Grrls.

Mr. Herschel, who had formerly tended to be in the office a

lot, was now often seen in the hall during change of classes, and a few teachers who were slow about getting to their duty stations got an imperiously whispered reprimand from him. Emily and Theo observed that while Herschel seemed unduly stressed out, he also seemed more *present* than before, and much more on top of things. He was quicker to move than usual, possibly because he was desperately trying to avoid Harriet, who always had her usual toothy smile and a hearty "*Hi*, Mr. Herschel!" for him whenever she saw him.

Female students got used to seeing Bethany being tended by Punkin in the girls' bathroom, and noticing the reflection in the mirror, where Punkin appeared to be combing the air. Since Bethany was unable to reflect in mirrors, Punkin often had to perform the services of a mirror, checking Bethany's hair and occasionally applying lipstick and mascara. Bethany preferred that Punkin do this; since Frankie did not use makeup she didn't know how to apply it properly, and Harriet not only eschewed makeup in general but had too broad a sense of humor to be allowed to tend Bethany. When Punkin was not able to Theo did it, since Emily was not really tall enough.

"What do you think they do at night?" asked Theo. She was over at Emily's house one evening doing homework, and talk had turned to the subject of the Grrls, as it usually did.

Emily put down her science textbook. Mrs. Parkinson had hinted about a pop quiz on the periodic table, and Emily was making sure she was prepared. "I don't know," she said. "I mean, they're monsters. What do monsters do at night?"

Theo considered this. "Roam around town. Drink blood. Eat people. Things like that."

"Oh, come on!" said Emily. "Frankie's nice. She wouldn't do anything like that. And Bethany drinks *bottled* blood." She looked thoughtful. "Though I don't know where she gets it or anything."

"I know," said Theo, putting down her book. "See, that's the thing. They're not like I thought they would be. They're real nice all the time, but I keep thinking, they're *monsters*. And then I feel bad, because it's like I'm *judging* them. It's weird."

Emily stared out the window. The moon was high in the sky, and was heading into first quarter. Theo had been right; she often found herself doing the same thing. "Maybe they're different when they're in Morlock Heights," she said.

"That's where they live?"

"Yeah. I guess it's like monster land, or something. I've never heard of it. Probably they're doing homework just like us."

"Yeah," said Theo. "Or maybe they're *not* doing homework, and they're out at some freaky monster party or something." She looked sad. "I kinda wish *we* could have a party with them."

"Well, I don't think Frankie would. She has her homework every day, and sometimes she does *extra*. And none of them act like the rebellious type."

"There's Bethany," said Theo.

"I don't think so," said Emily. "She's nice to us like the rest of them are. And she said they'd take us to Jessica's party. That's something to look forward to."

"It depends on whether Jessica has it or not," said Theo. "I overheard in the hall today that her parents are having trouble getting a flight for their vacation, so she's had to put it off. She was really upset about it."

Emily put her head on one side. "Bethany didn't mention that today. Do you remember her saying anything about it?"

Theo looked at Emily. "No."

The two stared at each other, then out the window into the dark night. They sighed together, and bent over their homework.

Five: Strangeness

The next morning, Emily and Theo found the Grrls in the courtyard, seated around a table covered in books and papers. Frankie was quoting off the elements of the periodic table, as Bethany, her sunglasses perched down her nose, prompted her, using Frankie's science book. Harriet and Punkin seemed to be furiously copying homework, and Punkin was writing so hard that the top of her hat quivered. Emily and Theo looked at each other, and approached the table. Both were wondering if their suspicions about the Grrls' nocturnal activities were true.

"What's up, guys?" asked Theo, trying to sound light.

"Oh, just studying before that pop quiz we're supposed to have in Science class," said Frankie. "Did you study, Emily? I spent three hours going over this stuff last night."

Emily gulped. She and Theo had worked together for only an hour, then called it a night. "Um, yeah."

"Cool," said Frankie. Emily noticed that she wore a pair of lightning-bolt-shaped earrings. "Those earrings are neat, Frankie," she said. "When did you get those?"

"Thanks, Emily," smiled Frankie. "I got them yesterday. I had to pierce my ears myself, though, so my lobes are a tiny bit sore."

Theo gaped at her. "You--you did that *yourself?*"

"Yeah, with a knitting needle," said Frankie. Noticing the girls' horrified expressions, she added, "Sorry, but my dad would have been shirty about using one of his hypodermics, and that's the only other thing that would break my skin. I must have broken about ten sewing needles before I thought of using it." She smiled. "I still ended up bending it, anyway."

"D-did you bleed much?" quavered Theo.

"Nope," said Frankie. "My blood's a special mix. See, Dad had developed this special coagulant--"

"*Can* we get on?" asked Bethany, a bit peevishly. "Not to be rude, but it's only five minutes before homeroom."

"Oh, sure. Um, boron, carbon, nitrogen, oxygen, flourine, neon, mag... mag..."

"Mag-*nesium*..."

"Magnesium! Darn! I *always* miss that one!"

Bethany clucked her tongue. "Good study habits always pay off, darling."

"Oh, yeah?" said Frankie snidely. "What about all that algebra homework Mr. Glass gave you yesterday?"

Bethany solemnly produced three pages of figures. Frankie, surprised, took them and examined them. "Oh. Well. I guess you know what you're doing, then." She returned the pages to Bethany. As she took them, Theo heard her hiss, under her breath, *"Simple."*

"What's up with you and Harriet, Punkin?" asked Emily.

"I had *Coven meetin'* last night," muttered Punkin. She was nervous; her usually soft accent had taken on a slight twang. "My *hateful* ol' cousin Bevadelia wants me to start reportin' what I'm doin' at school to the Coven once a week, so they won't be worried about my Power gettin' out of hand. So I didn't get all my homework done." She sighed. "Stuart's lettin' me copy his homework."

Theo smirked. "How much did he charge you?"

"He didn't charge me nothin'. He's probly scared of me 'cause I'm a witch." She huffed. *"Everbody's* scared of me 'cause I'm a witch. Even *other* witches."

"Well, *we're* not," said Frankie.

"What happened to you, Harriet?" asked Theo.

"Oh. Um." Harriet looked embarrassed. "Well... I'm thinking about trying out for basketball, and my little brother had one, so we went out and started playing with it, and we had such a good time that... well, I forgot." She looked sheepish. "But it was just this one History essay thing. I had everything else done in class."

Punkin flung down her pen. *"There.* I wish we'd get to doin' *somethin'* in Mrs. Carson's class other than these dumb ol' worksheets, like maybe growin' *flowers* or somethin'.."

There was a sudden inrush of air, and a rumbling sound. Everyone looked up. The table was surrounded by a thick, densely growing ring of daisies and buttercups. The group stared at the flowers, then stared at Punkin.

"Oh, *durn*," said Punkin, hanging her head. "I'm sorry."

"No, actually it's very nice," said Bethany. "This courtyard could use a little color."

"Smells better, too," added Harriet.

"Well, at least it's simple for you guys, since you're new," said Emily. "You can copy each other's homework, since you all have classes together."

"Huh?" said Harriet. The Grrls all stared at Emily and Theo.

"None of us have any classes together, Emily," said Frankie. "We don't see each other until lunch and break and after school, unless it's in the hall."

Theo looked puzzled. "But new students, or transfer students, *always* get scheduled together," she said. "Even if their homerooms are different. That's been going on since forever."

The Grrls stared at each other. "Wow," said Harriet, "what's *that* about?"

The discussion was interrupted by the bell for homeroom. Emily's brow furrowed in thought. "Everybody bring your class schedules to lunch. I want to see them."

At lunch, a comparison of schedules showed that none of the Grrls had classes together at all. In fact, there seemed to have been a concerted effort to keep them as far apart on the school campus as possible. There was some discussion about this.

"It's all part of Mr. Herschel's Plan For A Better Education," said Emily around a mouthful of hamburger. She chewed and swallowed. "It *always* works that way. He approves the final schedules every year, and he always changes them around two or three times, and everything always gets messed up."

"Well, I don't know," said Frankie, sipping her chocolate milk. "Dr. Adams told us that there would be some opposition to us."

"Opposition?" asked Theo.

"You know," said Bethany. She hooked her hands into claws and made a face. "*Monsters. OOOOooo.* Big spooky. Call in the four kids and the dog from the cartoon show."

"What cartoon show?"

"The one you told us about. Scooby-Doobie or something."

"Yeah!" said Harriet, who stopped eating momentarily to respond to this. "I saw that when Dr. Adams took me shopping for *high-gene* stuff. It was like that game Clue, except that instead of Colonel Mustard in the parlor with the rope, it was Mr. Henderson in the carnival with the robot thing."

"Thank you, Sherlock," quipped Bethany. "Anyway, there's bound to be someone who doesn't want their kids going to school with monsters. I mean, I even had a lock on my locker the first day."

"I did, too," said Frankie.

Punkin stared at both of them. "You, too?"

Emily looked from one to the other. "Did you have a lock on your locker, Harriet?"

"Mmm-hmm," said Harriet. She swallowed her mouthful of food. "Tore it off."

Everyone looked at each other. There were similar unpleasant thoughts going through everyone's head. "Well," said Emily, "sometimes a lock gets left on a locker, that's all. It's probably not anything we should worry about."

"Yeah, but four locks on four lockers, all assigned to the *new* students?" said Frankie. "That's a little too close for coincidence."

"And whoever put them there," said Bethany darkly, "knew how to Uninvite a vampire."

The Grrls all traded a furtive look. Emily got the distinct feeling that all of them knew something that they didn't want to talk or think about. She was worried for them, but she was also curious.

Harriet broke the moment. She raised an eyebrow and said, "It's a mystery. Maybe we should call in the four kids and the dog from Scooby-Doobie."

There was laughter from everyone as Bethany flung a spoon at Harriet, who ducked under the table. But Emily and Theo still wondered if the Grrls hadn't been hiding something.

Classes droned on as the students fell back into the order of school. Frankie and Emily enjoyed their Science class with Mrs. Parkinson, who proved to be a witty and wise teacher. Punkin dutifully completed worksheets in Mrs. Carson's class, and looked forward to the free time afterward when she could continue computer studies with Stuart. Harriet coached Theo in P.E., which caused Theo to gain some self-confidence, for Harriet was a much better coach than Coach Simpson, who drove the class through endless exercise drills and then let them play games on their own. Because of this, she discovered that she did have some athletic ability, and she began to get picked more often for teams.

Bethany enjoyed Literature class with Mr. Harrington, for she was an avid reader and often had several library books with her in addition to her textbook. The only bad spot for her was having to endure Jessica, Heather and Tiffany, who seemed to take up useful space and oxygen. For their part, Jessica and her clique seemed to accept Bethany as a best friend without trying to understand her. Though they often acknowledged an inherent strangeness in her, they still did not understand that she was a vampire, which Bethany supposed had to do with their continued attention to nothing except themselves. With the exception of Stephanie, the Clique hated Mr. Harrington, and made constant complaints about not getting the grades that they felt they deserved, or not understanding the lesson.

During one particularly virulent period of this Bethany said crossly, "The reason you don't get it is because you don't pay attention and you don't read the... stuff." She refrained, at the last minute, from using the word *material*.

This made them stare at her. "Jeez, mom," quipped Heather, "does this mean I can't go out this weekend?" The others laughed.

Bethany sighed to herself, and said, "Well, you *don't*."

"It's really weird that you read so much," said Jessica. "How come you read so much?"

"Yeah!" piped up Tiffany. "I mean, I've read *all* the Sweet Valley High books, but I don't read *nearly* as much as you do."

Bethany turned her best vampire stare on all of them, and said quietly, "It passes the time."

Something in the way she said this made them unusually quiet. The subject was never brought up again.

"*Why* do you put up with them?" Bethany asked Stephanie one day as they changed classes.

Stephanie smiled the slightly haggard smile that Bethany had seen her first day. "Jessica's mom and my mom were best friends and sorority sisters in college. I've known Jessica for as long as I can remember."

"Well, I'm sure glad *I* can't say that," snapped Bethany.

"You just have to get to know them, Bethany," said Stephanie. There was resignedness in her voice. "They're not all that bad, really."

Bethany put her head on one side. "You know, if there's something you ever want to talk about, you can always talk to me, you know."

Stephanie smiled. "Thank you, Bethany."

"Do you want to get together at the daily break?" The break was a ten-minute period between classes, just before lunch, when students were allowed to gather in the courtyard. It was something Herschel had instituted that supposedly made Clearwater progressive. "You could meet my friends."

"I can't," said Stephanie. "I'm meeting Jessica. Um... she needs help with notes for history class."

"So skip it."

"No, I really can't," said Stephanie. "Thanks anyway, Bethany. Maybe... maybe some other time."

Bethany stared after her as she walked away.

"I don't understand Stephanie," said Bethany when she was with the group at break later. "We seem to be friends, but she refuses to be away from that horrid Jessica and her little friends Tweedledum and Tweedledummer."

"It is curious," said Frankie. "She won't hang out without them at all?"

"No! And they treat her so terribly. It makes no sense to me. It's as though Jessica has her *mesmerized* or something."

Emily shrugged. "That's Jessica," she said. "She just has this weird control over her clique. They all do what she says. She's like a general, or something."

"They're so *stupid*," spat Bethany. "None of them like Mr. Harrington, and he's one of the best teachers here." She had a rather risqué smile. "Also, he's one of the *yummiest* men I've seen in at least seventy years."

"Yeah, Mr. Harrington's a hottie," said Theo. "I've got him at sixth period and I'm one of only four girls in the class, and he treats us like *ladies*. Wish *boys* were like that and not just men." She frowned. "Wish I was older."

Bethany glared at her.

"Okay, maybe not," backpedaled Theo.

"Mr. Harrington's really *dreamy*," sighed Emily. "He should have been here sooner."

"Sooner?" asked Harriet.

"Yeah. Last year we had Mrs. Gibson, and she was horrible. She knew her subject, but she was *really* mean, and she would snap at you if you made a mistake." Emily sighed again. "This is Mr. Harrington's first year here. He's a really great teacher."

"Jessica doesn't seem to think so," said Bethany. She suddenly looked thoughtful. "First year?"

"Yes." Emily put her head on one side, observing Bethany. "Did he teach at Graf Orlok?"

"Oh, no," said Bethany. "Human teachers wouldn't last five minutes at Graf Orlok." She frowned. "Unless they were..." Her voice trailed off.

"Unless they were what?"

"Nothing," said Bethany quickly. "Anyway... have you ever gotten the feeling you know someone, even though they're a stranger?"

"Yeah."

"Well, I've repeatedly felt that I *know* Mr. Harrington from somewhere," she said, looking at Frankie. Emily noticed that something was passing between them. "Do you know what I'm talking about?"

"Good afternoon, girls," said a voice behind them. Emily looked up and saw Mr. Harrington. Her mouth fell open.

"Oh, *hi!*" she said. "We were just--" She caught herself at the last minute. "We were just discussing the Lit lesson." Out of the corner of her eye, she saw Frankie looking fixedly at Mr. Harrington.

"Really," said Mr. Harrington. His amused tone indicated that he didn't believe that for a minute. "I'm sure Bethany must have led that discussion in her usual excellent manner. She's one of my better students." Bethany contrived to look humble and did it very badly.

Theo cleared her throat loudly.

"I did say *one* of," smiled Mr. Harrington. Theo beamed. "And how are the rest of you girls doing?"

"Oh, we're great," smiled Theo. "You're not going to give us a pop quiz tomorrow, are you?"

"If I could tell you that it wouldn't be a pop quiz," said Mr. Harrington, giving her a comically stern look. "*Read* the material and you'll be prepared." He looked at Harriet. "I don't believe I have you in my classes, Miss..."

"I'm Harriet," said Harriet, grinning. "No, sir, I'm not. I'm in Mr. Greeley's English class. It's nice to meet you, though." She put her head on one side. "People said you were a dreamy yummy hottie and they were right."

Theo and Emily immediately went red-faced. Bethany, unable to truly blush, seemed instead to turn paler than usual. Frankie and Punkin looked away, grinning.

Mr. Harrington's mouth quirked. "Thank you for the compliment, Harriet," he said. "Obviously you're very observant, and you listen well. I'm sure Mr. Greeley appreciates those qualities." He nodded to the others. "Must go. See you in class, ladies." He walked away, whistling.

Emily, Theo and Bethany all released the breath they'd been holding, and turned outraged glares on the giggling Harriet. "*Get her*," hissed Bethany through clenched teeth.

The three of them chased the werewolf across the courtyard as Punkin turned to Frankie with a serious expression. "I see what Bethany was talkin' about," she said. "What do you think?"

Frankie frowned. "I don't know. He could be. But *anyone* could be a member of the Shadow League." She shrugged. "I don't think Mr. Harrington *is* one of them, personally. He's too nice."

"Yeah," said Punkin. "You know, they were right. He *is* awful cute."

They watched the scuffle taking place at the other end of the courtyard, which gave way to the four collapsing into laughter. Punkin stared at her shoes. "I feel bad not tellin' Emily and Theo about the Shadow League. It probly ain't no different from the stories humans tell their young'uns about monsters."

"I know," said Frankie. "I do too. But it's better if we don't." She sighed as the bell rang for classes. "At least, not right now."

At dismissal time that evening, Emily and Theo waited with the Grrls for their bus.

"Where's Morlock Heights, exactly?" asked Theo. "I've never heard of that neighborhood."

"It's not exactly a neighborhood," said Frankie. "It's... kind of like a special place for monsters." She thought a moment. "What was that place we learned about in History today? Where the Pilgrims stayed?"

"Plymouth Rock?" asked Emily.

Frankie shook her head. "No, no. It was--oh, yeah. *Settlement.* Morlock Heights is a settlement for monsters."

"You mean like a gated community?" said Emily. "My mom's best friend lives out in California, and she's in one of those. It's like only people who live there can get in, and everybody else is a guest."

"Hmm," mused Frankie. "Yeah. That's pretty good, Emily. Yeah, we live in a gated community for monsters." Emily looked pleased.

"Well, where is it?" asked Theo.

"It's--well, it's not exactly close," said Frankie. "It's sort of *outside* Clearwater. You have to ride our bus to be able to go in."

Theo and Emily looked at each other. Both tried to picture themselves riding in the same bus with Mr. Sabbat. "Well, I guess that rules out any sleepovers at your house," said Theo dryly.

"You know, maybe some time you could all come over to my house," said Emily to Frankie. "We could have a sleep-over here or something."

"That'd be nice," said Bethany. "But not anytime soon."

"Why not?" asked Theo.

There was a general uncomfortable look. "Well," said Frankie slowly, "there's a curfew in Morlock Heights right now."

"A curfew?"

"Yeah. There's been some... weird things happening lately."

Theo stared at Frankie. She said, "You guys are *monsters,* and you live with *other* monsters. Define *weird.*"

"It's hard to explain," said Frankie, looking embarrassed. "Look, I can't come over right now. None of us can. No one who lives in Morlock Heights can go out after dark."

The bus roared up then. "Well," said Frankie, "see you tomorrow, OK?"

Emily and Theo watched as the girls got on. They noticed the sad looks on the faces of the Grrls as they boarded the bus. As the door closed and the fog enveloped the bus, they saw Punkin wave to them. Her eyes were filled with tears.

"So what do you think that was all about this afternoon?"

They had walked to Theo's house and were in her comfortably messy room doing homework, or at least they had been. They'd decided a break was in order and were now lounging on the perenially unmade bed with Oreos and milk.

"I don't know," said Emily. "You don't think they're just pretending to like us, do you?"

Theo considered this. "Nope," she said. "I mean, think about it. None of them pretend anything. It's almost like they don't know *how.*" She swigged milk. "And if *Bethany* didn't like us she *sure* wouldn't hang out with us. You've heard what she said about Jessica, and she tried to get Stephanie to come hang with *us* instead of *them.* She really hates Jessica, and from what she said I think Stephanie does too."

"But they *know* something we don't, Theo. There was that thing about Mr. Harrington, and Bethany thinking she knew him. And there were the locks on their lockers."

"Yeah, but that doesn't have to do with *us,* Emily."

"Well, I don't understand it. They're our best friends at school, but we don't know much about them *beyond* school."

Theo stared thoughtfully at the *Attack Of The Lurchin' Dead* poster on her wall. Her mother managed the movie theater in town and had gotten it for her; it was Theo's favorite horror movie. She said, "Maybe we're not supposed to."

"What do you mean?" Emily asked curiously.

"Well, Morlock Heights is like a gated community for monsters, right? Like your mom's friend lives in."

"Uh-huh."

"Okay. So maybe if everybody knew where it was and could get in, maybe there wouldn't be any monsters anymore. Maybe they're afraid people would hurt them or kill them or something."

"Isn't it usually the other way around?" asked Emily. Theo was considered the monster expert between them since she'd seen more horror movies than Emily, but she couldn't imagine the Grrls being hurt or killed by humans. Especially *Bethany*. "You know, them... um, hurting or killing humans?"

"Not with the Grrls," said Theo, munching an Oreo. "They're too nice. I mean, Bethany drinks blood and snaps a lot, and sometimes Harriet eats raw meat for lunch, and Punkin acts like the girl in *Carrie* or something, and Frankie has to do that charging thing. But they're all really nice to us."

"But they won't come to our houses, Theo. They won't stay after dark."

"Well, do you want to go to Morlock Heights? Where the monsters are?"

Emily swallowed. "N-no."

"Well, okay, then. Maybe it's the same way with them." She smiled. "Boy, what could *monsters* be scared of that they'd have a curfew?"

There followed a few moments of reflection upon this. Sunset was beginning, and shadows were lengthening in the room. After a moment Emily said, "Maybe I should get home before it gets dark."

"Um..." Theo reached into the bedside table's drawer for a flashlight. "I'll walk you."

Theo got back home just before dark. She slammed the door and leaned against it, panting. She had run most of the way back.

She locked the door, and checked the other doors and windows in the house, to make sure they were locked. Her mom was working late at the theater and she was alone in the house, so it made sense to double-check everything. She looked out the living room windows at the darkened street.

Somewhere out there were the monsters. And they lived in shadows, she knew, because that was how monsters had always lived. People couldn't see what was waiting for them in the dark, which was better if you were a monster. But she remembered Punkin's behavior on the bus that afternoon, and she believed that they also lived there because they were *afraid*.

What could scare a monster?

The phone rang. She jumped, and after gathering herself, went to answer it. "Hello?"

The phone crackled briefly. "Hi! Can I speak to Theo, please?"

Theo recognized the voice. "Is this *Harriet?*"

"Yeah! Hi! Um, I was wondering if you'd come with me tomorrow to tryouts after school. There was a sign thing up today that said they're having basketball tryouts."

"Uh, yeah. Sure. Uh, how are you calling me? Do they have phones in Morlock Heights?"

"Mordecai's got a cell phone thing. He's letting me use it. Thanks a lot for going with me." The voice sounded guilty. "Look, you know you guys are our friends, right?"

"Well, yeah."

"Well, things are really strange in Morlock Heights right now, because we're all going to the human school. That's why there's this curfew and everything." There was a pause. "You're not mad at us or anything?"

"What? No, we're not mad. We're just curious, is all."

The voice sounded resigned, and a little sad. "Well... we just can't tell you everything right now. But we will soon." There was another pause. "I'll see you tomorrow."

"Sure." Theo suddenly had a thought. "Hey, how can you go to tryouts tomorrow if you have a curfew--"

But Harriet had already hung up. Theo stared at the silent phone in her hand.

Six: Tryouts

Damon checked out the potential team members. There weren't a lot of new people trying out. Most of them were people from last year. All the girls had come back, but Coach Edmund had told him how to deal with that, and as team manager, he was prepared to follow orders.

Coach Edmund was an excitable man, and he had not reacted well to the budget cuts, or to Herschel's suggestion of a coed team. A coed team, he felt, would foster loss of *discipline.* And Coach Edmund had a traditionalist streak that rivaled the most dedicated Mad Scientist or the most staid Vampyre,[4] and he also felt that none of the administration knew *jack* about basketball. So he had quietly discouraged the idea of any girls trying out for the new team.

And so Damon went around planting stories about how Edmund planned to run the new coed team until they dropped, how he planned to drill incessantly because he was determined to have a winning season, how there would be *no* water breaks until after the *first* hour of practice, and so on. This last had been a bit farfetched, but he'd been surprised at how many bought it.

He watched the players moving in a ring, shooting baskets.

Of *course* Coach Edmund would *have* to have some *mamacitas* on the team, just to keep the numbers up and satisfy Herschel. But that didn't mean they'd get to play.

He smiled to himself, and made a note on the clipboard. He became aware that someone was walking up.

"'Scuse us," said a female voice. "Hi, Damon."

Damon glanced up briefly. It was Theo MacKenzie, whom he vaguely remembered seeing in one of his classes. Being a typical teenage male meant that Damon spent time in classes not paying attention to much except girls, cars, girls, sports, girls, new basketball sneakers, and girls. Theo qualified as a girl, and while he thought

---

4   Even the ones who spelled their names with *umlauts* attached.

she was relatively cute, she hadn't made his short list of hotties. He hadn't known she was interested in basketball. Might have to take a second look.

"What up, Theo," he said easily. He smiled and made another note on his clipboard. "Didn't know you were gonna try out for the team."

"I'm not," said Theo, pointing. "Uh, she is."

"Hi there!" said Harriet, bouncing up.

Damon was so surprised that he backed up and tripped over his own feet. His clipboard bounced out of his hands and fell to the floor. He stared at Harriet, who was standing over him, and gulped.

The girl (*girl?*) was like something out of those old lame horror movies his little brother liked to watch. *Wolf Man*, yeah. That was it. This must be his... daughter. She was *grinning*. Damon saw the teeth, and sweat broke out on his forehead, even though it wasn't that warm in the gym.

"You dropped your clipboard," said Harriet, recovering it. She took his hand and pulled him to his feet, and Damon felt a muscle pull in his shoulder. She had some... *furry*...arms on her, that was true. And what a *grip!*

He brushed himself off and took his clipboard. "Uh, hey," he said. "Hey." He noted the fur on her hands and the clawlike nails, and swallowed. "Uh, you trying out for the team?"

"Oh, yeah!" said Harriet. "I'm Harriet." She pumped his arm vigorously, and Damon again experienced the grip. He looked at Theo, who smiled and shrugged.

"I saw your sign thingy in the hall," continued Harriet, "and I thought I might like to try this. What's basketball?"

Both humans stared. "You've never played?" Theo said.

"*Never?*" asked Damon, shaking the feeling back into his arm.

"Nope," said Harriet cheerfully. "But I can learn. What do I do?"

Damon relaxed. This was going to be fun. "Yo," he called to one of the players, "Toss me a ball, dawg." The player complied.

"Now," said Damon, smiling, "this is a basketball." He held it up in front of Harriet. Theo saw the look in Damon's eye, but couldn't bring herself to say anything.

"Okay," said Harriet.

"Now," said Damon, "what you gotta do is take it, and throw it through that hoop right there." He pointed to the basketball goal at the far end of the court. "Understand?"

"Oh, yeah," said Harriet. "I can do that." Theo winced at this.

She took the ball from Damon, eyed the hoop, and tossed. The ball *swooshed* through the net. Theo stared.

Damon's mouth fell open. "You... you did it."

"Yeah!"

He stared at the net. "Except... that you did it from center court." He rubbed his eyes and looked down at the floor. "Uh, yeah. Center court."

"Where we're standing," said Theo, smiling maliciously.

"Yeah," said Harriet, putting her head on one side. "Was that wrong?"

"No!" said Damon. "That was good. Uh, that was... *real* good. First time... and everything." He swallowed. "Uh, let me go get the ball." He walked shakily down the court.

Harriet grinned at Theo. "This is fun."

Theo, noting Damon's discomfort, was grinning herself. "Yeah, it is."

Damon returned with the ball, and handed it to Harriet. "Now, you think you can do that again?" He smiled.

"Sure," said Harriet, eyeing the hoop, and tossed.

Swoosh.

Damon stared at the ball bouncing beneath the net. He stared at Harriet, who smiled innocently. "I did it again," she said. "How was that?"

Damon looked past Harriet to Theo, who smirked. He felt heat rise in his face. "Okay. I'm gonna go get the ball, and I want you to do it again. In fact," he said, looking hard at Theo, "I *bet* you can't do it again."

He retrieved the ball, and this time he tossed it from his position beside the goal to Harriet, who caught it easily, and threw it back toward the net.

Swoosh.

Parts of Damon's brain stood behind other parts of Damon's

brain and shouted at them. *"Okay,"* he said, trying to ignore the desperation in his voice, *"this* time I'm gonna have you try it from the *end* of the court, instead of the center." He retrieved the ball, and walked to the other end of the court, where the players were. Harriet and Theo followed.

"Okay," said Damon loudly. The other players turned to stare at them, saw Harriet and continued staring. Harriet smiled and waved to them.

"Now," said Damon, looking furtively at the watching group, "I'm gonna have you, *who have never played basketball before,"* he said, enunciating each word clearly, "take this ball, and throw it into that net." He pointed to the opposite end of the court. "That one. *Right down there."* The group of players stared.

"Oh," said Harriet. She took the ball and squinted, eyeing the net. "That might be a little harder."

Damon smiled. "Yeah. Might be." *This'll do it. Even* Jordan *couldn't pull this off,* he thought to himself.

Harriet tossed.

Swoosh. Thump-thump-thump. Silence fell over the group.

"Guess it wasn't," said Harriet. "Is this all you have to do in basketball? It's kinda fun, but I thought there was more going on than this." She waved at the group. "I mean, you've got all these people here and I--"

"Okay!!" shouted Damon. "Okay." His voice became calm, but there was still a discernible quaver. Coach Edmund would have to deal with this, and even then there seemed *no* way they could keep this... *girl* off the court. "Let--let me go get the coach."

The group waited. Once in a while raised voices came from the direction of Coach Edmund's office, just off the gym. Then a door banged back, and Coach Edmund, followed by Damon, stalked onto the court.

He was a large, florid man with a massive build that was only slightly fat. He strode over to Harriet and glared at her. Harriet smiled. The fact that Coach Edmund did not smile back did nothing to dissuade Harriet. Theo eyed Coach Edmund, who did not look like he was in a good mood, and debated whether to drag Harriet off the court.

Coach Edmund finally broke the silence. "Damon tells me that you made four shots in a row, three of them from center court and one from the opposing team's goal. He also says that you have never played basketball before."

"That's right, sir," said Harriet, still grinning.

"So you want to be on the team."

"Yes, sir."

Coach Edmund smiled a tight smile. "And we should let you play even though you've never played before?"

Harriet's smile never changed, but Theo sensed that things were about to happen. "I can learn the game, can't I, sir? I pick up stuff pretty fast."

"Oh, *sure*," said Coach Edmund. "Anyone can *learn* the game. I'm sure *dogs* can learn the game." There was murmuring among the other players, who decided that this was low even for Coach.

Harriet's eyes were a deep, warm brown, with a strange golden quality about the whites. Now Theo saw a momentary glow flicker across them--something *predatory*. Her smile never wavered. "Gonna teach me?" Her voice had only the mildest hint of a challenge.

Coach's eyes narrowed to slits. Damon stepped forward, hands raised in a conciliatory motion. "Now hold up, Coach--"

"*Okay*, little... whatever-you-are," Coach said, between clenched teeth, "I guess I will." He motioned to the players. "On the court. *Now.*"

The players moved onto the court, splitting into groups of five and getting into position. "All right," said Coach. "What you're going to see here, uh..."

"I'm Harriet," said Harriet.

"Okay, Harriet. This is a basketball game. Watch *carefully.*" He tossed the ball to Damon. "You referee, *manager*," he said coldly. Damon gulped, and went to center court. Harriet squatted beside Coach and watched.

The ball went up, and the game started. Theo watched Harriet, who sat perfectly still. Her eyes never left the court. Theo was aware of an enormous, awesome sense of *focus*.

107

The ball flew into the net, and Coach blew his whistle. Everyone stopped.

"Okay, Harriet. Do you see the point guard?"

"Which one is that?"

Coach pointed angrily to one player, who instantly left the court. "Get in there and take his position. Since you can handle the ball so well, I'm going to see how you play in that position."

"Yes, *sir*," said Harriet. She grinned, and Theo felt a chill run down her spine. Most of the time Harriet's happy, friendly nature was so far removed from what Theo thought of as werewolfish behavior that it overshadowed her appearance, but now, even though she had the same grin, there was an added element of *hunting*.

Harriet bounced out onto the court. The ball handler on the sideline looked uncertain, then saw Harriet's look. He straightened himself.

The ball flew into play.

Theo watched Damon's face. While she would admit that Damon was cute in a sort of cocky way, she did not really like him; he was too jokey, too stuck on himself, and a bit unmannerly with girls. Now, as Harriet bounced and jumped around on the court, she saw shock, grudging admiration, and cold terror flicker across his face, and felt a warming sense of vindication.

Coach, on the other hand, had at first been quietly enraged that someone who claimed to know *jack* about basketball was playing on *his* court, but was slowly changing his mind. As the game progressed and Harriet sailed through play after play, common sense eventually kicked in. He saw the other players on Harriet's team, inspired by her natural prowess, slide into place like parts of a well-oiled machine. He saw visions of a championship season flickering in the distance as Harriet leaped and slammed the ball through the hoop.

He blew his whistle. The winded players stumbled off the court. Harriet sauntered up to Coach, smiling. "So, do I get to play?"

Coach pursed his lips. "You got some game, wolf girl," he said, glaring at Damon. "You should have told me when she made her *second* shot from center court," he growled.

Damon cringed. "Y-Yes, sir."

"Be here tomorrow, same time," said Coach to Harriet. "I've got to go through the rest of what I got here today. But I think you can play. The only thing is, you got to learn how the game works. Positions and everything."

"Damon can teach her," said Theo, with a wicked grin.

Coach, noticing Theo for the first time, smiled from the corner of his mouth. "Not a bad idea." He turned to the wide-eyed Damon. "This girl's education in the game is *your* responsibility, manager. Got that?"

Damon stared forlornly at Harriet, who grinned and said, "You're *cute.*"

Theo laughed all the way out of the gym. Harriet bopped alongside her, jumping up and down. "I'm gonna play on the *team!* Isn't it cool? Wait till I tell Frankie and the others!"

"How did you do it?" asked Theo. "You said you'd never played!"

"It wasn't that hard, really," said Harriet. "The team operates kind of like a pack, you know. It all felt pretty normal. Like I was running with Pop and the rest of the Clan on a hunt." She grinned. "Pop's gonna be so proud of me. I can't wait to tell him!" She bounced up and down excitedly.

"Yeah! And we'll all come see you at the games, and--" Theo paused. "Wait a minute. How are you going to play if Morlock Heights has a curfew?"

"Um--" Harriet looked uncomfortable. "Well, actually that's not the truth."

Theo eyed Harriet angrily. "So exactly what is the truth, Harriet?" She stared coldly at the embarrassed werewolf. "Me and Emily are beginning to wonder what the big secret is with you guys."

"What secret?"

"The one you're *keeping* from us. We'll be talking about stuff and suddenly you'll all have this look between you, like you *know* something. It makes us think you guys are just pretending to be friends with us."

Harriet's look of hurt was so profound that Theo felt

ashamed. "Why would we do something like that? We really like you guys. We wouldn't ever do that."

Theo frowned. She was a little mad at herself; Harriet had been so joyful about making the team, and she felt as though she'd spoiled it. "I'm sorry, Harriet," she said. "But it's not fair. Friends don't keep secrets from each other."

Harriet considered this. "Okay," she said, "This is the problem. There are monsterkind in Morlock Heights who don't want us to spend a lot of time with humans." She looked very embarrassed. "They're--they're afraid something will happen to us. Something bad."

Theo was unprepared for this. She had thought that someone would eventually say the same thing about the Grrls, but she'd never expected the monsters to do it first. "Why?"

"Because something happened before we came to school here." She shifted her feet. "Someone tried to get in."

"Get in? Why?"

Harriet shrugged. "I dunno. All I know is that they were bad people, and they tried to take something." She rubbed her arms nervously.

Theo had all kinds of questions, but she didn't think that Harriet could answer any of them. Harriet's behavior was very unusual, for her, and she felt that Harriet couldn't explain what was going on because she was *frightened*.

"Look," she said finally. "I'm sorry I got mad at you. But... well, you're the first people to accept me and Emily for what we are." She looked downcast. "We're not popular kids. And we think you guys are something really special. Really... *weird*, but special." She looked away, embarrassed.

"So are you," said Harriet softly. "To us, anyway." She looked thoughtful for a moment. "I meant the special part. You're our first human friends, you know."

They smiled at each other, and Theo gave Harriet a hug. "I'm sorry I spoiled the good news," she said.

"'S okay." Harriet looked sheepish. "I'm sorry you felt bad. I didn't mean it."

There was a loud rumbling. Theo looked up and saw a slim,

long-haired, bearded young man dressed in a black leather jacket, black jeans and engineer boots, standing next to a black Mustang waiting at the curb.

"That's Mordecai," said Harriet. "I gotta go." She looked uncertain. "Still friends?"

Theo, in spite of all her questions and discomfort, couldn't help smiling. "Yeah, still friends."

The two hugged again, and Harriet ran to the sidewalk to meet her brother. Mordecai looked directly at her, and Theo saw saw the kinship to Harriet. Mordecai was not a true werewolf, but the intense, burning gaze he gave to Theo definitely meant he had werewolf in him somewhere. His look seemed to mark her, and she felt cold.

She saw Harriet speak to him, and point at her. He looked at her again, and seemed to relax. He raised his hand and gave her a wave. She slowly waved back.

The door of the car opened by itself. For some reason, this did not surprise Theo at all. Harriet and Mordecai got in. The car gunned its engine and drove away.

Theo told Emily what had happened that evening. They agreed that they would not tell other people what Harriet had said, partly because they really had no idea what to tell. Neither of them could figure out what humans would want to steal from monsters. To them, it seemed that humans would stay as far away from Morlock Heights as they could. They both decided to wait and watch.

Later on, it seemed to Emily and Theo that, from the way things happened, both of them were really *destined* to be friends with the Grrls, because no one else they could think of would have been willing or able to do what they did. But they firmly agreed that the friendship between themselves and the Grrls didn't really gather steam, apart from seeming like any other typical school friendship, until the evening of Jessica's party.

SEVEN: PARTY OUT OF BOUNDS

Tiffany nervously approached Bethany at her locker.

She didn't like her. She had tried to, but Bethany *scared* her. Sometimes Tiffany would watch Bethany's eyes when they were in class, and she would see something scary there. Something *red.*

And Bethany was just so… *weird.* And *pale.* She really should go to a tanning booth or something. And she dressed, well, *kind* of stylish, but it was like she thought she was Dracula Girl.

She was about to tap Bethany's shoulder when she turned around, and Tiffany saw the *red* thing. She wanted to scream, but that wasn't *cool.* Instead she fought to keep her composure.

"Yes?" said Bethany.

"Um, Jessica told me to tell you that her party's this weekend, and to remind you to come."

Bethany took out a textbook and closed her locker. "Sure. I didn't know if you were still going to have it or not. None of you have said anything about it since the first day of school."

"Oh, yeah," said Tiffany, relaxing. "Jessica's parents just had problems, you know, getting a flight to Club Med and everything, so Jessica had to put it off, but it's definitely this weekend." She grinned excitedly. "And *all* the *cute* boys are coming, too. You've just *got* to be there, you know. *Everybody* always comes." She smirked. "Or *wants* to come."

Bethany sighed to herself. She felt sorry for Tiffany, who really *needed* something beyond Jessica and high school, but at the same time it seemed that any misfortune wished upon her was somehow deserved. She put on a polite smile and said, "Well, it sounds like fun. I'll be there."

"Oh, cool!"

"And so will my friends," said Bethany, walking away. "I'll be sure to tell them."

Tiffany remembered that she'd seen Bethany with a couple of little nerd girls. She didn't know their names, but privately she had referred to them as Four-eyes and Beanpole. And sometimes she'd seen Bethany hanging out with some other girls that were, like, *so* last Halloween. *Monster* girls. One of them had a lot of hair, and one of them had a bunch of *stitches* and looked like a zombie or something, and the one who wore the big hat was supposed to be a witch.

She wondered if Bethany would bring *them* to the party. Maybe she would. And then maybe Jessica and Heather and Stephanie would see how *weird* Bethany was, and dump her. *Finally.*

She went off to her next class with a rather nasty smile on her face.

The night of the party arrived. Emily and Theo waited outside Emily's house, by the mailbox. Fall was approaching, and the night was slightly breezy. Leaves had begun to fall.

"So they're meeting us here?" said Theo. She wore a denim jacket, girly T-shirt, baggy jeans and a baseball cap turned backwards on her head.

"Yeah," said Emily. "They'll meet us here and we'll walk up to Jessica's. It's just a few blocks." Emily, who was more conservative in dress than Theo, had worn a nice sweater, blouse and skirt.

"We're gonna *walk* to the coolest party of the year?" said Theo, a little disdainfully.

"Well, no one *said* anything about a car." Emily shrugged. "It'll be okay. I mean, we're actually getting to *go*, aren't we?"

Theo shrugged. "I guess so. I mean, some of the kids on her block'll be walking over, right?"

"Right. So it's okay if we walk."

They waited. Shadows seemed to deepen around them. The sidewalk was lit by streetlights, but between them were patches of darkness. Emily could not help thinking of night creatures.

She looked at the mailbox, and remembered the night when the raven had been there. She stared into the darkness at the end of the street. "Do you see them?" she whispered to Theo.

Theo strained to see into the gloom. "No," she replied, also whispering. She paused. "Why are we whispering?"

"Don't know," said a deep, hollow voice.

They jumped, and whirled around to see Frankie, Punkin and

Bethany standing behind them. Frankie grinned. *"Didn't know I could do this Voice, did you?"*

"Don't *do* that!" said Emily.

"Okay, okay," said Frankie. "Sorry. Are we ready?"

"Yeah," said Theo. "Where's Harriet?"

"Late as usual," sighed Bethany. "Harriet's been late to every party I've ever been to with her." She wore a blood-red velvet minidress and black leather boots that matched her small chainstrap purse. Around her throat was a black choker, with the Eye Of Azrael affixed to it. She crossed her arms and stared into the darkness at the other end of the street.

"I feel underdressed," said Emily, examining Bethany's dress.

No worries," said Bethany. "This is just a simple party frock."

"Simple?" queried Theo.

"Do you think we could leave our stuff on your front porch?" said Frankie. Emily saw that each Girl had her school backpack, and that Frankie was carrying her generator case.

"Oh, sure," said Emily. They started toward the porch.

"What was that?" said Theo.

They became aware of heavy breathing headed in their direction. Emily and Theo moved closer to Frankie. Something was *moving* through the shadows.

"What?" asked Frankie.

"Something's out there," breathed Emily. "And it's *big.*"

The bushes along the sidewalk rustled. A blur of hair and teeth leapt out at them.

"AAAAAAHHHHH!!!"

"Hi," said Harriet. She leaned over, panting. "Sorry I was late. We had kind of late practice this evening." She stared at the girls. "How come you guys are hanging on to Frankie like that?"

The two girls slowly let go of the amused Frankie. "We were... it was... we heard something," muttered Emily.

"Let's go," mumbled Theo.

After leaving the Girls' belongings on the porch, the group proceeded down the street, chatting as they walked along. Harriet kept running ahead and sniffing the air, obviously enjoying herself.

"You keep staring at us, Emily," said Frankie. "What's wrong?"

"Oh, nothing's wrong," said Emily. "It's just, you guys seem more... I don't know, *vital* or something."

"More *there*," said Theo.

"That's the night," smiled Frankie, looking up at the stars. "Monsters are made for the night. It's our time to live."

"Or unlive," quipped Bethany. "But she's right. Monsterkind are, by nature, night people. Night time is a better time for us."

There was a clang and the sound of a cat yowling up the street. Harriet's voice drifted back to them. "Okay, *okay!* Jeez, I'm *sorry* already!" Up ahead they saw Harriet race out from behind a group of shrubs, sniffing the air. She threw back her head and howled.

"AAARRRRROOOOOOOO!!!"[5]

"I hope she doesn't wake up anybody," said Emily.

Bethany rolled her eyes. "Just excuse her, Emily," she said. "It's going to be full moon soon."

"Oh," said Emily. "Um. Should we worry?"

"No," said Frankie. "The werewolves hunt in Morlock Heights during full moon. She'll be out of school a couple of days, though."

Punkin stood on her tiptoes, looking up. "Someday I'm gonna be up there on a broom. I wish I could tonight. It's wonderful flyin' weather."

This statement was so unlike the quiet, deferential Punkin Theo was used to that she wasn't sure how to answer. She noticed that Punkin was wrapped in a shawl knitted of multicolored yarn, in deference to the beginning fall chill. She'd never seen anyone of Punkin's age in a shawl, but somehow it fit her. "That's pretty," she said, touching it.

"Thank you. Aunty Grimadene made it for me. She says every witch worth her hat has a good shawl." She sighed. "And a good broom."

"So how come you don't have a broom?" asked Theo.

---

[5] The howl is the most basic element of werewolf language. Even though it has fearful connotations, most of the time it means the same thing as "party *on,* dude!!"

115

Punkin sulked. "Cause ol' Cousin Bevadelia talked Mama and Aunty into keepin' me off one. Said it wasn't *safe*, and that she didn't want nothin' happenin' to the new *Adept*." She sighed. "It's 'cause there ain't been an Adept among the witches for awhile, so they worry more than they would otherwise."

Theo was not sure what to say. She settled for, "Well, you'll get one soon. You're still young, right?"

"*Watch* that," said Bethany.

Emily was thinking about what Frankie had said about the curfew. "So how did you guys get out of Morlock Heights?"

"We didn't go home," said Frankie. "I got Mr. Sabbat to let us off downtown, in that little place where all those shops are."

Emily stared. "You were down in the *square?*"

"Of course we were," said Bethany. "Where do you think I got this outfit?"

Frankie shrugged. "It was no big deal. We got a few funny looks, but that was to be expected."

"Well, there was that little man at the newsstand," said Bethany. "He seemed to think we were some sort of gang." She took a tin of Altoids out of her bag and opened it. Paper rustled. "I don't know what he was talking about. All the kids who looked like gang members left as soon as they saw us coming." She dropped one in her mouth and offered the tin to Emily and Theo. "Want one? I've found these are the only things that really work against blood breath. Everything else is like taking candy."

"Blood breath?" said Emily.

"When you're a vampire fresh breath and general mouth care become rather important," said Bethany archly.

Theo and Emily considered this, and solemnly took two Altoids each. Bethany returned the tin to her bag with a quiet smile.

Harriet ran up from her latest short excursion. "I think I found it. There's a big house up ahead with a lot of cars and people, and there's loud music and lights. Come on." She ran back the way she had come.

Frankie looked at Emily, who nodded. "That sounds right. We're on Jessica's block now."

Bethany eyed the surroundings.   "Well,   it's   a   nice

neighborhood, but it doesn't seem so upscale. Most of these houses are as nice as yours."

They rounded the corner to view an old and rather ostentatious pseudo-colonial house, surrounded by a low stone wall with an iron gate. Cars were pulling up along the sidewalk, and several groups of people were entering. Music thudded in the air.

"Jessica lives in the biggest house on the block," said Emily to Bethany.

"Of course the little whelp would have such," muttered Bethany in a low voice.

"Whelp?"

"I was thinking of another word." She strode forward briskly. "Come on, darlings. No rest for the wicked, I'm sure."

There were some stares and whispers from people as they entered. Emily waved tentatively at some of these as they passed through. She could tell that Theo was nervous, because she had a look that she referred to as her "game face" on, and was not looking around much. The Grrls were gazing curiously at their surroundings, and Harriet had wandered off to chat with some kids she recognized from basketball practice; Emily heard them complimenting her on her prowess. *I bet seeing her play will be really something,* she thought.

She looked at the other Grrls. Frankie was smiling brightly, and Punkin was shyly waving at people in the crowd. Bethany's expression was haughty, and Emily wondered if she was expecting problems with Jessica sometime this evening.

A blonde girl approached them. "*Hi,* Bethany! It's *so cool* you could come, and... *oh.*" She had seen Frankie, and was openly staring. Frankie smiled politely.

"Hi, Tiffany," said Bethany. "It's... good to see you." Emily noted that it took effort for Bethany to say this. "I'd like to introduce my friends, Frankie, Punkin, Theo and Emily. And Harriet's over there-- ah, here she comes."

"Hi, there!" said Harriet, coming up. "I'm Harriet." She gave Tiffany a big smile.

Tiffany swallowed at the sight of Harriet's teeth. "Ohmi*god,*" she breathed.

117

Harriet looked at Bethany, then said to Tiffany, "No, my name is *Harriet.* I just said so."

"Um..." This temporarily derailed Tiffany. She recovered herself and said, "I'll... I'll tell Jessica you're here." She moved off quickly.

Harriet stared after her. "Was that the dumb one?" she asked Bethany.

"No, *Heather* is the dumb one," said Bethany. "Tiffany's the stupid one."

"Mmm." Harriet scratched her chin. "So what's the basic difference?"

"Heather has fake red hair instead of fake blond hair."

"Oh."

"Well, she wasn't very friendly," said Frankie. "She didn't talk to any of us much."

"I know," said Bethany. "I'm wondering if maybe this wasn't a bad idea--"

"Hi, Bethany!" Stephanie appeared out of a crowd of people. "I'm so glad you're here. Are these your friends?" She looked curiously at the group.

Introductions were made. Stephanie eyed Harriet and said tentatively, "I had heard that there was a--a wolf girl on the basketball team, but I didn't quite believe it."

"That's me," said Harriet proudly. "Coach says I'm probably gonna be one of the starters. He says I've got game." She grinned. "Which is true, 'cause we went on a hunt last weekend and I got *plenty* of game. Some deer, too."

"I see," said Stephanie after a moment. "And you're the science whiz?" she said to Frankie.

"Yes," said Frankie. "Sort of hereditary, what with Dad being a Mad Scientist and all."

"And you're really a witch?" she said to Punkin.

"Yup," answered Punkin, adjusting her hat. "I wore my *best* hat, since it's a party."

Theo said, "How do you tell?"

"This one," said Punkin authoritatively, "came from Balrog And Soggoth's Of London, and it's real dragon's-wing silk. Mama had to order it special. All my other hats are standard daily-wear models from their Extended Service Outlet on Maim Street in Morlock Heights."

"*Maim* Street?"

"It's very nice," said Stephanie. "It suits you, really." She turned to Emily and Theo. "I've seen you around school, but I haven't ever gotten to meet you. Do you guys hang out with them a lot?"

"Uh, yeah," said Theo. Her defensiveness had been disarmed by Stephanie's friendly behavior. "I'm with Harriet in P.E. She's actually a better teacher than Coach Simpson." Harriet looked pleased.

"And I've got Science with Frankie," piped up Emily. "She's the best Lab partner I've *ever* had."

"Thanks, Emily," smiled Frankie. Her cheeks were a bit deeper green than usual, and Emily realized that she was blushing. She grinned happily.

"So then it's true," said Stephanie. "There really are monsters at Clearwater."

The Grrls looked at each other. "I take it that news does not travel fast at *all* in our school," said Frankie. "If the Clique are supposed to be so popular at school, how come you didn't know? Couldn't you *tell?*"

Stephanie rolled her eyes. "That's just Jessica," she answered. "She's not interested in anything except *her*. Just like the others."

Theo raised an eyebrow. "Sounds like some of Bethany is rubbing off on you," she said. Stephanie smiled.

"And how is that a bad thing?" shrugged Bethany. Everyone laughed.

"*OhmiGOD!!*"

The shout came from behind them, and everyone turned. Heather was standing there, weaving slightly. A can of beer was in her hand. Beside her were two boys dressed in lettermen's jackets, staring at the Grrls. Tiffany entered behind them with an evil grin on her face.

Heather was drunk. She staggered over to the group, and Harriet recoiled instantly from the beer smell, nostrils flaring.

Heather pointed at Frankie. "She looks like freakin' Frankenstein's *daughter* or something!" People turned to stare at this, saw Frankie, and continued staring. There was some laughter from the crowd of kids.

Frankie looked offended. "I am not! My father's name is *Franken!* And who are you?"

"Thad's th' *dumb* one," said Harriet, holding her nose. "Thmells *horrible.*"

"Scuse me?" said Heather, whirling on Harriet. A fog of alcohol hit Harriet's nose, and she began growling, a low, warning sound.

"You want some?" shouted Heather belligerently. *"Bring it ON!!"*

"Heather, you're drunk," said Stephanie, trying to take control of the situation. Out of the corner of her eye, she saw that Harriet had advanced one step forward, her hands hooked into claws. "You need to just calm down a bit--"

"Are you kidding me?" shouted Heather. "We got a friggin' freakshow in here and you're telling me to calm down? *Come on, Wolfy!*" she shouted at Harriet.

"Yeah," said one of the boys. "We don't need their kind in here." He pointed at Emily and Theo, who recoiled. "Bunch of little *Halloween* people. With pet *nerds.*"

"I think we should throw the nerds out," said Tiffany evilly. "What do you think, Bradley?" she said to the boy beside her.

Emily looked at Bethany, and trembled. Bethany was glaring at Tiffany, and her eyes were glittering bright red. Emily could see her fangs extending. *"Get behind me,"* hissed Bethany. Emily obeyed. Punkin moved protectively beside Theo, wearing an uncertain but determined expression.

"Good idea, babe," said Bradley, grinning. Tiffany simpered.

"Yeah," said the bigger of the two boys, who was next to the drunken Heather, and looked a little unsteady himself. "Let's rush 'em!"

"No, Cam, it's cool," said Bradley. He swaggered up to Frankie. "Think you can take me, little girl?"

Frankie drew herself up to her full height. She was nearly two heads taller than Bradley. "Take you where?" she asked quietly. There were some titters from the watching group.

Bradley smiled and turned away. He suddenly whirled back, and planted a fist on Frankie's jaw. There was a loud crunch.

Frankie never moved.

Bradley's eyes widened. *"OWWWWW!!!!!"* he screeched. He clutched his hand and screamed in pain at his own touch. *"OWWW!!! She broke my hand! She broke my friggin' hand, man! OWWW JEEZ!!!"* He ran toward the kitchen.

Stephanie gaped at Frankie, who turned to her and said calmly, "Friends of yours?"

"JEEZ GET ME SOME ICE!!! CALL 911!!! OWWWWWWWW!!!!!"

"They're on the football team," breathed Stephanie, her eyes wide with shock. Frankie sighed, and stepped over to get between Harriet and Heather; Heather was, rather inanely, squaring off against the amused Harriet, and weaving with her fists up like a boxer.

"I really don't think you should pick a fight with a werewolf," Frankie said, gently lifting Heather away with one hand. Heather gaped at Frankie. Harriet sniggered.

Bethany, her hands clenched into fists, strode menacingly toward Tiffany and Cam, who were backing away in terror. "I have *never* seen so much *rudeness* to guests," she hissed. Her voice deepened into a snarl. "I *swear* I think you planned this whole little scene."

"Now hold on, babe--" said Cam uncertainly.

"I'm not your *babe*," snapped Bethany. Her hands were a sudden blur of movement, and Cam fell to his knees, clutching his stomach.

"Now w-wait a minute, Bethany," Tiffany said, in a wheedling tone. "It--it was just a little joke, you know, just for laughs--"

"You sniveling little *rodent*," spat Bethany. Her eyes reddened. "You're going to be laughing out of the other side of your *face* when I'm through with you, because I'm going to tear the *first* side *off*--"

121

"What's going on here?"

Jessica had entered. Silence fell over the room.

"Well," said Bethany. "Nice to see you." Her face had, in an instant, reverted to its usual humanlike appearance. "Some of your guests, here, are getting out of hand."

Jessica stared at Tiffany, who was cowering in fear next to Cam, tears rolling down her cheeks. "They *started* it," she wailed. "It was all *their* fault, I *told* you not to invite her, but you wouldn't *listen* to *meee--*"

Heather staggered up. "Yeah, Jess, it was *them,* they're all *crazy--*"

There was a cracking sound.

The group turned. A large mirror was hanging on the wall. The glass within the mirror had an enormous crack running through it. It seemed as though the mirror was cracking by *itself.* Jessica's mouth opened in shock. "What the *HELL*--my mom's gonna *kill* me--"

Harriet nudged Frankie and pointed. "Uh-oh."

Punkin was staring angrily at Tiffany. "You're *lyin',*" she said. The soft country twang in her voice was suddenly more prominent. The pupils of her eyes were swelling, and the air seemed to crackle. "Ain't *nobody* here done *nothin'* except *you.*"

"Back off, Punkin," said Frankie.

"Yeah," said Harriet nervously. "I mean, there's no need to get violent here or anything--"

"I ought to *kill* you!" screeched Jessica. "You *broke* the mirror! My mom's gonna *know* I had a *party* here now!"

"That's not *true!*" shouted Emily. "We weren't doing anything except talking to Stephanie, and then *Heather* came in *drunk* and started *yelling* at us!!!"

Everyone turned to stare at this unexpected outburst. Emily swallowed and looked a little sheepish. "Well, we *weren't,*" she muttered.

"Wow," said Harriet admiringly, "you've got some *lungs* when you want 'em."

Theo, who had been staring blankly at the uproar, snapped out of her stupor. "Yeah! What they said! I mean, we weren't doing anything," she finished lamely. "And--and I don't know how the mirror got broken. *Whatever.*" She moved to stand beside Emily.

"Who the hell is *THAT??*" shouted Jessica. "And what is she... it... *them,*" she raged, waving wildly at the group, "doing at *my* party?" She whirled on Stephanie. "Why are *nerds* at *my* party?"

"*They,*" said Bethany in tones that dropped the room temperature by several degrees, "are *my* friends, and *I* invited them to this party. *That,*" she said, pointing at Tiffany, who cringed beside Jessica, "was supposed to tell you. Right?"

There was silence. Then Heather seemed to remember something. "Well, *yeah,* of *course* I'm drunk," she said. "I mean, you're s'posed to be drunk at a party."

Harriet stared at her, and then said to Bethany, "You were right. She *is* the dumb one."

"*Tiffany didn't tell me ANYTHING!*" shrieked Jessica. "She sure didn't tell me you were bringing the *Munsters* over!!"

"Monsters," said Harriet. "It's *monsters,* not Munsters."

"*Shut up!*"

"Hold it," said Frankie. "Look, Stephanie can tell you. We were all standing here talking, and Heather came in and started yelling at us. And she called *me* Frankenstein's daughter, and I take exception to that because *everyone* knows that Shelley what's-her-name got it wrong." She looked around at the crowd, who were staring at her. "Er... don't they?"

Jessica turned to Stephanie. "*Well??*"

Stephanie's throat worked. "Er. Um, I--I don't know what they're talking about." She swallowed. "Um. Frankie broke Bradley's hand. They were trying to start a fight."

There was dead silence in the room. The MonsterGrrls stared at her, horrified at the enormity of the lie. Bethany looked even paler than usual, and her eyes were blazing. Frankie said, in a low voice, "I did not. That's not true."

"*Get out! OUT!*" shouted Jessica, pointing a shaking finger at Bethany. "*And take them with you!!!*"

Bethany stared at Stephanie as if seeing her for the first time. "Don't worry," she said, her tone deadly. "I'm *delighted* to leave." She turned on her heel and strode out. Frankie stared angrily at Stephanie and followed. Emily and Theo followed behind her, eyes wide and staring. Harriet put her head on one side and looked at Stephanie, who seemed to be gazing with rapt attention at the floor. Then she sniffed, and left.

Punkin's expression was grim. She looked at the broken mirror, and then flapped her hand at it as she walked out the door.

The crack in the mirror vanished. Jessica's eyes widened. She walked over to the mirror and rubbed her hand across the glass, mystified.

Stephanie watched them go. She turned toward the kitchen doorway, where Tiffany was standing with a pleased smile. "Well, I guess *that's* over, and we won't have to worry about *them* anymore--"

"Shut up," snapped Stephanie. "I'm going to check on Bradley." She pushed past Tiffany into the kitchen.

Heather watched her go. "Wow," she said to Tiffany, "what's wrong with *her?*"

"Well, that's all for that, then. What do we do now?"

"I have *never*... in my *life*... or *unlife,* even..."

"Was it you who broke the mirror, Punkin?"

"Yup, but I fixed it. She *should* be grateful, the ol'... ol' *meanie.*"

"Is there somewhere to eat around here? I'm hungry."

"...seen such... *rude*... *stupid*..."

"I can't believe she said that about me. That was... that was a *lie.*"

"...*miserable*... I should, I should have *throttled her--*"

"WILL YOU ALL STOP IT!" Emily shouted.

The others stared at her. "Well, gee," said Frankie, "what are you yelling at us for?"

"BECAUSE... because..." Emily began to cry. "Because I just got *thrown out* of the biggest party of the year," she sobbed. "I feel so s-stupid, and everybody s-saw me there, getting thrown out, and I don't know how I'm going to face anyone at school next week."

"Yeah," grumbled Theo. "Everyone thinks we're *real* nerds now."

The Grrls looked confused. "I don't understand," said Frankie. "Why do you want to *stay* at a party with those people? I mean, they *lied* about me," she said, looking hurt. "I never touched that guy, and *he* started it. Why do you want to hang around someone like *that?*"

"They're *dumb*," said Harriet. "And they smelled funny. I think it was that stuff they were drinking. Maybe it was making them dumber."

"Why would you care about what *they* think?" asked Punkin. "They're all *mean.*"

"But--but haven't you guys ever wanted to be *liked?*" wailed Emily.

The Grrls looked at each other, and Frankie said, a bit uncertainly, "Well, *you* like us."

"Yeah, but this, this is *different.* I mean..."

"What you're saying," said Bethany coldly, "is that you want to be *popular.* And this thing of being *liked* all has to do with being around the *popular* people, right? Is that it?"

"Well, yeah." Emily wiped her eyes. "I mean, don't you?"

"No," said Bethany. "I've lived long enough to see that there's not much point. Quite a bit longer than *you*, really," she added haughtily.

"Oh, well, that's just *great*," snapped Theo. "I guess it doesn't matter. No one likes vampires anyway, so what's the point of trying, right?"

"Now *wait a minute*--"

"No, *you* wait a minute," snarled Theo. "It's all right for *you* guys, not being popular, not being noticed, not having any *friends* or anything. Having to stay home all the time because you can't go out on dates, because no one will pay any attention to you, because you're not a *babe* like Jessica. Being *nerds. Monsters* don't have to deal with that. But *we* do. And we'll catch it next week from everybody. *Including* Jessica."

The monsters all looked at one another, and then Harriet said, "If you don't have any friends, then what are *we?*"

"You won't catch it from *us*," said Punkin. "We wouldn't tease you, or call you nerds or anythin'."

"It's not fair," said Emily. "It's just not fair. We could have gotten them to like us..."

Bethany exploded. "Oh, *come off it!*" she shouted. "Those *idiots* don't like *anybody but themselves!* And you're telling *me* about unfair? *I'm a vampire!* Do you think I asked to be this way? Do you think it's such a great life having to drink *blood* to *live?* Do you think that being a monster is all about being weird and wearing black and hanging out in crypts and old castles and graveyards? I mean, *really!* How *melodramatic* can you *get?"*

"This is wrong, Emily," said Frankie. "You're not being fair to us, and you're not being fair to yourselves, either. I mean, maybe they have all this popularity and everything, but they're still just a bunch of jerks. And you guys are really cool. Cooler than they'll *ever* be."

"Well, if we're your best friends and everything, how come you guys didn't come clean with us about what was going on in Morlock Heights?" said Theo. "Why didn't you tell us that some bad people tried to get in and take something?"

"Theo!" said Emily.

Bethany and Frankie recoiled in surprise, and then all eyes turned to Harriet, who shrank inward. "You *told,"* said Punkin.

"Sorry, guys," mumbled Harriet.

"Oh, whatever," sighed Bethany. "Werewolves can't be expected to not tell the truth. It's not in their nature." She hugged the embarrassed Harriet. "It's okay."

"Well, what's the big secret?" asked Emily.

Frankie sighed. "Okay. We didn't want to tell you this, but the truth is that humans are not allowed in Morlock Heights. And we're not supposed to be out with you guys at night, here in your world."

"*Our* world?" said Theo.

"Yeah. Morlock Heights is--a *different* place. And because these bad people tried to break in, the Council Of Monsterkind said that we could only go out to go to school. I mean, there was a big row because Harriet got on the basketball team."

"Yeah," said Harriet. "Pop settled it, though. That's one of the good things about being the daughter of the Baron of all the werewolf Clans." She smiled softly. "I showed him some of the basketball stuff I'd learned, and he was *so proud* of me. He and Mom are gonna try and come see me play."

Theo stared. "Your father's a *baron?*"

Harriet nodded.

"Anyway," said Bethany softly, "we knew that you really wanted to go to this party, and we were curious, I guess. We've all been to parties, but we've never been to a human one before." She sighed. "So we deliberately didn't go home so that we could take you to Jessica's, and… well, it's my fault, I suppose. I should have *known* that silly little trollop Tiffany would have tried something."

"Oh," said Theo in a small voice. "Um. What's a trollop?"

"A prostitute," answered Bethany flatly. "Or lady of the evening, if you prefer."

"Oh." Theo grimaced. "Ouch. Well… I hope I didn't make you mad at me." She looked ashamed of herself.

"No," Bethany said. "You're rather a brave girl, getting in an argument with a vampire. We don't like losing, as you probably figured out tonight."

Emily felt childish. "I'm sorry, Frankie," she said. "I didn't mean to get so upset. I was being stupid." She sighed. "I guess Jessica isn't such a good choice for a friend. I mean, look at Stephanie, and the way *she* acts around her."

"Let's not," said Bethany, wrinkling her nose.

"It's okay," said Frankie, grinning.

Theo sighed. "I'm sorry, too. I didn't mean to be such a jerk. I just got excited with the party, and everythin g--"

"You were so nervous at the party you barely enjoyed yourself at all," Bethany said pointedly.

"Yeah," said Theo, looking embarrassed.

"Well," said Bethany, putting an arm around her, "I was nervous, too."

"You were? Really?"

"Really really," said Bethany, smiling. "There were a few seconds where I thought I was actually going to *kill* Tiffany and Cam." She looked thoughtful. "Mind you, it's still not too late to go back."

"It's still not too late to do *anything*," said Punkin. "I bet we could have a better party than mean ol' Jessica and her friends ever could, anyway."

"Why don't we?" said Frankie.

"Yeah!" said Harriet.

"Yeah!" echoed Emily. "Er… where?"

"Your house," said Bethany, starting in that direction.

"*My* house?" said Emily. "Wait! Wait a minute! I… well, I suppose I could ask my mom…"

"Especially since we can't go home," said Punkin. "Mr. Sabbat's bus was the only way back into Morlock Heights."

The two humans stared at the Monster Grrls. "Well… you did say you wanted to have a sleepover, Emily," said Theo after a moment. "But this is *real* short notice."

Emily looked thoughtful. "No," she said. "It'll be okay, Theo." She began to grin. "I'm going to have a party and invite all my friends. It'll be really *cool.*" The grin faded. "Except that I don't have any food at my house."

"I think we can take care of that," said Frankie. "We'll go back to the square. It's still early evening, and a lot of the food places will still be open. We'll get some things and bring them back to your house."

"Wow! Er, you would do that?" asked Emily.

"Sure," said Bethany. "Anything for friends, you know. I mean, I'll never spend *all* the money I've got, even if I hang around another two hundred and twenty-five years."

"Two hundred and *fifty*-five," said a chorus of voices.

"Yes, *do* rub it in, will you?" scowled Bethany.

"Gosh. Thanks, guys," said Emily. "I'm *really* sorry I got so mad."

Frankie smiled. "It's okay. Just square things with your mom, and we'll take care of everything else. See you back at your house in a few minutes."

The MonsterGrrls headed off into the night. Harriet stopped and looked back at Theo. "Um… still friends?"

Theo ran up and hugged her. "Still friends, always."

Harriet grinned and ran after the MonsterGrrls, howling. The sound was nearly ear-splitting.

"*OOOOWWWW-RRRROOOOOOOOOOO!!!!!!*"

"She's really going to be a handful around full moon, I bet," said Emily.

"Yeah," said Theo thoughtfully. "It's probably a good thing we won't have to deal with it."

They looked at each other, and high-fived. "Wow! We're going to have a party!" shouted Theo, as they started back toward Emily's house.

"Uh-huh," said Emily. "And we deserve it. After all, we have to do something that's even harder than trying to be friends with Jessica."

Theo looked at Emily. "Wow," she said, "what's harder than that?"

"We have to get permission from my mom."

"Oh."

Joanna Peters looked up from her book. The clock on the living room wall said seven-thirty. She wondered if Emily was having a good time.

She'd been, in a way, as excited about the party as Emily had. Ever since Malcolm had left, Emily had been a bit withdrawn. She'd had Theo, and they were together almost constantly, but Joanna worried about her daughter. The divorce had hurt Emily almost as much as her.

And, of course, Emily is going through that time when having school friends means everything. She seemed really happy tonight. In fact, she's been much happier lately. She talks constantly about these new friends of hers at school. Wonder what they're like.

She didn't seem anxious for me to meet them right away. I suppose that's something I'll have to deal with, too. After all, she's at the age when moms are not cool.

She looked at the clock, and sighed. She supposed Emily would be a bit late tonight. But that was okay; Emily was a responsible child, and knew to call if there were problems. And she had Theo with her, and then there were these other girls as well. Safety in numbers, then.

The door opened, and Emily entered with Theo, who waved hello. Joanna raised an eyebrow. Both of them had slightly nervous looks, which meant that something had happened.

"Hi," she said. "You're home early. Much earlier than I expected." She put her head on one side. "How was the party?"

"Oh, it was okay," said Emily. A silent alarm went off in Joanna's head, but she gave nothing away.

"Yeah, it was okay," said Theo. "It was nice."

"All right then." Joanna counted down to herself. It usually took five seconds for Emily to come clean about something.

"Um... Mom?"

Just two seconds. What on earth could have happened? "Yes, dear?"

"Um... would it be okay if Theo stayed over? She's already called and asked her mom, and her mom said it was okay."

Joanna relaxed. "I guess so, dear. Your brother's away with his father, so there's plenty of room."

"Oh, thanks, Mrs. Peters," said Theo.

Joanna watched them. There was quite a bit of discomfort between them. She began counting down to herself again. "Is there something else, Emily?"

"Um, could some *other* girls come over? Maybe?"

"Please?" said Theo.

"These girls wouldn't be these friends you've been telling me about, would they?" Joanna smiled. "I've been wondering when I would get to meet them."

The doorbell rang.

"How about now?" said Emily, as Theo raced for the door.

"*Now?*" said Joanna, watching her daughter leave the room. She got up and followed. "Exactly how *many* other girls are we talking about sleeping over? That *is* what this is about, isn't it?"

"Um..." Emily stopped. "Yes, Mom."

Joanna eyed Emily. "I was not really *prepared* for a sleepover, dear. What happened to the party?"

"Well, it--it wasn't all that great." She sighed. "Mom, there were these guys there, and they were drunk, and they started bothering us, and Frankie got accused of breaking Bradley's hand and Jessica got really mad at us, so she threw us out. And the Grrls don't have any way to get back home and they don't have any other place to stay, so could they *please* stay here tonight? They're even bringing food and everything…"

"You were at a party with *drinking* going on? And you were *thrown out?* What kind of girls are these that you're… *oh.*"

They had entered the kitchen. Frankie and Punkin were arranging food on the table, while Bethany, cradling two large paper bags in her arms, was standing just inside the outer doorway, looking perturbed. Theo was standing by the door, and when Emily entered, she pointed at Bethany and mouthed "Invite", which she immediately ceased when Joanna entered behind Emily. Frankie and Punkin saw her and paused.

Joanna stared at them for a long time. Her eyes kept returning to Punkin's hat, then to Frankie, and then to the table. There were several bags of chips, cookies, and fast food. A large sack of hamburgers stood next to a box labeled FINLEY'S FRYER BARN. The smell of broiled beef and chicken grease filled the room.

"Hi, guys," Emily said uncertainly. She looked at her mother, whose eyes were riveted on Frankie, and said, "These are my friends. That's Frankie, this is Punkin…"

There was the sound of someone clearing her throat from the doorway.

"… and that's Bethany," Emily finished. She finally caught Bethany's gaze. "Oh! Oh, yeah. I Invite you in."

"It can't be you," muttered Bethany. "Your mother has to do it. It's *her* house."

"Do what?" said Joanna.

"Invite her in," said Theo.

"Please?" said Bethany. "These bags are getting heavy."

Joanna stared at the vampire, and then sighed, letting her motherhood reflexes take over. "Please come in, dear."

"Thank you," breathed Bethany gratefully, and entered, setting her bags on the table with the rest of the food. Joanna saw that the bags read WONG'S CHINESE TO GO.

"We didn't know what you liked, exactly," Frankie said, "so we got some of everything."

Joanna stared at the MonsterGrrls, taking in Frankie's electrodes, skin color and stitches, Punkin's hat and Bethany's pale

131

skin. "Emily," she said, "was the party a... costume party?"

"Um, no, Mom. It--it wasn't."

"I see." Joanna leaned on one of the chairs. "Well. It's not quite Halloween yet..."

"No, ma'am," said Frankie.

"We can't wait," Punkin said happily, and then realized that she had said the wrong thing. She crossed her hands over each other and stood looking at the floor.

There was an uncomfortable silence. Joanna stared at the Grrls, fully taking in their general appearance. She said, "This is a lot of food. It must have been quite expensive..."

"I have money," said Bethany, just a shade too quickly. "Vamp... I mean, *Father* gives me an allowance. He's a very generous man."

"We'd be happy to share," said Frankie. "There's plenty for everybody."

"And of course Mr. Peters could have some as well," said Bethany.

"Oh... no. No," said Joanna, smiling tightly. "There is no Mr. Peters."

They looked at Emily, who said, "He left." She looked down at the floor. Joanna looked at her daughter, but didn't say anything. The silence returned.

The Grrls exchanged a look. Then Bethany removed a carton and some chopsticks from the Chinese food bag and opened it, stirring. "This dim sum isn't as good as the kind I had when I was in China," she said, "but it's not bad. Would you like some, Mrs. Peters?"

Joanna looked at Bethany. She took the chopsticks and plucked a dumpling from the carton. "You've actually been to China?"

"Yes--I mean, yes, ma'am. Twice." She shrugged. "The Great Wall and the countryside were beautiful. But it was long ago."

Joanna chewed and swallowed. "Well. I was not aware that Emily's new friends were such... *singular* people." She looked at her daughter. "She said there were some problems at the party--"

"That's *my* fault, Mrs. Peters," said Bethany, before anyone else could speak. She held up a hand at the Grrls, and continued. "I was originally invited to the party, and I was told that I could bring friends. Unfortunately, I wasn't aware that Jessica was so *selective* about *her* friends."

"It was *Jessica Hardin-St. James's* party?"

"Yes. I mean, yes ma'am."

"Ah," said Joanna. "That explains everything." She turned to Emily. "If I had known it was *that* party, I wouldn't have let you go. I suppose I should be thankful for these friends of yours, taking care of you."

Frankie looked confused. "Don't her parents ever know she has it?"

"No."

"Oh." Frankie pondered this. "I don't understand--"

"Jessica's parents don't know a *lot* of things about their daughter, and they wouldn't believe it anyway," said Joanna. She noticed that Bethany had a knowing expression, as if something she suspected had been finally confirmed. She eyed the group. "I'd heard that there were monsters attending the school. Are they talking about you?"

The Grrls looked sheepish, except for Bethany, who said, "There's not much gets past you, ma'am," with a hint of bad grace.

Emily, stepping to their defense, said, "Mom, they're my friends, and they're really nice people, even though they're monsters."

Joanna smiled. "I suppose they are. They're certainly generous people," she said, looking at the food. She looked at Bethany critically. "Let's see. Vampire, right?"

"I brought my own blood, ma'am," said Bethany, holding up her black leather bag. "It's bad manners to expect your host to take care of *everything.*"

"I see. So... I shouldn't worry, then."

"*No,* ma'am," said Bethany emphatically.

"And you're a Frankenstein," she continued, addressing Frankie.

"*Creature,*" said Frankie and Emily together. Frankie's expression was a bit sour.

"Ah. Sorry, dear," she said to Frankie. "And I can tell what you are," she said to Punkin.

"Yes, ma'am. It's the hat." She thought a moment, and said, raising her hands, "Blessed be this house and all who enter in."

"Very nice," said Joanna thoughtfully. She looked at Emily. "I suppose that it's all right if you have them over. But next time *tell me in advance.* And thank you, girls, for taking care of my daughter and Theo." She glared mildly at Theo, who hung her head. "And if you help clean up later, I won't tell *your* mother about what happened tonight. Kathleen would have had a *fit* if she'd known."

"Yes, ma'am," said Theo, sighing.

"It's okay, Mrs. Peters," said Frankie. "They're cool."

"Thanks, Mom," Emily said, a happy smile on her face. She hugged Joanna. "Thanks a lot. Hey, where's Harriet?"

"Late *again*," sighed Bethany.

"Who is Harriet?" asked Joanna.

"Harriet's the other girl in our group," said Frankie. "She said she would get some pizza."

"She's a werewolf," said Punkin.

Joanna's eyes widened. *"Werewolf?"*

There was a loud banging on the door. Bethany opened it. A large stack of pizza boxes clasped in a pair of furry arms bustled in.

"Hi!" said Harriet, setting down the food. "I'm sorry I'm late. I had to call my little brother and tell him where we were, and he said he'd tell Pop and that Pop would tell everybody else, and *then* I had to chase down one of those pizza guys and make him take me to the pizza store so I could get food. Is that your mom?" she finished, looking at the staring Joanna. "Hi, Mom. You have a nice house."

Joanna finally found her voice. She said, "Is... is all that pizza for us?"

"Oh, no, Mom," said Harriet, heading out the door. "That's for *me*. I've got some more for all you guys out in the pizza guy's car."

Eight: A History Of Monsters

There were, of course, some things to be cleared up.

"I want everyone, and that means *everyone,* in bed by twelve at least. No exceptions," said Joanna. "And bring down the trash when you're through. And *don't* leave a mess for me."

"Yes, ma'am," chorused everyone. Harriet saluted.

"I've put the rest of your... special food in the refrigerator," she said to Bethany. "No doubt you'll want some in the morning."

"Yes, ma'am," said Bethany. "I'm taking a bottle up. Thank you."

"Um. Is it *real* blood?"

"Yes, ma'am. O-positive."

"Um, do you know whose it is?"

"No, ma'am," said Bethany. She gave a small shrug. "Father gets it from a medical blood bank. I can only guess that it comes from a donor." She munched a taco chip.

"I see. And you drink blood, yet you're eating food."

"Yes, ma'am. I can eat most human foods." She sighed. "It's just not *filling,* if you know what I mean. But I do promise that you have nothing to worry about, and neither do Emily or Theo."

"She *wouldn't,*" Frankie said. "Really." The human girls nodded in affirmation.

Joanna considered this. The Grrls had related the whole story of Jessica's party, including the fight that Bradley had tried to start, and Emily and Theo had verified how the Grrls had protected them. "I think you've all proved that tonight," she said. "Thank you."

Bethany bowed slightly. "Yes, ma'am. You're welcome." The others nodded.

"We're going up, Mom," said Emily. Everyone was loaded down with food and drink. Harriet had most of the pizza with her.

"I don't suppose I have to worry about you, either," Joanna said to Harriet.

"No, Mom," said Harriet seriously. Joanna had, after some

deliberation, allowed Harriet to refer to her as "Mom," since it seemed that Harriet was going to continue with it. "Not with all this food. And besides, humans taste bad now." Theo had explained Harriet's grandfather's theory about junk food, and for once Joanna had had no guilt about helping herself to some of the party food.

"Ah. Well. Up you go, then. And remember, lights out at twelve."

Everyone headed up the stairs to Emily's room. Joanna watched them go. Harriet shifted pizza boxes and gave a little wave, and Joanna found herself waving back.

Well. This is interesting. My daughter's new friends are all monsters.

After her husband had left them, Joanna and Emily and her little brother James, and sometimes Theo, had spent occasional weekend nights together watching old Universal and Hammer horror movies on AMC. She had enjoyed them as much as they had, and she had often understood the monsters' dilemmas. Now, after having met the Grrls, she somehow felt that she was prepared to spend a night, and perhaps many more nights, being den mother for a bunch of teenage monsters. And yet, at the same time, the Grrls were nothing like the movies. The more she thought about it all, the more she felt the world *widening* somehow.

They all seem so much different from other children. And not just in the obvious. They seem to have no malice. They have kind hearts. They are innocent. Even Bethany is innocent, in her way; all the hauteur and worldliness is an affectation.

She realized that she had just named qualities that she admired, and taught to her daughter. She suddenly felt very proud.

She stood on the bottom step and listened to the voices drifting down from Emily's room. By the sound of things, Theo had gotten the Playstation from James's room and was showing them how to play it. She smiled to herself.

She went and got some food from the kitchen table and took it to the living room. Perhaps the dim sum was not all the way from China, but it really was very good.

In Emily's room, the Playstation lessons continued.

"So I press this button here, and… oh! It's started. What do I do?"

"OK, move the button forward."

"Which way is forward? I'm having to hold this thing so the little X-shaped button won't be a cross."

"Um, top right."

"OK. So, I'm heading down the highway, and here's a curve and… *Oh!!* I just hit someone in an ice cream truck!"

"That's OK. It's *Twisted Demolition Derby 4.* You're supposed to do that. Watch out, here comes the tank!"

"AHHH! He *hit* me! The *bugger!* Which way is left?"

"Top left!"

"BAM! Take that, you! Of all the *cheek!*"

"Fire the missile!"

"What missile??"

"You've got missiles, see them there? Push the red button!!"

"Ooh. I *like* this. BOOM! There goes the tank! Ooh, can I shoot the *kitty?*"

"Yeah! It's an opponent, see, it's driving a Cadillac…"

"BOOM! Ha ha ha! I'm telling Father I want one of these for my deathday!"

"You'd better get a joystick instead of a pad controller, though…"

More sedate interests were going on across the room. Frankie was lying on Emily's bed with a large bottle of chocolate milk, leafing through a magazine. Harriet sat on the floor with a pile of empty pizza boxes next to her, and was well into a fresh one. Punkin was examining Emily's desktop computer. "What's this here?" she asked.

"It's my computer," said Emily.

Punkin put her head on one side. "Stuart's computer don't look nothin like this."

"Yeah, but if it's *Stuart* you're talking about, he's probably got two or three of these at home. His dad works in electronics, and Stuart always has the latest thing, with computers."

"Well, maybe, but the one he always got with him in class is kind of like one of my Mama's spell-books at home. He can carry it around in his backpack." She snapped her fingers, remembering.

"Oh, gorry! We left our stuff on the porch!"

"That's okay," said Frankie. She put the magazine aside and got up. "Let's go get them, Punkin. I'm gonna need my generator in the morning, anyway." They stepped over Harriet and headed to the door.

"I'll go with you and help," said Emily, walking out behind them.

Bethany was enjoying herself immensely. "*Yes!* Two thousand points!!" A boom sounded from the TV screen. "Oh, bugger," she said. "My car blew up."

"That's okay," said Theo. "You can start it all over again, and you can choose a different vehicle even. See?" She demonstrated, using the pad controller to scroll through a selection of cars.

"How *pleasant*," said Bethany, smiling evilly. "I can pretend everyone on the road is *Tiffany*."

Harriet belched. "Yeah," she said. "You can get out all your violent urges that way."

"Oh?" Bethany turned. "And what would *you* know about violent urges, darling?" There was a vicious edge on this.

"Well, I guess we all *saw* 'em tonight," sneered Harriet around a mouthful of pizza.

"Oh, *well*. I didn't see the big *beastie* trying to hold me *back*. *You* were being somewhat laughably menaced by *Heather*, who looks *remarkably* like the slutty little kitty in the Cadillac on this video game."

"Well, I didn't wanna *hurt* her," snapped Harriet, dropping her pizza slice and glaring at Bethany.

Theo looked fearfully from one to the other. There was very little that made Harriet ignore food. "Uh, guys…"

"I mean, she was drinking stuff that made her *stupid* and everything, and she didn't know what she was doing. It wouldn't have been *fair*." Harriet's eyes were glowing bright yellow.

"And what do *werewolves* know about *fair?*" retorted Bethany, her own eyes deepening to red. She stood up angrily. "What about what happened at the Valley Of Bones?"

"Guys? G-guys…"

"*That was an ambush!*" shouted Harriet, bouncing to her feet.

"It was s'posed to be like that! All the darn *vampires* were coming out of the *sky!!* What did you *expect!?*"

"Uh, guys… hey guys, let's not…"

"*We* certainly expected something more *honorable* than being pelted with *rocks!*"

"Vampires had an *air* advantage at the Valley Of Bones! If *we* hadn't been hiding in the cliffs with the rocks, we'd have all *died!!*"

"*You weren't there!*"

"*Neither were you!*"

They were now nose to nose. Bethany's fangs were fully extended, and the fur on Harriet's shoulders was standing on end. Bethany hissed, "*Lycanthrope!*"

"*Deadbeat!*" snarled Harriet.

"*Beastie!*"

"*Rotbag!*"

"*Mongrel!*"

"Hey…" Harriet nudged Bethany and pointed.

"What? Oh."

Theo was huddled in her chair, staring wide-eyed at them. She had drawn her knees up and was hugging herself protectively. "You guys can fight all you want to," she quavered. "Just leave *me* out of it, okay?" Tears were in her eyes.

"Oh, dear," said Bethany. They went over and sat beside Theo. Harriet gently patted her on the back. Bethany took a box of tissue from the top of the TV and handed it to Theo.

"We're sorry," Harriet said. "We're just letting off steam, Theo. It's really okay."

"It's all this frustrated predator thing," said Bethany. "We sometimes snap at each other a bit. We didn't mean to scare you, Theo. I'm sorry."

Theo wiped her eyes. "It's…" She sighed. "See, I'm like Emily. My dad left too." Harriet looked very sad at hearing this. "He and Mom used to fight an awful lot, and sometimes they'd do it in front of me."

"Oh, dear. Darling, I *am* sorry," said Bethany.

"Yeah. It wasn't like they *meant* it or anything. Sometimes they'd get so worked up that they'd forget I was there, and…" She sniffled, and wiped her eyes furiously with the heel of her hand.

Harriet looked at Bethany seriously. "Okay. *No more fights* in front of Theo."

"Of course not," said Bethany. "Look, Theo, Harriet and I have known each other for quite some time. We've had a long history together. It's kind of why we bicker so much; we know we can do that with each other."

"Yeah," said Harriet. "Bethany used to babysit all my litter and me."

Theo considered this. "So Bethany's older than you?" she asked.

"I'm a vampire," sighed Bethany. "I'm older than *everybody* in this house. But Harriet and I are great friends."

"Yeah," said Harriet, smiling. "There's nothing I wouldn't do for Bethany."

"And there's nothing I wouldn't do for Harriet," said Bethany.

"And that's exactly," said Harriet, grinning, "what our friendship is all about."

Theo had an idea what was coming. They all traded a look, and said together, "Doing *nothing* for each other," and then laughed.

"I'm sorry I got so worked up," said Theo. "What was the Valley Of Bones?"

"Ancient history," said Bethany. "And probably best left alone, considering the circumstances. It's a story for another time."

"Yeah," said Harriet. "Course, it's not really *ancient* history..."

"What would *you* know about it?"

"A *lot!* It's only just *nursery school* werewolf history!!"

"Well, I'm *older* than you, and *I* learned about it from someone who'd *been* there--"

"*GIRLS!*" It was Frankie, doing her Voice. Everyone jumped.

"I thought Emily told you not to *do* that," muttered Harriet.

"Well, you guys need to be quieter," said Frankie hoarsely, lugging her backpack and generator case into the room. "Mrs. Peters is gonna hear you."

Emily and Punkin followed with the rest of the Grrls' things, closing the door. Frankie put down her things and massaged her throat. "Sometimes I wish Dad hadn't taught me how to do that," she said, looking at Theo. "What was it, the Battle at the Valley Of Bones?"

"Yeah," said Theo.

"You'll have to excuse them," said Frankie. "To werewolves and vampires, that's like the Revolutionary War is to humans. Or the Civil War." She looked thoughtful. "I read in the library at school that sometimes people dress up and re-enact old Civil War battles. Isn't that weird?"

"Well, not really," said Emily. "I mean, it helps people to see what things were like then, and how the battles were actually fought. It's very educational."

"Well, yeah, but why does it always have to be a *battle?* Why couldn't somebody re-enact the moment when some great invention was made, like the combustible engine, or the light bulb? Why couldn't re-enactments be used to show what was involved in *making* something, all the trial and error and creativity?"

Emily thought about this. "Wow," she said. "I never thought about it that way before, Frankie. That's neat."

"Yeah," said Theo. "That's pretty cool."

Bethany sighed. "It's probably not a good idea to re-enact the Battle of the Valley Of Bones, anyway."

"Nope," said Harriet. "But the only problem with your re-enactment idea, Frankie, is that some of those Mad Scientist guys have dumb ideas. Except for your dad, they're all kinda crazy."

"Yes, I know," shrugged Frankie. "Some of them like making things, and some of them just like to do Experiments around some idea they come up with, and then there's the ones like Doctor Thimk."

"Doctor *Thimk?*" said Emily.

"Oh, yeah," said Frankie. "Doctor Thimk is a *legend* in Morlock Heights. He blew up half the Guild's laboratories trying to turn gold into lead."

"*Huh?*"

"He just decided to do it one day. He said it would save time, because everyone knew you couldn't do it the other way."

"Was he the one who eventually started doing all the atomic

radiation experiments?" asked Bethany. "There's places you *still* can't go into in Morlock Heights without coming out glowing for a few days afterward," she said to Theo.

"I don't think so," said Frankie. "I think it was his son who did those. Giant insects and stuff."

"Yeah!" said Harriet. "Remember the giant tarantulas? It took Pop and all the Clans *days* to get them all herded up so they wouldn't tear up Maim Street, and then we found out they were really pretty tame. They were as scared of us as we were of them." She smiled. "I had one as a pet."

"You had a *pet giant tarantula?*" gaped Theo.

"Yeah," said Harriet. "I named him Toby. Rode around on his back and stuff, all the time. And *then* Dr. Thimk Jr. got mad because we tamed all the giant tarantulas, and so he started trying to breed giant chickens, and his test subject got loose and *ate* Toby. And *everybody* went after that one. I was sad for a long time after that, because I really loved Toby, and then Pop killed the chicken and brought it home and we all ate chicken for months and months, and everybody else got *sick* of chicken. But not me. I ate bones, skin, and *all.*"

Theo was not sure whether to be sympathetic or burst out laughing. She settled for, "Well, that must have been bad."

"I didn't know that Mad Scientists made giant bugs and things," Emily said. "I thought they just made Creatures, like Frankie."

"No," said Frankie. "A Creature--something like me--is an attempt at the original Experiment, the one that Shelley wrote about. It's kind of a trial run; if you can do that, then you can do *bigger* things." She sipped her chocolate milk. "I guess my dad was really lucky and got it right, or at least half-right, because the Guild was very enthusiastic about me when he first introduced me to them. They'd been thinking they might have to throw my dad out. But they all said I was terribly advanced, for a Creature."

"It was because he taught you," said Bethany. "He didn't waste his time making destructive giants like Dr. Thimk."

"Well, Toby was okay," said Harriet.

"The Guild was rather proud of Dr. Thimk for some reason,"

said Frankie. "Dad always said that the Thimks were idiots. He said that *any* Mad Scientist could take something and make it *bigger*." She smiled. "He said there ought to be chickens with *three or four* legs, so that no one would fight over the last drumstick. And he made some."

"Really?" said Emily.

"Yep. The problem was, the only way you could kill them for eating was to make them run themselves to death. No one could catch them." She sighed. "They were also *smarter*, and it got so that they'd run into the henhouse and hide whenever they saw Igor coming with the treadmill."

"There's an Igor?" asked Theo.

"Several," said Frankie. She looked sad. "And then Dad ended up being blackballed from the Guild because he fixed Igor."

Theo gulped. *"Fixed?"*

"Yeah," said Frankie. She reached around and patted her back. "Took off his hump, straightened him up. He wasn't even recognizable as an Igor anymore when Dad got through with him, and he was supposed to be an original model."

"Model?"

"Yeah." She sighed. "The Guild was so mad about that."

"Hmmph," sneered Bethany. "The reason Dr. Franken got blackballed was because the Guild was *jealous* of him, because he did such a good job with you. You know that." She broke out her bottle of blood and took a sip. "My father was on the Council Of Monsterkind then, and the Guild has to pass everything through them to be approved, and he *refused* to sign the order. And I remember that Dr. Corinthian wouldn't sign it either."

"I know," said Frankie, smiling. "If there hadn't been such a fuss, Dr. Corinthian would have probably been my mom." She smiled fondly. "She kinda already was, anyway. She said I was the best student she'd ever had in Mad Science classes at Graf Orlok." She turned to Emily. "Mrs. Parkinson reminds me of her, sometimes."

There was silence for a few minutes. Emily looked at Frankie curiously. "I thought everybody got along in Morlock Heights."

"Oh, we do," said Frankie. "But the Mad Scientists are just

the Mad Scientists.   And not all monsters are civilized like us. There's a lot of places in Morlock Heights that *we* won't even go to, because there's bad things and wild monsters there."

"That's true," said Bethany. "Not all vampires want to drink bottled blood."

"And not all werewolves want to hunt just animals," said Harriet. "There's still some wild Clans, like my cousins in Bulgaria. But they've learned since then not to challenge Pop." She smiled. "Pop's *tough*. You'd really like him, if you met him," she said to Emily and Theo.

"What about the witches?" asked Emily, looking at Punkin.

"Well," said Punkin slowly, "we sort of keep to ourselves. There's good relations between us 'n all the other monsters, but we don't meddle in other folks' affairs. Our Coven Of The Nine Stones watches over everbody in Witchhazel, and Mama and Aunty have been runnin' it for a long time. But we don't have nobody sittin' on the Council Of Monsterkind." She was beginning to relax, and her voice was slipping into a gentle country patois. "Mr. Grimm keeps askin' Aunty to join, 'cause she's Elder Witch. But she hasn't said yes yet."

"Who's Mr. Grimm?"

"He's our old principal from Graf Orlok," said Bethany. "He's Nosferatu."

"What's that?"

"There are two kinds of vampires," said Bethany. "There are Revenants, who resemble humans, and then there's Nosferatu. I'm a Revenant."   She settled herself on the floor.   "Nosferatu can shapeshift into different kinds of animals, and each has a totem animal that they shift into. They can also call that animal, in large numbers. Usually, the animal is a bat, a rat, a raven, or a black hound." She sipped her blood. "They also *look* like that animal. Mr. Grimm, for example, can call rats, and he looks a bit like a rat."

"Um," said Emily, a bit uncomfortably. "That's not exactly how Dracula does it."

"Oh, *that*," said Bethany dismissively. "I actually met Bram Stoker once, and read a bit of the first draft."

"Wow! Really?"

"Yep. He had a good imagination, and he'd researched his history well, but he didn't know a *thing* about vampires. And there was all that swooning about over long-lost-loves and everything. But he was a nice man." She sniffed. "Nicer than his wife, anyway. She was a real creep."

"Oh. So there isn't a real Dracula," said Emily sadly.

"Well, *I* know that Vlad Tepes IV ruled a good bit *longer* than history claims," said Bethany. "The Romanian government had to keep it secret for years. Does that count?"

"Who's Vlad Tepes IV?"

"An early ruler of Wallachia, who fought against the Turks. Vicious man. Stoker based his book on him."

"Oh," said Emily. "And he became a vampire?"

Bethany nodded. "It was bound to happen. He was called *drakul* by his enemies, which means demon. But he wasn't as charming as, say, Bela Lugosi. And he didn't wear a cape."

"Well, *you* wear a cape," said Theo.

"Well, vampires *have,* to some degree, been influenced by humans' popular culture," said Bethany. "And it's a good look for us."

"True." Theo looked at Bethany. "So, how long has Morlock Heights existed?"

The Grrls looked at each other. "*O-kay,*" said Harriet. "*Now* we're starting to get into the *history.*"

Bethany had a grave expression. "It would be easier for us to show you things than tell them to you. But it would be a rather different point of view." She looked at Punkin. "What do you think?"

Punkin looked nervous. "Well... I suppose I could. But I need a mirror, and four candles. And we'll need to dim the lights a little bit."

"Huh?" said Emily.

"Wait a minute," said Theo. "What are you going to do?"

"Well," said Punkin, "It's a scryin spell. But it ain't *dangerous* or nothin." She swallowed. "See, I'm an Adept. I can do magic naturally, just like some people playin' the piano when they're little babies."

"Like a prodigy?"

"Y-Yeah. But see, I have to be real careful, because I'm...I'm *real good* at magic. I don't never need to memorize spells; I just have to do 'em the one time. But sometimes ...stuff *happens* when I scry."

Theo and Emily looked at each other. "Like... you mean you can predict the future?" said Emily.

"No," sighed Punkin. "I mean that sometimes the images in the mirror start *doin'* stuff on their own." She hung her head.

"That doesn't sound like *not dangerous,*" said Theo.

"I know," muttered Punkin. "I ain't sure we should, anyway."

"What about a mist mirror?" said Bethany.

"Well--" Punkin thought a moment. "It ain't foggy outside. Will you help me?" Bethany nodded.

"A mist mirror?" asked Emily.

"Scrying with mist," said Bethany. "And I can take care of the mist part." She handed her bottle of blood to Frankie, who set it carefully on the desk. Bethany smiled at the human girls. "Revenants can't turn into animals, but we *can* become mist. Watch carefully, ladies."

She closed her eyes and concentrated. Her body faded, and then slowly dissolved. Within a few seconds there was a thin cloud where Bethany had been sitting.

"Wow!" said Emily. "That's *cool!*"

"*Thank you,*" said Bethany's voice from the cloud. "*I think so too, even if I do say so myself.*"

"Show-off," said Harriet, smiling.

"*Always,*" came the tart response. "*I learned how from you, anyway.*"

"That's the neatest thing I've ever seen," said Theo. "Can I--can I touch you?"

"*Well, let me flow around you, rather. Hold out your hand.*" Theo did, and the cloud drifted to her, swirling gently around her fingers.

"You're cold," said Theo. "And you're kind of *thick.*"

"*Yes. I'm not like fog on a rainy day, you see. This is actually an ectoplasmic form, like a ghost.*" The cloud left Theo's fingers and floated over to Punkin. "*What now, MacDuff?*"

Punkin smiled. "You'll need to spread yourself out a little bit." To Emily and Theo she said, "It's better if we do it this way anyway. Have you got some candles?"

"I've got some in the desk drawer," Emily said. "Mom keeps them here for emergencies and stuff." She took out four candles and a candle lighter and handed them to Punkin, who set each candle in one of the empty cups on the floor. "How come mist mirrors are better for scrying?"

"Cause if you use a mirror, then that's a physical entity. *Hard* stuff, like. If we do it this way," she said, arranging the candles in a circle under Bethany's mist-cloud, "then somethin' can't look back at us." She noticed Theo's look. "If you know what I mean."

"*Very prudent,*" said Bethany's voice. The mist-cloud seemed to swell above the ring of candles, spreading out into a rough oval shape. "*We're all systems go at this end. Are you ready, darling?*"

"Just need to light them up. Frankie, could you get the lights, please?"

Frankie dimmed the lights. Shadows deepened around the group as they moved to sit on the floor, gathering around the candles. Emily and Theo, who were both thinking about what Punkin had said, deliberately sat close to Frankie and Harriet.

"*Don't worry,*" said Bethany's voice. "*This method is much safer than using a mirror. Think of it as watching a documentary, with me as your host.*" The others heard a smile in her voice when she said this.

"All right, everbody quiet," said Punkin. "I need to concentrate." She lit the candles, and closed her eyes. The group watched the mist-cloud floating gently above the circle of candles on the floor. Punkin began to chant, and as she proceeded with the spell, her voice began to echo slightly.

> "*Orange sky and blackened trees,*
> *Pumpkin frost and firebrand leaves,*
> *Shadow's vision, vermilion red,*
> *To we who are seeking, show times long dead.*"

The mist swirled. Punkin's eyes opened. Emily and Theo saw the pupils swell and swallow the white of Punkin's eyes. They began to glow a bright sapphire blue, and the mist took on a gentle blue glow of its own. Emily nervously took Frankie's hand, and Frankie smiled and gave her a gentle squeeze. Theo moved closer to Harriet.

The shadows in the room thickened and closed around them. In the center of the mist, images appeared, flickering and twisting. Gradually they became clearer, deepening within the swirling cloud, until everyone saw a darkened room, lit only by candles and firelight. It was filled with men, dressed in clothes of the medieval period. All of them carried weapons, and listened intently to a man standing in the center of the room, waving a sword and shouting. The group could not hear what was being said.

"A long time ago," said Bethany, *"the monsters roamed the world much more freely than they do now. They stayed within shadow, but they had no fear of humans, and they took what they wanted and did what they pleased. They were not like we are now."*

The image shifted. A vision of a shadowy hill, lit only by the light of a full moon, spiraled out of the mist. A form melted out of the shadows into the moonlight, massive and red-eyed. It threw its head back and howled soundlessly. The image swirled, and lightning flashed as a dark shape groped and stumbled through black shadowy trees toward a distant ruined castle. It swirled again, and three women, their eyes bright with purpose, their faces wreathed in dark smiles, bent over a roaring fire, shadows playing over their features. Another swirl, and a coffin on a bier appeared, enclosed within a tomb. It opened slightly, and a pale, long-nailed hand crept out. Eyes glittered from within the darkness of the coffin.

"We had no quarrel with humans at first, but not all of us were as prudent as we should have been when we wandered the night," continued Bethany. Her voice had taken on regretful tones. *"Many of them were terrified of us, and in some cases, there was good reason. But the majority of us never meant you any harm."*

They saw a man, his face pale with terror, his mouth wide and screaming, running through darkened woods. In the distance, shadowy shapes with maddened eyes drew closer as he ran. Sharp teeth and claws glimmered ominously.

The image shifted to a couple walking by a cemetery. They stopped by the gate, and embraced tenderly. As they kissed, a horrible shadow rose and clutched the bars of the gate, staring hollow-eyed at the lovers. It pulled, and the gate opened. The couple screamed and ran.

"So the humans did what all humans do in times of trouble, no matter how disparate they may be. They banded together, and formed a society called the Huntsmen." The image shifted again, showing a group of hard-looking men with swords and clubs. There was no humor or kindness in their faces. Each one wore a badge of sorts: a black shield split with a golden cross. The men were glaring so intensely that Emily and Theo shuddered; they actually seemed scarier than the monsters. Frankie made a small, displeased sound, and Harriet growled quietly.

"And the Huntsmen took care of the humans, and protected them from the monsters." Three men ringed an enormous, wolf-like beast, jabbing at it with weapons. The beast roared and snapped at them, jaws slavering. Foam dripped from its mouth. The scene flickered, and men with torches poured into a tomb, shouting, splashing coffins with oil. The men touched the torches to the coffins, which burst into flame. Shapes rose from the blazing coffins, wreathed in fire, their eyes blackened holes. Their mouths screamed silently.

A long shuddering sigh came from the mist, and Emily and Theo felt ashamed. Emily said quietly, "Didn't any of them ever try to *talk* to any of you?"

"No," said Bethany. There were overtones of a sad smile in her voice. *"These were different times. People in early days were superstitious, and often they were made even more frightened by other people in positions of power."*

The image shifted to a church, with people kneeling before an elderly priest. A young, amply figured girl came and knelt before the priest, her cheeks rosy, her lips pouting and full. The priest gazed at her low-cut peasant's blouse, eyes shining. An evil smile played over his lips.

"Eeew," said Theo. "What a pervert."

"Not really," said Bethany. *"More like the wrong man for a very difficult job. But as time wore on, people began to question things and wonder about the world they lived in. Because of this, some of the Huntsmen began to attack the people they were supposed to protect. There's no telling how many humans were accused of being werewolves, witches, and vampires, and hunted down and murdered, or how much knowledge the*

149

world lost because of your ancestors' fear of knowledge replacing religion."

They saw a rather hirsute man fleeing through cobblestoned streets, with a mob behind him waving torches. Some of the men in the mob wore badges similar to the ones seen before. Other men broke into the room of a student, shoving him roughly onto the floor, smashing bottles and destroying lenses and equipment. Books and manuscripts were piled on top of a roaring fire, as scholars pleaded vainly with a gang of armed men. A trio of young girls were dragged toward three stakes with logs piled around them. They were tied to the stakes, and a large man in robes of office, his face red with anger, touched a burning torch to the woodpile. Flames flickered, and the girls screamed in anguish.

Emily looked at Punkin, and saw tears trickling from her glowing eyes. Theo stared, horrified. "Why... why did they start attacking *people?*"

The images vanished. *"Because they were jealous of each other, or because they were afraid of what they didn't understand. And they saw the changes in the world that were beginning to happen. Mechanical developments. Inventions. Science. Things you take for granted. Like, say, clockwork."*

"They were scared of a *clock?*"

"Yes, some were. It was new. But what scared them the most was that they might have outlived their usefulness. That was even worse than the world being overrun by monsters." There was a snicker in her voice. *"But by this time, they were so busy fighting against each other and jumping at shadows that they weren't really paying attention to us anymore. So we retreated.*

"We drew deeper into the shadows. And reason among humans prevailed eventually, because the world is made so that people cannot survive in a vacuum. Superstition no longer reigned. There was growth, and change, and learning. And the Huntsmen moved underground, to wait, and be called upon whenever they were needed. And we began to watch humans."

"Watch us?" asked Emily.

"Yes. We watched you advance, develop, and grow. We watched how you conducted yourselves, how you interacted with each other, even how you raised your children. We wanted to know who and what you were."

The image shifted again, showing the window of a lighted house. A mother sat beside her child's bed, reading a story from a book of fairy tales. Outside the window stood a vampire. It made no movements of attack, but instead appeared to be listening. The child smiled at a certain point in the story, and the vampire also smiled. Its expression was the look of someone who had never heard a fairy tale before, and was enjoying an unexpected pleasure.

"Some of the braver of us began to move among you, so that we could learn more." The mist showed a party within a well-lighted drawing room, with people dancing to a small orchestra. One of the couples was moving a bit haltingly around the floor. As they drew nearer, Emily saw that both partners were slightly hairy, and had glowing yellow eyes. They were watching the other humans carefully, copying their movements. Near a small console table, a man poured goblets of red wine from a decanter and handed one to a smiling woman. They clinked the glasses in a toast, and drank, moving away. Another couple, rather pale-faced, moved into view. Each held a goblet filled with a liquid that was a much deeper red. They smiled at each other, exposing fangs, and clinked their glasses in imitation of the previous couple. They drank.

"Did you want to be like us?" asked Emily.

"Not quite," said Frankie. "It was easier for the vampires and werewolves to be among you, because they were actually able to pass for human. They already had their own cultures, in a way, but they wanted the experience more than anything else."

"Mm-hmm," said Bethany's voice. *"Sometimes being immortal can be a little boring."*

"Are you immortal, Harriet?" asked Theo.

"Nope," said Harriet. "Werewolves are just long-lived. My Grandpop's been around, gosh, I don't know how long. He's an old wolf."

"He's at least as old as me, if not older," said Bethany's voice.

"Yeah," said Harriet. "And Pop's lived nearly two centuries and just started slowing down a little bit." She sighed. "It's being Baron that caused that, mostly. Having to run everything, and keep the peace."

"Okay, so all this is part of your history," said Theo. "But

151

what happened to make all of you settle in Morlock Heights?"

"We're getting to that," said Bethany's voice. *"Even in the enlightened times, the Huntsmen were still hunting us, but we were being more discreet and making ourselves harder to find. But the man who changed everything, for both monsters and humans, was Tobias Cochrane."*

The image shifted. A stocky bearded man, dressed in a white shirt, suspenders and trousers, stood lecturing to a group of younger men. He wore an armband with the insignia of the Huntsmen. The man did not speak with the venomous hatred that the girls had seen earlier; instead he spoke as a teacher to a class of students. His eyes were steel-blue, and possessed a fierce, hungry intelligence.

"Tobias Cochrane was different from the average Huntsman," said Bethany's voice. *"He was curious about monsters, and wanted to study them, learn about them. He thought that some sort of peace could be arranged between our peoples. And that was the reason the Huntsmen tried to get rid of him. They didn't want peace between our kinds; they wanted to destroy us, because they thought we were evil."*

"But some of you are," said Emily. "Or were, rather. I mean--"

"No. That's true. I don't deny that there are monsters among us who are vicious, and bullying, and power-hungry, and unscrupulous and mean-minded. The early monsters were wild and untamed and had no use for humans. But when they began watching humans, they sort of grew and learned along with them. Monsters discovered, just like you, that it was a bigger, wider world, and that how big it could actually be was all up to us."

"So what did they do to Tobias Cochrane?"

"They sent him alone to hunt down a pack from the Vrolok Clan," said Harriet, her nose wrinkling. *"No one,* not even *other* werewolves, had much to do with them. Still don't. They're like the early monsters. They haven't changed with the times, or anything." She growled softly. "They're also *mean.*"

"Right," said Bethany's voice. *"Look."*

The mist swirled again, and Tobias Cochrane appeared on a hillside in the midst of a pack of massive, snarling werewolves, their corpse-gray fur glowing in the moonlight. They had cornered him against a clump of dead trees, but he was slashing at them with a huge axe, and apparently holding his own. Blood flew and spattered as Cochrane drove the pack further away from him. The axe shone brightly in the moonlight; its blade was plated with silver.

The lead werewolf, who was larger than the others, rushed forward and bowled Cochrane over backward, claws slashing. A gash appeared on the back of Cochrane's axe hand. Cochrane roared in pain and slammed the flat of the axe against the beast's head. As the werewolf drew back, shaking its head, Cochrane sprang to his feet and drove the axe through its neck. The head flew out of view, and the body fell to the ground. The other werewolves, seeing the demise of their leader, fled howling into the darkness. Cochrane wiped his axe hand across his forehead, and winced, staring at the gash on his hand.

"It was only a scratch," said Bethany's voice. *"And it would have taken at least until next full moon to tell if he would shift. Most likely he wouldn't have, because it takes a serious wound from a werewolf in order to become one. But the Vroloks were pretty strong, and one scratch was all the Huntsmen needed to rid themselves of him."* There was a sigh.

"Don't anybody get any ideas about *me,*" said Harriet sharply. "I know what you're thinking, but I'm *not kindred* to the Vrolok. We don't run with *wargabas* like that."

"Well… of course not, Harriet," said Emily.

"What's a wargabas?" asked Theo.

"Warga-*ba.* Werewolf swear word," said Harriet. "It means a werewolf with no family, no alpha, no pack. It's a bad thing to call a werewolf that, and it's grounds for war between Clans in some cases. But Vroloks *deserve* it."

"The Huntsmen dismissed Cochrane shortly after that," said Bethany's voice. *"And in those days, being dismissed meant that you were left somewhere where monsters had been sighted, so that you would die. The Huntsmen hoped Cochrane would be found again by the Vroloks, so they could finish him off. But it was the Lunas-Gaia Clan who found him first."*

In the mist, Tobias Cochrane sat on the floor of a cave beside a tall, gentle-looking female werewolf with honey-colored fur. Other werewolves clustered around them, all listening, as the two spoke in conversation. Emily and Theo saw that Cochrane's ears had become pointed, and his hair now had a vaguely fur-like appearance. Cochrane raised his hand to make a point, and they saw the now-healed scar left by the Vrolok. His fingernails had lengthened a

153

bit.

"So he did become a werewolf?" asked Theo.

"No. He gained some heightened senses, and there were a few physical changes due to the deepness of the wound. But he never fully shifted. He lived among the werewolves for many years, and gradually, he met other monsters, as well. Look."

The scene shifted, and Cochrane stood at the door of an old castle, with three werewolves surrounding him. Two of the werewolves had the honey-colored fur of the Lunas-Gaia Clan. The third was an enormous, hulking beast who towered over the others, and seemed to be totally muscle and sinew. It had fur that was the same color as Harriet's. Cochrane and the big werewolf turned into view, and the group saw a distinct resemblance to Harriet. One corner of the mouth was quirking into a smile, and the eyes sparkled with warm humor.

"That's Pop," said Harriet, smiling proudly. "Artemus Von Lupin of the Clan Of Romulus. This was way before he became Baron."

Cochrane knocked at the door. It opened, and two vampires stood there. One was a handsome, jovial-looking man dressed in an Elizabethan-era riding costume, whose black hair was combed back from his forehead and whitening at the temples. The other was bald, thin and gaunt, dressed in a long dark coat and trousers. Its eyes burned with a feral intensity. The fangs protruded from the front of its mouth, giving a ratlike appearance. It held a small white rat gently in one clawed hand.

"Nosferatu," breathed Emily.

"Yes," said Bethany's voice. *"That is Mr. Hieronymous Grimm, now the principal of Graf Orlok, and the Revenant is my father, Count Andreas Leonidas Ruthven."* There was a hint of grudging pride in her voice.

"Wow," said Theo. "Your dad's *hot.*"

There was a pause. *"Yes,"* said Bethany's voice, mildly irritated. *"He does attract attention from the ladies, that's for sure."*

Ruthven smiled at Cochrane and shook hands vigorously with him. Artemus waved a hand at Grimm, and spoke to Cochrane. Cochrane held out his hand. Grimm looked surprised, and tentatively shook hands with Cochrane. His expression hovered somewhere between pleasure and curiosity. The white rat ran up his arm and perched on his shoulder, gazing at Cochrane.

"Eventually, Cochrane came to know all the different monsterkind, including the witches, Creatures, Mad Scientists, and so forth. He saw that while we lived differently, sometimes even violently, most of us meant no harm to mankind. And eventually, he decided to return to the Huntsmen and tell them what he'd learned."

There was a sigh from Punkin. The group saw that she was swaying slightly. The glow in her eyes flickered. *"Tired,"* she sighed.

"So am I, darling," said Bethany's voice. *"I'm almost done. Cochrane eventually convinced most of the Huntsmen that monsters and humans could live companionably, to some degree. And thus began the great project--a place where monsters could live quietly alongside humans with all they needed. This was the beginning of Morlock Heights, and the great Partnership that eventually became our ruling body--the Council Of Monsterkind."*

They saw a large stretch of overgrown forest-land, dominated by a high hill with a single enormous oak tree at its top, all underneath an overcast sky. On top of the hill stood Cochrane, Artemus, Ruthven, and Grimm, with a tall, middle-aged woman in a red robe. The woman's hair was a stark white, with a single red streak of hair down the center of her head, and she carried a large broom with a red-varnished handle. She leaned her broom against the tree and helped Artemus to hang a somewhat weatherbeaten board onto a low-hanging limb. On the board was written in large letters:

MORLOCK HEIGHTS.
HERE THERE BE MONSTERS.

"Rasputina," said Punkin in a whisper. *"My Great-Granny."*

"And someone else, too," said Bethany's voice. *"Look, Frankie."*

Another woman, wearing a white laboratory coat and carrying a large roll of blueprints, strode confidently into view. The woman was starkly pale and beautiful and had hair that was even whiter than Rasputina's; it almost glowed. She unrolled a blueprint

155

and began discussing it with the group.

"That's Dr. Anais Corinthian," said Frankie, pleased. "It makes sense, really; she was the only one who could get the Mad Scientists to act sensibly, most of the time. But I never knew that she helped found Morlock Heights."

"You said that most of the Huntsmen followed Cochrane," said Theo. "What happened to those who didn't?"

"That was the bit we didn't tell you about," said Frankie. "We don't like to talk about them, and sometimes we wonder if they're not still around."

"Even so," said Bethany's voice," *"the question deserves an answer. They became the Shadow League, Theo. Outlaws and mercenaries without sanction, who hunted down not only monsters, but humans and Huntsmen who were sympathetic to them. They had no faith in Cochrane and no wish to change with the times, and they were consumed by fear and loathing."*

The scene shifted. A man dressed in a dark leather coat stood haranguing a gathering of men. He was disguised by a black mask that fit tightly over his face, revealing nothing but his eyes, which blazed with rage as he shouted ferociously at the group of men. Behind him was a large banner with the Huntsmen insignia. He strode to the banner and tore it away, revealing another banner: a black shield with a red lightning bolt running diagonally across. A cheer went up from the assembly. The man held up a clenched fist, shaking it at his audience.

"They will not survive," he hissed. *"They will retreat into the shadows, but we will be waiting there for them. There will be no safety in the shadows--only death. DEATH!!"* he shouted.

"Wait a minute," said Emily. "We couldn't hear other stuff. How come we can hear *him?*"

"Huh?" said Frankie.

"I don't know," said Bethany's worried voice. *"Punkin, what's going on?"*

Punkin's body heaved suddenly. Her breathing quickened, and the glow from her eyes spread through her body. *"I... don't know... help...me..."*

"DEATH TO MONSTERKIND!!" shouted the man. His voice

was becoming clearer. The girls could hear the shouting men. *"ONE BY ONE WE WILL TAKE THEM!!"*

"Punkin!!" shouted Bethany's voice. *"Something's wrong! Stop!!"*

The man had stopped speaking, and seemed to be listening. He turned his head slightly. Emily and Theo clutched each other, afraid.

He was looking right at them. His eyes widened. *"Someone here…"* He brought his fist down, over his heart, and clenched it.

There was a squeal of pain from Bethany within the mist. *"OWWW! PUNKIN, STOP IT! BREAK THE SPELL NOW!!"*

Punkin's body wrenched horribly. Emily and Theo screamed. Harriet sprang to her feet and crouched, growling, hovering protectively over Punkin. Frankie seized Emily and Theo, pulling them away from the mist.

Bethany screamed, and the mist rippled dangerously. The man's voice raised to an angry echoing roar. *"WHO DARES??!"*

Punkin shrieked in terror. The glow faded from her eyes.

The candles went out.

Joanna was curled in her easy chair with a good book when she heard the noises above.

Well. They must be having a good time.

She got up and walked to the foot of the stairs. She glanced at the clock, and noticed that it was 11:30. Time for them to start preparing for bed.

Then she heard her daughter and Theo screaming.

Joanna was an exceedingly tolerant woman. She had kept her cool when her husband Malcolm had first shown signs of cheating; after he'd confessed his discretion she'd handled the divorce proceedings in as businesslike and calculating a manner as her emotions would allow, and she'd done her best to help her children through the transition. She'd met Theo when Emily had brought her home the first time, and though she'd thought at first that Theo was a little wild for Emily and maybe had more time without supervision than was healthy, she'd recognized a kindred spirit between them, and had instantly got on with Theo's mother Kathleen. And tonight, she had met the Grrls and recovered quite well from the first shock of seeing them, and despite all she knew about monsters from movies, despite all her initial fears because of their terrible differences and inhuman aspects, she'd *allowed* them in her house. *Her house.*

The screams banished all pretensions of tolerance and replaced them with cold panic. She raced up the stairs.

The door to Emily's room was closed. She heard a shriek, and then a loud thump, as of a body hitting the floor. Terrible scenes of the children, the children she was responsible for

(*oh dear God my daughter and Theo don't forget Theo Kathleen would be devastated if something happened to Theo*)

being eaten, bit, clawed, drained of blood, *murdered,* surfaced in her mind. She rushed to the door and kicked it open.

"What in heaven's name is going on?!" she shouted without thinking. Then her vision cleared, and she saw the scene before her.

The room was not dark as she had expected, but was fully lighted. Harriet was crouching over Punkin, who looked pale with fright. Frankie had both Emily and Theo in her arms, and was clutching them protectively. Bethany appeared to have taken a fall and was lying on her back in the middle of the floor, amidst a mess of paper cups.

Bethany saw Joanna first and shouted, *"Bloody mouse!"*

"I suppose I'll have to buy a mousetrap in the morning," Joanna said wearily.

Theo and Punkin had been dispatched to the kitchen with the dishes, and Joanna had ordered Theo to perform part of her penance; Punkin had gratefully offered to help. Frankie and Bethany had gone down the hall to get sleeping bags and extra pillows, and were arranging nests for everyone on the floor. Harriet was dutifully sniffing about the room, searching out possible locations for the "mouse's" lair. She had rounded the room and was now halfway under the bed.

"It wasn't anything terrible, Mom," said Emily. "It was just really… unexpected."

"*Very* unexpected," echoed Frankie.

Harriet pulled herself out from under the bed. "I think he

might have hidden somewhere in this corner, over here by the window. I guess that's where the trap should go, Mom."

"Thank you, Harriet," said Joanna. "That nose of yours is rather handy, I expect."

"Yes, Mom. The nose knows," said Harriet, laying her finger aside it.

Bethany had a contrite expression. "I'm sorry about the swear word, ma'am," she said. "It just surprised me so that I tripped and fell. I didn't mean anything by it."

"It's all right, dear," said Joanna, patting Bethany's shoulder. Out of the corner of her eye, Emily saw Harriet roll her eyes and receive a smack from Frankie. Joanna's back was to them, and she never noticed.

Theo and Punkin returned from the kitchen. Punkin still looked dazed, and Emily supposed that her spell must have been very tiring. Joanna gave her a concerned look. "Are you all right, dear?"

"Yes'm," said Punkin. "It was just real sudden, is all. The mouse just ran across the floor so quick that I didn't know what was happening." She rubbed her arms, as if she were cold. "I just got scared, was all."

"Well, I wasn't scared of it," said Harriet.

"Mom," Emily said, hoping to distract her mother from the glares Harriet was receiving from the other Grrls, "I think everything's okay here. I'm really sorry I scared you. I didn't mean to."

"Neither did we," said Frankie and Bethany together.

"Sorry, Mom," said Harriet. Punkin hung her head, shamefaced.

Joanna looked slightly ashamed of herself. "It's all right. That's what mothers do, you know." She gave Emily and Theo each a hug, and went around and hugged each of the Grrls. "Good night, everyone. Time for bed. Lights out in five minutes, understand?"

"Yes, ma'am," said everyone. Joanna closed the door, and the group heard her footsteps descending the stairs. There was a general sigh of relief.

"Well, that's all for that, then," said Harriet, a bit sulkily. She glared at Bethany. "I thought someone said tonight that werewolves aren't good at lying. Well, they *aren't*."

"It wasn't a lie, Harriet," said Bethany tiredly. "We just didn't tell her *everything*, that's all. And you did a *very* good job pretending to sniff out the mouse."

"Well, it wasn't all pretending," said Harriet. "There actually was a mouse in here once." She looked at Emily. "It might be a good idea for your mom to get a mousetrap in here, for awhile."

"Oh," gulped Emily. "Okay. Thanks, Harriet."

Frankie was staring at the door. "Your mom's really cool, Emily," she said. Her voice was quiet.

"Yeah," said Theo. "Mrs. Peters is a good mom."

There was a moment of quiet among the group. "Thanks, guys," Emily said softly. "It was a good party."

"What do you think all that... stuff was about?" asked Theo. "I mean, what *happened?*"

"What happened," said Bethany, "was that something looked back. It was definitely the Shadow League we saw, but I'm not sure about anything else."

"But what if he knows where we are now?" asked Emily. "What if he tries to hurt us?"

Frankie went to Emily and took her shoulders. "The Shadow League," she said, "will not bother us. Cochrane and the Huntsmen who followed him drove them away a long time ago. And even if they did come, we would protect you."

"It's like Punkin told you," said Bethany. "She's an Adept, and a very powerful one. It was probably one of those cases where the images take on a life of their own, which sometimes happens even with mist-scrying."

"*I* dunno," grumbled Punkin. "All I know is I'm *real* tired and I wanna go to *bed.*" She flopped down on the floor and began to undo her shoes. "Too powerful. Can't do *nothin'* without it becomin' somethin' *big*. Sometimes it's a pain in the tailbone bein' an Adept."

"I guess so," said Emily. "Anyway, it was really neat, even if we did get a scare." On this note, the other Grrls began preparing for bed.

"Um, Emily?" said Bethany. "Do you think your mother

would mind if I slept on the bed in your little brother's room?" She looked slightly embarrassed. "It's sort of an... Undead, vampire kind of thing."

"Oh. Um... sure," said Emily. "It's just down the hall. Will... will you be okay? By yourself, I mean."

"Yes, I will. Thank you, Emily," said Bethany gratefully. She turned to Harriet. "Will you come and close my eyes?"

"Sure," said Harriet. Bethany gathered up her sleeping bag and a pillow and left the room, with Harriet following. Emily stared after them.

"She's embarrassed about you and Theo seeing her in deathsleep," said Frankie, by way of explanation. "She thought you might be a bit iffy about sharing a room with someone who's Undead."

"Oh. Oh, dear." Emily looked downcast. "Poor Bethany."

"It's okay," said Frankie. "It's a vampire's way of manners. They're particular about that kind of thing, anyway."

"Why did she ask Harriet to close her eyes?" asked Theo.

"Because when they enter deathsleep, vampires can't move at all," answered Frankie. "And it's not so great to come out of it later with your eyes glazed over."

"Ooh," said Theo. "Yuck."

"Yeah," said Frankie. "It's why vampires keep a human servant, to take care of things like that."

"Well, she was really sweet to show us everything tonight," said Emily. "So were you, Punkin," she added. There was a mumble of acknowledgement from the exhausted witch.

"Yeah, thanks," said Theo. "It was cool. But we didn't see much about the Mad Scientists or anything."

"Well, I c'n only show so much," mumbled Punkin, snuggling down into her sleeping bag. "And Frankie knows more about 'em than I do, anyway." She yawned.

"The Mad Scientists began migrating to Morlock Heights around the 1800's," said Frankie, stretching out on her sleeping bag. "They came in pretty steadily until about the end of the 1950's, I think. We haven't seen too many since then."

"Hey," said Theo thoughtfully, "were any of them, like, Nazi scientists? We learned in history class that the Nazis had a bunch of scientists that did all kinds of weird stuff, trying to build super soldiers and things. What about that?"

"I dunno," said Frankie, shrugging. "A few of them were German, I know. But I don't think any of them were Nazis." She snickered. "Nazis wouldn't last too long in Morlock Heights."

"Why not?" asked Emily.

"Cause if you're gonna live 'n be neighbors with Creatures 'n werewolves 'n witches 'n vampires, you can't go round castin' aspersions on folks 'cause of how they are if you want to survive for too long," mumbled a voice from underneath a pointed hat. "Now can we *please* go to sleep?"

"Okay, okay," said Frankie. "Here comes Harriet."

Harriet sauntered into the room. "Your little brother's room is cool," she said. "All those sports posters and things."

"Is Bethany all right?" asked Emily. Theo looked up from the floor.

"Yeah, she's fine," said Harriet, grinning. "She said to tell you thank you and good night." She began bedding down.

"Who's getting the lights?" asked Theo.

A hand waved in the air from Punkin's pile of bedclothes. The room plunged into darkness. "G'night," she mumbled, and turned over.

"Good night, everybody," said Frankie, and closed her eyes. Harriet was already in place on the floor and snoring.

" 'Night," said Theo, shifting in her bag.

Emily lay in bed and looked out the window at the night. She definitely felt a lot safer with the Monster Grrls now, after having seen the Shadow League. She supposed that humans could be even scarier than monsters at times, or maybe even *become* monsters without trying very hard. She turned over in her bed and looked at the dark shapes on the floor, watching them. Her eyes grew heavy.

It had been a strange party, and even a little bit scary. But it had been a *good* party. Her *first* party.

There was a smile on her face as she drifted off to sleep.

NINE: THIS IS WHAT WE ARE

Morning came, and sunlight streamed into the room. Emily blinked, and rubbed her eyes sleepily.

Her first thought was of school, and then she remembered that it was Saturday; she didn't have to go to school. She smiled and wondered what time it was.

She rolled over to look at the clock, and sat upright in bed, staring.

Punkin was gently floating about three feet in the air. Her blanket lay over her sleeping body, and her pillow, positioned under her head, also floated. Her hat lay on the floor below her. Punkin was deeply snuggled into her blanket with a dreamy and somewhat ecstatic smile on her face.

Emily watched for a moment, then smiled to herself. She got out of bed and went over to Punkin, picked up her hat, and set it carefully on the dresser. She padded quietly around the room, looking at her sleeping friends.

Theo was snoring nasally, buried in her sleeping bag. Frankie was lying stiffly on top of her bag, her arms by her sides and her feet together; occasionally, her hand spasmed, and her electrodes crackled softly. Harriet had made a sort of nest out of her sleeping bag and blanket and had pulled pillows around her, so that she appeared to be sleeping in a doggy bed. She lay curled in a fetal position and was snuggled deep into one of the pillows, snoring gently. One of her legs began to twitch, as if she were running.

She's dreaming, thought Emily. *And in her dream she's running with the full moon. And Punkin dreams of flying. And Frankie dreams of lightning.*

She remembered something her mother had told her. Sometimes, her mother had said, she would come into Emily's room at night when Emily had been a baby, and she would watch her sleep. It was not because Emily had been a difficult baby, she knew; James had been the one who cried a lot at night. It was because she derived pleasure from seeing her sleeping child. Emily had not understood this at first.

Now, as she watched her friends sleep, she had an insight into what her mother had meant, and she felt her heart swell a bit. She looked around at them all: the kindhearted, infinitely gentle and curious Frankie; sweet Punkin, well-meaning, sometimes so painfully shy that your heart bled for her; Harriet, heart as golden as her eyes, rowdy and wild, who made them all laugh with her jokes and playful nature; and Emily's best friend Theo, who had weathered the storms of boring school days and no friends and no fathers and divorce with her, who would be her friend forever.

And there was also Bethany. The dark one.

Emily went to the door, lost in thought. She stared down the hall at the closed door of James's room.

Bethany was the paradox of the Monster Grrls, she thought. Bethany came across as worldly, jaded, decadent, more adult than she should be. She'd lived, of sorts, for a *long* time, longer than anyone Emily had ever known. She, of all the Grrls, was probably the most dangerous, the most *monstrous,*due to being a vampire.

Except that... well, sometimes the actions didn't *fit* with the picture. Bethany *could* be amazingly peevish and self-centered at times, but she was terribly generous and kind to them. She was often very impatient with Harriet, but there seemed to be a long and shared history between them, as well as the others. She seemed to possess boundless hatred for Jessica and her cronies, and at the same time it was more exasperation than real hatred, as if she were waiting impatiently for them to realize that they were being *stupid* and needed to get on with things.

She wondered what would have happened if Bethany had misted at Jessica's party, during the fight. An image rose unbidden in her mind: of Jessica, Heather, Tiffany and their friends all swathed in a swirling, peculiarly *solid* mist, falling to their knees, clutching at their throats, gasping, *choking.* And just above them, a face forming out of the mist; an *angry* face with red eyes, a grimace of rage twisting its mouth, fangs protruding...

She shook herself. Bethany was not like that.

Emily had watched the Grrls since the first day she'd been

with them. Oh, Bethany could get *mad*, all right, but she had never behaved badly or seemed particularly *evil*. In fact, she often strived to be better than what she was. All the Grrls did.

Emily glanced at Frankie, sleeping on her bag. There was no question that Frankie was the leader; something about Frankie *said* that. But Bethany was the moral compass, the instigator, the lieutenant, and though she could be a leader in her own right, she deferred to Frankie. That was not vampire behavior as Emily knew it.

Bethany also keeps their secrets. Their history.

She blinked.

This was silly. There was no room for such dark thoughts, not on a Saturday morning with no school. There were things to do, and the Grrls would wake up soon, and they'd all have breakfast with her and Theo and Mom. Maybe Mom would make toaster waffles. She usually did on Saturdays. Maybe they could have waffles too.

And since it was Saturday and such nice things were going to happen, she was going to skip out on these dark thoughts, go down the hall to her little brother's room, and check on her friend.

Her *vampire* friend.

She swallowed. She quietly opened the door, as wide as possible, and tiptoed down the hall to her brother's room.

The door was closed. Emily debated on whether to knock, then remembered that Bethany couldn't move. Which meant she probably wouldn't *hear*.

Frankie said she couldn't move in deathsleep.

Deathsleep. Ooh, what an awful name. It sounds like a horror movie, almost. Deathsleep. Deathsleep II. Return of Deathsleep.

Stop it!

She shook herself again. She felt a chill, and rubbed her arms. She turned the knob, and gently opened the door.

The curtains had been drawn, and the room was shadowy and dark. The sleeping bag had been placed over the mattress, covering the comforter and pillows.

In the gloom, Emily could see Bethany lying on the sleeping bag, on her back. She wore a black T-shirt and black underpants. Her

165

hands were folded over her chest, and her feet were bare. Emily saw black toenails gleaming dully against her white skin.

The picture struck Emily as odd at first; she had never seen Bethany wearing anything *that* casual. She saw Bethany's dress and cape hanging on the knobs of James's dresser. Her shoes and bag were on the floor.

There was no sound of breathing at all. Bethany was dead.

Emily felt cold. She rubbed her hands on her legs, trying to make them warm. The *room* seemed cold.

She began to move toward the bed, her heart pounding in her chest. She was terribly frightened, but she had come this far, and she was going to see it through.

She stood beside the bed, and looked at the dead girl. Bethany's skin seemed to glow in the dim light, as if she were a statue carved from alabaster or pearl. She saw the Eye Of Azrael around Bethany's neck. The image of the eye swam forward, appeared to blink curiously at her, and then vanished.

Bethany's face was expressionless. Peaceful. Emily wondered if she dreamed.

Probably not. Not like this.

The full horror of Bethany's condition struck her, and it was all she could do to keep from screaming. But she had to see. Had to *know*.

She steadied herself, reached out, and gently tapped Bethany's shoulder. No response.

She swallowed, and tried again. Still no response. She gripped Bethany's shoulder, and shook. Bethany did not move.

Well, what to do now, she thought. Maybe one of the others knew how to wake her up. Which meant she'd have to wake *them* up. She sighed and sat down on the bed beside Bethany.

The mattress was old and creaked when she sat down. Emily arranged herself, trying to find a good sitting position. The creaking sound prevented Emily from hearing a soft *chuckh* sound, like someone's tongue clucking against the roof of their mouth. She took one last look at Bethany, then put her chin in her hands, wondering what to do.

A horrible apparition roiled up from the bed, spitting and

hissing, its clawed hands flailing the air. The eyes were a burning red, sunken deep into the skull-like face, and its fangs were fully extended. Black hair flew wildly as the thing shook its head back and forth.

"HHhhhraahhhhhrrrrrhh!!!" it screeched.

Emily's heart slammed into her throat. She flung herself off the bed and scrambled on her behind along the floor, her legs backpedaling furiously. She wanted to scream, but her voice was stuck; all she could manage was a terrified, hyperventilating squeak. Emily felt her back hit the wall, and froze in terror.

The thing seemed about to hurl itself toward her. It stretched out its claws.

Then it blinked. It put its head on one side and seemed to recognize her. *"Oh, bollockth,"* it lisped. *"I'm thorry, Emily. Juth give me a minute..."*

It stretched and shook its head, like a cat. The fangs receded, and in a moment Bethany was sitting up on the bed, her face normal, her eyes blinking. She pinched the bridge of her nose, sighing heavily. Emily saw, dully, that Bethany's T-shirt seemed to advertise some sort of rock band. Three cartoon girl heads floated above a logo in slashing letters: INTERPLANETARY SUPERHEROES.

Emily slowly got up from the floor, shaken. "What was... was..."

Bethany looked extremely embarrassed. "I'm *so* sorry, Emily," she said. "I *never* look my best when I've just woken up. *Unh.*" She rubbed her forehead. "You shouldn't have had to see that. I didn't think you'd be up so early." She gave Emily a miserable look. "I didn't think you'd come to wake me up, either."

Emily watched Bethany for a moment, then went and sat back down beside her. Bethany moved to sit on the edge of the bed and stared at the floor. Neither of them spoke.

"What's Interplanetary Superheroes?" asked Emily after a moment.

"Hmm? Oh." She looked at her T-shirt. "It's one of my favorite bands. They play around Morlock Heights a lot. You'd like them." She sighed sadly. "Would you mind handing me my blood, please? It's in my purse." Her mouth tightened. "I should probably have my Altoids, too," she added.

Emily got the bag and handed it to Bethany, who rummaged through it. She took a long, deep swig of blood first, and then popped three Altoids. The silence returned.

After a moment Emily said, "I'm sorry. I probably should have let you wake up on your own. It's just--Frankie told me about... last night, and, well, I was worried."

Bethany smiled. "Good old Frankie." She sighed. "I guess I should have, well... explained myself last night. Which is something I'm not used to doing."

"But you weren't comfortable with explaining. About deathsleep."

She hung her head. "No, I wasn't, Emily. I... I never wanted to go to human school, you know. But Father is trying to move further up in the High Court of Vampyr, and... well, it'll look good for him if his daughter gets along with humans. So I'm going to school with the humans. And I didn't want to." She sniffled. "Not at first."

"Oh."

"I didn't expect to meet someone like you. Didn't think that humans would behave like you, or Theo. You're... you're both so sweet." Her eyes filled with red tears, and she wiped them away furiously. "I think, God, I shouldn't let them see this, shouldn't tell them this, because then they'll see I'm a *monster* and they'll *hate* me, and you never *do*, never act how I *expect*, and... I keep forgetting that you aren't... I mean, you've been so *tolerant*, and..."

"Why not?" asked Emily. "We're friends."

"Y...yes... but, but..." Bethany was trying to decide how to word her thoughts. "Humans aren't ordinarily so accommodating of vampires. They... they burn coffins, and stick stakes in them, and..."

"And vampires normally bite humans and drain all their blood," Emily said. "But *you* don't act like a regular vampire, so why should I act like a regular human?"

Bethany frowned and looked away. "You're right," she said. "It's very annoying."

"What, vampires biting people and draining their blood?"

"No, that you're right."

Emily grinned. After a moment, Bethany smiled. "I'm sorry about that bad scare I gave you, Emily," she sighed. "Most of it is, well, force of habit."

"Huh?"

"Oh, *you* know. It's nearly dawn, and you've had a pleasant evening's feeding, and you've just settled down into your coffin, all comfy and cozy, with the lid on good and tight, and then just before you really slide into deathsleep, your coffin opens and there are all these *silly* little peasant people standing around with crucifixes and garlic and stakes, and..." Bethany noticed Emily's blank stare. "You've never experienced what I'm talking about, have you?"

Emily wordlessly shook her head.

"Oh. Well, then." She lapsed back into a sad silence.

After a moment, Emily said haltingly, "W-when I went to summer camp once, some of the girls put a frog in my bed."

Bethany stared at her for so long that Emily became embarrassed, and decided she had *really* said the wrong thing. Then she noticed the corner of Bethany's mouth quirking. After a moment, Bethany snorted, then began to snigger. Emily smiled, then began giggling.

Within moments the two of them were convulsed with laughter, leaning on each other. Bethany laughed so hard that she fell off the bed, which caused a fresh spate of laughter. Little by little, they regained control of themselves.

"Whoo," said Bethany, grinning. "I haven't laughed *that* hard in a while. Thank you, Emily."

"No, thank you," said Emily. "Thank *all* of you. You guys are really great friends."

Bethany put her head on one side and smiled gently at Emily. "Well, I should think it works both ways," she said. "And thank you for being such great friends of ours." She got to her feet. "I've got to get dressed," she said, pulling out socks, black sneakers and a pair of red shorts from her bag. The socks had a pattern of small black bats.

"You carry clothes with you?" asked Emily.

"Yep, and a toothbrush," she said, producing a black-handled one from her bag. The bristles had a pinkish stain. "Might I borrow some toothpaste?"

"Oh, sure. That's kind of cool. I mean, carrying the clothes."

"The motto of the Boy Scouts is also the motto of the vampires: Be prepared. Especially if you do a lot of the night life," Bethany said, smiling. She pulled on her shorts. "I'm dying for some coffee." She sat on the bed and pulled on her socks and sneakers.

Emily stared at her. "Vampires drink *coffee* in the morning?"

"This one does. The blood is the life," said Bethany, tying laces, "but the caffeine makes it worth the effort. Shall we?"

"I guess we should get the others up," said Emily. She heard a sudden thump and a squeal from her room. "Ooh. I wonder if that was Punkin."

"Was she...?" Bethany held her hand out, palm down, and moved it up and down, in the manner of someone levitating. Emily nodded.

"Probably was, then. Let's go see."

"Oh, shoot!" shouted Punkin. "Durn, durn, *durn!*"

Everyone was up, and preparing to go downstairs for breakfast. There had been a sort of mild clearing away of various bedclothes, and a groggy Frankie had stumbled sleepily downstairs with her generator case to do her morning recharging outside in the back yard. There had been various morning rituals, and Punkin had recovered her hat. Then they discovered that something was wrong with the room lights; the switch did not seem to be working, and the lights wouldn't come on. Punkin, since she had used magic to turn them off last night, was trying to turn them on again. She flailed her hand again and again at the switch. Nothing happened. Finally she squealed in frustration and sat down on the bed.

"It's not anything to worry about, Punkin," protested Emily. "This is an old house. It's probably just a blown fuse or something."

"It's not *fair*," wailed Punkin. "It's always the *same*. I do a spell and then it's like everythin' switches *off* for a while. I don't know *what's* wrong with me." She leaned over and pulled the brim of her hat around her head. "I'm *never* gon' be able to fly a broom."

"That's not true, darling," said Bethany. "You *know* witches have to be at least sixteen before they can apply for a broom license, and just because you're an Adept doesn't mean you can get around that. It's Council Law."

"Witches have broom licenses?" asked Theo.   Bethany nodded.

"But I *don't understand it!* I *turnt* the dang thing off last night! How come I can't get it back on?" Her voice was twanging dangerously, and can't came out as *cain't.*

"Maybe you need some breakfast," said Harriet. "Everything always works better after a good breakfast. Well, for *me,* anyway."

Frankie entered the room, carrying her generator.   She surveyed the group. "Still nothing?"

Everyone shook their heads.

"Hmm," said Frankie. She reached into a side pocket of her generator case and brought out an electrical cable, with a plug at one end and a stripped, bare wire at the other.

"Don't anyone touch me," she warned. She plugged it into the wall socket, and then put the other end in her mouth,[6] causing everyone in the room to wince. There was a soft hum, and Frankie's electrodes sparked.   "Hmm.   Ith not elethtrithal," she said, unplugging the wire. "Your house current's fine. Kind of yummy, really."

"Yummy sounds like a good idea," said Bethany. "I move we all go downstairs and have breakfast. No doubt the problem will resolve itself then."

There was a loud, low-pitched growl. Everyone looked at Harriet, who grinned sheepishly. "Sorry," she said. "My stomach's rumbling."

Emily briefly wondered if there was enough food to feed Harriet. "Bethany's right, Punkin," she said. "Mom's got waffles. C'mon."

"*One* more time," grumbled Punkin, standing up.   She straightened her hat and took a deep breath. Sticking her tongue in the corner of her mouth, she gathered herself and flung her hand at the light switch as if she were pitching a fastball. The air crackled, and the light switch glowed briefly.

The lights snapped on, blazing brightly, and both bulbs in the

---

[6]   Notice to readers, electricians, small children, daredevils, and the incredibly stupid: *DO NOT TRY THIS AT HOME, OR ANYWHERE ELSE, EVER.*

light fixture promptly shot out of their sockets and exploded. Glass showered the floor, making everyone duck. Punkin stamped her foot and crossed her arms over her chest, pouting.

"I think you put too much pepper on that one," said Harriet. "But at least you got it to work again."

"Oh, well, that's no worry," sighed Emily. "Mom bought tons of light bulbs from the Lions' Club last year. C'mon, everyone. Breakfast time." She headed for the stairs.

Joanna was already in the kitchen, and had just finished making coffee when Emily, Theo and the Grrls appeared. There was a chorus of good mornings, and Bethany quickly broke out a fresh bottle of blood from the refrigerator. "Is there any coffee, Mrs. Peters?" she asked, her eyes shining.

"Of course, dear, help yourself."

"*Thank* you." Bethany immediately dashed to the coffee maker, poured herself a cup, tipped the sugar bowl into it, and added a hefty dollop of blood. She stirred and sipped her coffee. "Mmmmmm," she said. "That's *lovely*. French vanilla blend and O-positive."

The humans among the group were unable to keep from grimacing. "No offense, Bethany, but make sure you keep *that* cup with *you*," said Theo.

"It's an acquired taste," said Bethany, smiling.

Joanna moved past the group, all helping themselves to coffee, and pulled out two boxes of toaster waffles from the refrigerator. "I thought that you girls would like toaster waffles for breakfast. It's sort of a Saturday morning tradition in our house --"

There was a loud growl from Harriet's stomach. Everyone, including Joanna, stared at Harriet, who immediately gazed at the ceiling. Emily saw her lips moving silently, and realized that Harriet, in an attempt to appear nonchalant, was counting the tiles in the ceiling.

"Um." Joanna had already gathered that two boxes of toaster waffles probably would not satisfy the needs of a growing werewolf. She looked at Emily, who smiled nervously and shrugged. "Well," she said, "I suppose I could go to the store--"

"Ma'am?" said Punkin. "Um, do you mind if I try somethin'? I might be able to make 'em enough to go 'round, if I use a duplication spell."

"Spell?" asked Joanna. The group, remembering the episode upstairs, all traded a nervous look.

"Yes, ma'am. I was real good at duplication spells when I took Remedial Spells out at Graf Orlok. Madame Abyssinia gave me top of the class."

Joanna smiled, thinking of the Sorcerer's Apprentice in *Fantasia*. "Were you able to get the brooms to stop getting water from the well?" she asked jokingly.

Punkin looked surprised. "How'd you know, ma'am?"

Joanna stared at Punkin for a minute, and then sighed. "All right. What do I need to do? And *please* don't mess up my kitchen."

"Yes, please," said Theo, thinking of her still-unfinished penance.

"Oh, no, ma'am. Um, I need to have one of the boxes, please."

Joanna handed her a box, and walked over to the group. Punkin moved to the center of the kitchen, examining the box curiously. "I've never had these before. Huh. They even make 'em with little bits of strawberry and blueberry in 'em," she murmured. "Okay. The power center of the kitchen is right about *here*," she said, standing beside the table. "I'm gonna need everybody to be quiet for a minute, and let me concentrate."

She stood straight and clasped the box in her hands, then closed her eyes and concentrated. After a moment she began to whisper, as if to herself. The group watched her.

The whisper began to echo slightly, and the air began crackling, as if filled with lightning. The group had a sensation of something *gathering* itself. The lights slowly began to dim, and a blue glow appeared, spreading itself gently over Punkin's figure.

"What's happening?" whispered Joanna.

"She's gathering power," said Frankie in a low voice. "That was the reason she was moving around the room. She was looking for the highest concentrated spot of magic power."

"Oh." Joanna looked uncomfortable. "I suppose I'll have to rearrange the kitchen."

"I've got a good feng shui book I can loan you," said Bethany. There was a low rumbling sound. "Stop that, Harriet," she said. "We'll have breakfast in a minute."

"It's not me," said Harriet.

"What?"

"It's not me," repeated Harriet. The fur on her shoulders was hackling slightly. She pointed.

The room was beginning to tremble, and the hanging light fixtures over the kitchen table began to sway back and forth. The blue glow now completely enveloped Punkin's body. Her grip on the waffle box tightened, and furrows appeared in the cardboard. Sweat beaded on her forehead. The rumbling grew louder, and glasses and dishes began jittering and clanking in the cupboards.

"Is that supposed to happen?" asked Joanna nervously. Harriet started to growl softly, and everyone began to back toward the door.

Punkin's eyes snapped open. The whites of her eyes were completely swallowed up by her brightly glowing pupils. The blue glow began to turn into a blazing white.

"Run?" suggested Bethany.

Everyone fled to the safety of the living room as the white glow filled the kitchen, obscuring everything.

There was a loud BAM. Blue smoke billowed from the kitchen, gradually clearing.

Joanna gave Emily a very clear look of "we will *talk* about this *later*" and tentatively re-entered the kitchen, her heart pounding. The group followed behind her and stared.

Punkin was standing in the middle of nearly two hundred boxes of waffles, piled on the table, the floor, and along the kitchen counter. Most of them were plain, but some were strawberry and blueberry. The box she held was a charred, smoking mass. As the smell of charcoaled waffles wafted through the room, there was a small blue flash, and onto the floor dropped a large bottle of syrup. Punkin's eyes opened, and she blinked at the group.

"Did I do it?"

In the end Joanna was given a chair and a very large cup of coffee (sans blood) while the Grrls prepared breakfast. Frankie devised a quick way of toasting the waffles by holding a cookie sheet full of waffles in her hands and sending a gentle electrical charge through it. It took a few tries to get it right, but there were plenty of waffles to work with, and soon everyone was enjoying perfectly toasted waffles with syrup.

There was also milk for everyone, and enough to go around of that as well; after some thought Punkin duplicated the milk carton at the rate of three at a time, rather than doing a lot all at once. Harriet was given her own carton, under the condition that she drink it by glassfuls. To the surprise of everyone, she complied with this. "Werewolves may eat a lot more than the rest of you," she said, "but that doesn't mean we have *bad manners* or anything."

Emily and Theo tried some of the blueberry and strawberry waffles. They found them quite strange-tasting until they both realized, with some fascination, that what they were eating was not the imitation-flavored bits in toaster waffles, but *real* blueberries and strawberries. "Mmm," said Emily. "These are *wonderful*, Punkin."

"Mm-hmm," said Theo, her mouth full. Punkin blushed.

"Oh, yes," said Joanna. "I'll have to keep some of these, if you don't mind."

"No, ma'am, not at all," said Punkin happily. "Just glad to help." She tucked another bite into her mouth. "Just glad it all went *right* for once," she muttered.

Joanna eyed Bethany, who had a plate of her own as well as a glass of chilled blood, with some curiosity. "I still don't quite understand how you eat, dear," she said. "I thought that vampires never had anything but blood and didn't eat food."

"Not true," said Bethany, swallowing. "Some vampires were superstitious for awhile about that, but we got over it, by degrees." She forked another bite of waffle. "Blood is... well, *necessary* to vampires in a way that ordinary food and drink is not. I can eat pretty much whatever, really. Except, of course, for garlic." She chewed and swallowed. "These blueberry ones are lovely, Punkin."

"Thank you."

"So no garlic at all?" asked Joanna.

"Well, in small amounts. It's not harmful in a dilute solution, though it does taste bad. But don't ask me to eat a raw clove or anything." She ate another bite of waffle. "The big thing, though, is that I have to watch how *much* I eat, because my body doesn't work the same way as yours. The digestion," she said thoughtfully, "is a bit slow in the Undead. It often takes a long time for my body to absorb food."

Emily and Theo traded a look. Both were thinking the same thing. "I'm not gonna ask her," said Emily. *"You ask her."*

"Ask me what?" said Bethany, sipping blood. Joanna looked away.

"Well," said Theo hesitantly, "when was the last time you went to--"

"Six months ago."

"Oh." Theo's expression was of someone who, having brought up the subject, was desperately trying not to contemplate certain aspects of it. "Um…"

"Clean thoughts," said Bethany primly.

Theo nodded. "Sorry," she said, a bit sheepishly.

"Especially at table," said Joanna.

"Yes, *ma'am,"* said Frankie. "I see a lot of gross things in Dad's lab every day, but I'm not going into them." She drank her milk.

"I'm also curious about you, Frankie," said Joanna. "Why do you charge yourself with the generator before you eat?"

"Because the electricity powers my central nervous system," said Frankie, "and also my metabolism. If I didn't charge before I ate I'd never burn off the food, and I'd get sluggish, and my brain wouldn't work right. I'd be walking around here going *uuurrrnnnnhhhh* and stuff just like in your monster movies." She looked thoughtful. "You know, I'd really like to see *Frankenstein* some time. The old one, with Boris Karloff. My dad won't let me watch it."

"I saw it--" began Bethany.

"When it first came out in 1931," said Frankie and Punkin together.

"There is *no* respect for experience," sighed Bethany, finishing her blood.

"Why won't your father let you watch *Frankenstein*?" asked Joanna.

"Oh, all Mad Scientists hate that book and anything connected with it," said Frankie. "There's a whole section of Mad Scientists that do nothing but research it and show that Shelley didn't know what she was talking about. I read it, and I thought most of the *science* was right, anyway." She munched waffles. "But please don't tell Dad I read it, if you ever meet him."

There was a soft burp at the other end of the table. Harriet covered her mouth with her hand. "'Scuse me, Mom," she said. "Boy, that was great, Punkin."

"It should be," said Bethany. "You ate nearly four dozen."

"Mm-hmm," said Harriet, grinning. "I'm a growing werewolf."

"Which probably means four dozen is normal for you?" asked Joanna.

Harriet shrugged. "Dunno, Mom. Werewolves just eat until they've had enough. But Pop and Mom--*my* Mom--always say I shouldn't gorge myself, so I watch it. I could eat another four dozen, but that'd probably be too much."

"Speaking of parents," said Bethany, "we should probably get going. Probably half our parents are going to kill us, staying out with the humans all night."

"Your parents don't know where you are?" said Joanna, shocked.

The Grrls looked shamefaced. "No, Mom," said Harriet.

"I see," said Joanna thoughtfully. "Well, if any of them need to contact me, I'd be happy to give them my phone number."

Six faces stared at her, and Joanna realized the potential folly in what she had said. "Oh. Well, perhaps that's *not* the best idea right now. I'm sorry, girls."

"No, actually, it was a nice gesture," said Bethany. "But I'm not sure our parents would trust you right away. And anyway, my father probably is not worried, mainly because... well, he just doesn't pay a lot of attention."

"What about your mother?"

"Well..." Bethany frowned. "No one really knows where she

is. She left Morlock Heights a few years ago. She's a bit dotty. Even for a vampire." She sighed. "She showed up long enough recently to talk to Dr. Adams about some things, when we were getting enrolled in school, and that was about it."

"At least *your* parents would *talk* to him," said Frankie. She had a disgruntled look. "*My* dad was working on new research and *wouldn't* leave the castle. He said the school would handle all of it. We couldn't even get him to go sign the forms; I had to take them home. I think Igor finally signed them. He signs a lot of things for Dad."

"There's an Igor?" asked Joanna.

"Several," answered Frankie. "But we only have the one." She sighed. "Dad will probably be very upset."

"I *think* Mama and Aunty Grimadene met with Dr. Adams," said Punkin. "Mama mooned around the house for awhile afterward, I do know that." She shrugged. "Mama's got an eye for the menfolk, Missus Peters. She can't help it. But they won't be worried about me much."

"Oh?" answered Joanna, frowning.

"I don't mean they don't *care* or nothin', ma'am," said Punkin quickly. "I mean they won't be *upset*. Witches *expect* their young'uns to be curious, and they teach 'em how to take care of themselves." She drooped. "The one *I'll* catch it from is my ol' cousin Bevadelia, who has been in a snit ever since I started goin' to human school, and *she'll* make them upset."

"At least *your* parents didn't think Dr. Adams was the postman," said Harriet. "Sometimes I worry that Pop has too much animal instinct." She looked at Emily and Theo. "Hey, what's wrong with you two?"

Emily and Theo had been staring at the Grrls all through this conversation. "I hope you won't take this the wrong way," said Emily, "but you are the *last* people on earth we *ever* expected to hear this kind of talk from."

"Yeah," said Theo. "We thought *your* parents were, like, a little more cool about stuff like staying out all night."

"This is a bit different," said Frankie. "We've been out with... well, no offense, but we've been out among humans all night. So it's going to be iffy."

Joanna looked at the Grrls, and reached a decision. "I want you to explain to your parents," she said, "that my house is a safe place for you in Clearwater. If any of you should need to stay here, for any reason, you most certainly can."

The Grrls all smiled gratefully. "Wow, Emily," said Harriet, "your mom's so *cool.*"

Emily smiled. "Yeah, she is," she said, and hugged Joanna. Theo smiled.

"All right, then," said Joanna. "I think we need to clean up." She began to delegate responsibilities. "Harriet, there's a phone in the hall. I think you should try to contact your brother after we clear the table. Punkin, after I set aside a few of these boxes, I'll leave the clearing of the rest to you; I'm sure you know how to best go about... that. Frankie, I think those rubber gloves over there will insulate you from water, and you can help us rinse dishes. Theo, you *will* load the dishwasher. Your penance, remember?"

Theo looked sheepish. "Aw, Mrs. Peters--"

"I'll help," said Emily.

"We'll all help," said Bethany. "And besides, Theo, you need to stay on good terms with your mother. For *us,* at least." She sighed. "After all, we can't expect to gain the trust of *every* human at once."

"Of course, dear," said Joanna. "And please rinse your glass *well,* if you don't mind."

"Yes, ma'am."

And so it was done. Harriet called Mordecai, who agreed with some trepidation to meet them a short distance from Emily's house. Theo, with the help of the others, performed her penance, and in a short while the kitchen was clean, with the exception of the remainder of waffles. Joanna and Theo both claimed a few boxes, and Punkin, whose Power seemed to have settled itself due to the morning repast, was able to very easily send the rest away.

"But where did you send them?" asked Joanna, after the boxes were gone.

Punkin had an embarrassed look. "Well..."

"Well, what?" asked Bethany nervously.

"I don't know," Punkin said. "I mean, I *know* they went *somewhere*... I just don't know *where*, exactly." She hung her head.

The group considered this. Theo said, "Well, wherever it was, I hope they like waffles."

Emily went upstairs with Frankie and Bethany to recover the Girls' belongings. She carried a broom and dustpan up and swept up the broken glass, with Bethany monitoring the dustpan. Frankie helped replace the light bulbs by holding Emily up to the fixture while she screwed the new ones in. "Are you guys really going to be in trouble?" she asked.

"I don't know," said Frankie, as she lowered Emily gently to the floor. "Dad may or may not have missed me. It depends on how far along he is in research." She handed Emily her generator case. "Will you take this, while I get the schoolbags?"

"Sure," said Emily.

"I'll take mine, Frankie," said Bethany. She collected her dress and shoes. "I doubt *I* will be in much trouble, either. Father has, no doubt, been off somewhere being *social.*" She smiled, and the smile was not particularly nice. "As have I. Because we're vampires, our house rules are a bit flexible, so it's pretty much not a problem. What'll be a problem is if the wrong person finds out about it, such as someone on the Council Of Monsterkind, or the boogeymen's patrol."

"Boogeymen's patrol?"

"Yes. They're sort of our police force. Mr. Sabbat is an honorary sheriff of Morlock Heights."

"Oh. Er, he won't be with Mordecai when you get picked up, will he?"

"No," said Frankie. "He only drives our bus, and today is a day off for him. And besides that, he let us off last night after we made him promise he wouldn't tell anyone. Mr. Sabbat is actually very nice. You just have to get to know him."

Emily thought about Mr. Sabbat and shuddered. Then she remembered Bethany coming out of deathsleep and decided that perhaps she was being unfair. "I guess that's true, maybe," she said. "I don't really know him all that well. No one does, except for you guys. He's always there and gone as fast as possible."

"He doesn't like the sun," Frankie said. "Maybe you'll get a chance to get to know him sometime."

"Maybe so," said Emily nervously. Openmindedness, she was discovering, was sometimes hard. She looked at Bethany, who was smiling, as if she had read her thoughts.

"One step at a time, Emily," she said, as they went down the stairs.

The group said their goodbyes, and stood outside on the sidewalk, waiting for Mordecai to come. Harriet ran up the street, doing a last bit of exploring. There was a general air of glumness among the group, the sort that usually turns up when a good time has been had by all and the desire to continue is keenly felt, even though it's obviously time to leave.

"I'm sorry you have to leave," said Emily. "I mean, it's Saturday and everything. We could go down to the square and hang out or something, if you could stay."

"We are too," said Frankie. "But it was really nice. And we'll definitely do it again."

"I feel bad, a little bit," said Punkin. "I'm sorry we kept what happened last night a secret from your mama. She's really a sweet lady."

"I'm sorry, too," said Bethany, adjusting her dark glasses. "Your mother is quite a prize, darling," she said to Emily.

"Yeah, she is," said Emily, smiling.

"Yeah," echoed Frankie softly. She had a sad, longing expression, and Emily supposed that she was thinking of Dr. Corinthian. She said, "You guys can always borrow my mom, you know. Theo does, all the time."

"Yeah," said Theo, grinning. "And I'm willing to share."

"Thanks," said Frankie, smiling gratefully.

"Good thing you're willing to share," said Bethany. "Between all of us, there may be a line." She looked a bit pensive. "I've not felt this kind of respect for a human in years. Maybe I'm getting older."

"You're already old," said Emily.

Bethany put on a mock indignant expression. "Bloody *cheek!*"

181

she shouted. Everyone laughed.

Harriet ran up the sidewalk, panting. "Wow! You guys, you gotta come see! Emily's got a *haunted house* on her block!"

Everyone except Emily and Theo looked interested. "Can we go *see?*" asked Punkin.

"Um," said Theo. "If it's what I think she's talking about --"

"Oh, come on," said Bethany. "You survived your first bit of magic last night, so a haunted house ought to be a snap. What is it?"

"It's the old Pritchett place," said Emily. "It's this old house up the street, and no one lives there anymore. But people have seen lights in the windows at night, and heard things." She shrugged. "That's what they say, anyway."

"It's really cool," said Harriet. "Nobody's lived there in a long time, the way it looks."

"Maybe we should take a look, at least," said Frankie.

"Oh, no," said Theo. "I'm not going in there, not for anything."

"Me neither," said Emily. "And Mom told me not to go around there anyway. No telling what's in there."

"Well, let's at least *look* at it," said Bethany. "We won't go in, and I'd like to walk about a bit. Come on. I promise we'll stay on the sidewalk." She waved at Harriet. "Lead on, MacDuff."

The Pritchett house was a short walk up the street.

Emily and Theo had never liked it. It had once been a large white two-story Victorian, with a fenced-in yard, a second-story balcony, and a large front porch. Now it was in a horrible state of disrepair. Ivy vines grew up the west side of the house and were visibly working their way into the wall. The front steps sagged, and the white paint had peeled like an old scab in many places, showing dead-gray weatherbeaten boards. Some of the windows were broken. The front yard was overgrown, and grass poked up through cracks in the sidewalk leading up to the house.

The group stood outside the rusted gate, examining the house critically. "Shame for this old place to be in such condition," remarked Bethany. "That was once a nice house."

"It's not haunted," said Punkin.

"It's gotta be, looking like that," said Harriet. "It looks just like haunted houses in Morlock Heights."

"It *ain't,*" said Punkin. "I can't feel anythin' like a presence around."

"Presence?" said Theo nervously.

"Yeah. Witches can *sense* ghosts, even if they can't always see 'em. It's one of the first things we learn." She shrugged. "There's nothin' here that's harmful."

"But what about all the lights and stuff?" asked Emily.

Frankie frowned thoughtfully, staring at the house. "Maybe someone's just spreading tales, or something. Trying to scare people." She grimaced. "It makes sense. This place doesn't look like a safe place to be. Little kids could get hurt playing around in there."

"Well, there's only one way to find out what's up," said Bethany. She started toward the gate. "I'm going to take a look."

"Wait! What if something tries to get you?" said Theo.

Bethany sighed. "How soon they forget," she said. She bared her teeth, and her fangs lengthened. She hissed, and Theo jumped back. Smiling playfully, Bethany entered through the rusty gate, which squeaked as she opened it. Strutting up the walk, she called back to Theo, "Nothing here's scarier than me at the moment, darling."

Theo turned to Harriet. "You're right. She *is* a show-off."

Frankie entered in behind her. "I'm going to look, too," she said. "You guys stay here. Your mom said not to go in here anyway."

"Just be careful," said Emily.

Frankie headed up the walk behind Bethany, who was already on the porch and peering through a dusty window. "Huh," she said. "Have a look at this, Frankie."

Frankie came to the porch and peered in. The window viewed into the living room of the house, which was filled with furniture. All of it had been covered with sheets. "What's all that doing here?" she asked.

"You tell me," said Bethany. "Who abandons a house and leaves all their furniture behind? And for this long a time?"

"That *is* strange," said Frankie. "You don't suppose someone's *in* this house, do you?"

Bethany and Frankie looked at each other, and both came to the same decision. They left the porch quickly.

"All of it?" asked Emily. The two had reported to the others what they had seen.

"Seems to be," said Frankie. "Maybe someone's moving in."

"In *this* house?" said Bethany. "It's in a horrid state, Frankie. I don't think anyone would buy this house as a fixer-upper." She eyed the porch. "In Morlock Heights, maybe, but not here."

"Well, at least it explains all the lights and everything," said Emily.

"I don't know," said Theo. "Maybe it's just there or something. Maybe it's always been there and no one ever knew about it." She looked at Punkin. "Are you sure you don't feel anything?"

"Nothin's here, livin' or dead," said Punkin. "'Cept us."

Harriet was unwilling to believe that something strange was not going on. "What if someone's in there watching us right now?" she asked.

The group stared at the silent house. The windows all resembled glaring eyes, and it was not hard to imagine that someone or something could be in there, looking out at them. *Watching.*

There was a loud rumble, and everyone jumped.

Mordecai's black Mustang pulled up to the curb beside them. The door opened, and out stepped Mordecai, his black hair pulled into a ponytail and tied with a cord. He wore jeans, a black shirt and engineer boots. His face was lean and fully bearded, and both Emily and Theo saw the werewolf characteristics; the bushy grown-together eyebrows, tough-looking skin, pointed ears and golden eyes. They noticed that Mordecai was somewhat *old*, to be Harriet's little brother.

Mordecai crossed his arms and stared at the group. "I am so *fed up* with you," he said to Harriet, who grinned. "You *said* you'd be in front of the house. I've been driving around looking all over for you."

"Sorry, Mordecai," said Harriet. She grabbed her brother in a hug, and he returned it, smiling. His face was not so intense and became quite pleasant when he smiled. "We were exploring."

"Yeah," sighed Mordecai. "I know." He waved to the others. "Hey, guys. Are we ready to go?"

"We'll have to go back to get our things--" Frankie began.

"I got 'em already," said Mordecai. He seemed to notice Emily and Theo for the first time, and pointed at Theo. "I remember you," he said. "Theo, right? And this must be Emily."

"Hi," said Emily. "It's nice to finally meet you."

"You're Harriet's *little* brother?" asked Theo.

Mordecai rolled his eyes at this, and Harriet giggled. "Yeah," she said. "See, we were born in the same litter, but he was the smallest male. So I've always called him my *little* brother."

Theo and Emily looked at each other, and then at Mordecai, who shrugged. "What can I say?" he said. "She's my sister. As far as I know, she's always had this problem." Harriet punched his shoulder, and Mordecai laughed.

"Gee," said Emily. "I wish you guys didn't have to go."

"I know," said Frankie. "But don't worry. We'll see each other in school Monday."

"And we'll do this again," said Bethany. "Promise." Punkin nodded, smiling.

"Come on, ladies," said Mordecai. "I've got to find a back way in so we don't get caught by the boogeymen. *And* I'm sure your parents will want to know where you've been all night."

Bethany sniffed. "Not *mine.*"

The Grrls began to get in the car. "Do you two want a ride back?" said Mordecai to Emily and Theo. "It'll be a little crowded, but I'm sure I can squeeze you in."

"No, thanks," said Emily. "We'll walk back up. It's not too far, anyway."

"I had a great time," said Harriet. She hugged both Emily and Theo. "You guys be careful, okay? See you in school." She got into the car, and it purred off down the street. Emily and Theo waved at them as they drove away.

"Well, that was nice," said Theo. "We had our first party."

"Yeah, it was," said Emily. "Let's get back to my house, Theo. Mom would kill us if she knew we were here."

Theo looked at the Pritchett House as they headed back down the street. "You don't think somebody's really in there, do you?" she said.

"I don't know," said Emily. "I've realized, ever since meeting the Grrls, that I don't know a lot about a lot of things. You know?"

"Yeah," said Theo.

They walked in silence for awhile. "What do you think things will be like in school Monday?" asked Theo.

Emily shrugged. "Dunno. But I know one thing; I'm not worried about it." She smiled. "We've got some really good friends, Theo. Even if they are monsters."

"Yeah," said Theo, smiling. "Yeah, we do."

The two friends headed back down the street and into their weekend, away from the old house with its darkened windows and fearful promise.

In a larger town a few miles away from Clearwater, a transport truck arrived at its destination, which was the Sav-A-Lot Foodmart. The driver entered the Foodmart with the manifest for his load and was met by the manager of the store.

The manager congratulated the driver on his efficiency in getting the items to the store. Among the items on the manifest had been a consignment of frozen toaster waffles. As he listened to the manager, the stunned driver realized that his load of waffles, minus a few scant boxes, had somehow arrived several hours before *he* did.

So, as Harriet would have said, that was all for *that*, then.

Except that it wasn't. Not quite.

The man in black stared down from the window in the upper room of the Pritchett House, watching the two girls walk away. He had seen them, as well as the four young monsterkind who had ridden away with the new-moon wolf, and had watched them carefully, studying their movements. He had vaguely hoped they would try to come into the house; a bit of exercise would have been useful. This current spate of inactivity made him restless.

But he was not sure that they were the ones who had seen him. So for the moment, he would wait, and watch. And search.

He reached into his coat, removed something and shook it out. It was a black mask, one designed to cover a person's whole head and face. He pulled it over his head, adjusting the eyeholes to fit properly, so as not to compromise his vision.

Then he moved away from the window into the darker areas of the house, and melted into the shadows.

It was Monday morning in Mr. Harrington's homeroom, and a council of war was underway.

"How *dare* that weirdo Bethany bring those nerds and those other weirdos to the party, Jessica," said Tiffany, filing her nails. "Who does she think she is, anyway?"

"Yeah," said Heather. "Though I don't remember much about it." She smiled. "I was drunk."

"I'm still trying to figure out about the mirror," said Jessica crossly. "I mean, one minute, it was broken. Busted. My mom would have killed me. And then the next minute, it's like it *wasn't*." She shrugged. "Anyway, you're right. Bethany's *finished* at this school. I mean, having friends like *that*. I mean, that Frankenstein chick *broke* Bradley's hand. Did you see his cast?"

"Yeah," said Tiffany, smiling. She was very pleased with herself; things were turning out okay after all. "I signed it, too. Did you?"

"Yeah. Poor Bradley." Jessica looked at Stephanie, who was giving her fingernails a lengthy examination. "You OK?"

"Hmm?" said Stephanie. "Oh. Oh. Yeah."

"Good." She gave Stephanie a hard look. "Don't *you* go getting weird on me or anything. We don't need someone like Bethany in our crowd."

"Yeah," said Stephanie miserably. "Whatever."

"How are we going to do it?" asked Tiffany. "Should we give her the basic snub, or should we pretend to be her friends for awhile and then dump her?"

"I'm not wasting *that* on Bethany," said Jessica. "We're just doing the basic snub with her. There's no need for any kind of spin on it."

"Oh," said Tiffany, disappointed. "Well, whatever."

"Good," said Jessica. "Now remember, when she comes in and says good morning, *nobody* talks to her. OK?"

"OK," said Heather.

"OK," said Tiffany happily.

"I don't think we should," said Stephanie. "I mean, I think we should try to talk it out--"

"*Talk it out?*" sneered Jessica. "Look at little Miss Touchy-Feely. You didn't *use* to be so *sensitive* and all that crap. This girl is bad news, and I'm not talking out *anything* with her." She frowned at Stephanie. "You know, you've been acting weird ever since they showed up."

Stephanie's cheeks burned. "All right," she snapped. "Let's just get it over with."

"Smart girl," said Jessica. "All right. We all know what to do." The Clique turned to face the door expectantly. Stephanie had a glowering expression. Tiffany's smile was positively evil.

Bethany strode into the room. She wore a short black jumper-style dress with bat-patterned knee socks and bright red Mary Jane heels, which caused a few of the boys in the room to stare. Her jaw was set, and she held her chin high and proud. As one, the group of girls fell to their books, appearing to be reading intensely and deliberately ignoring her.

Bethany did not acknowledge them at all. She strode past them, heels clacking in businesslike manner, to an empty desk on the other side of the room, where she sat down. She opened her textbook and began to read in a relaxed manner.

The Clique looked up. The absence of Bethany among the Clique was palpable. Everyone traded a puzzled look. Finally Jessica whispered, "Did we miss something?"

"She didn't sit with us," responded Heather, confused. "She *always* sits with us."

"What *happened?*" whined Tiffany. Stephanie said nothing.

The other three stared at one another, perplexed. Finally, Heather said slowly, "I think she snubbed *us.*"

Everyone considered this. Jessica's eyes widened. "That... little...."

"*Bitch!*" hissed Tiffany vehemently.

"I don't believe this," said Heather. "I am *so* not believing this."

"She snubbed *us!*" spat Jessica. "*Us!*"

"I *told* you she was *weird*," said Tiffany, stretching out "weird" to fit at least one more syllable. "We should have *never* had *anything* to do with her."

Jessica nudged Stephanie. "Go over there and find out what's going on."

Stephanie stared at her. "*What?*"

"You heard me!"

"I thought you didn't want to talk to her!"

"I *don't*," hissed Jessica. "That's why I'm sending *you* to do it. Go on."

Stephanie had had enough. "I am not! If you have something to say to her, *you* need to do it!" She crossed her arms and sat back.

Jessica's eyes narrowed. "Are you *crossing* me?"

"Oh, *God*," said Heather. "*I'll* do it." She got up and ambled over to an empty desk in front of Bethany. "Hi, babe. What's doing?"

Bethany reached out and smacked Heather hard on the back of the head with the flat of her hand. She did this without looking up from her book.

Heather flared. "Why, you little--"

She stopped. Bethany stared at her over the top of her book. Heather saw the violet pupils of her eyes swirl and glow bright red. Bethany slowly lowered the book, and Heather saw red lips twisted into a snarl, with sharp fangs fully extended.

"*Move*," snapped Bethany.

Heather gaped. She stuttered, "O-okay, okay, I know you're still mad about the party and everything--"

"*Get out of here!*"

Heather fled back to Jessica's group. She quickly got in her seat and sat down, shuddering.

"What?" asked Jessica.

"Leave her alone."

"*What?*"

"*Leave her alone!*" Heather was trying to keep from shouting.

"What do you *mean*, leave her alone?"

"I mean she went *freaky* and stuff like she did at the *party!*" Heather's voice was a terrified squeak. "I'm not going back over there!"

"Well, *I* will, then," said Tiffany, seeing an opportunity to score brownie points approaching. She got up and went over to Bethany. Less than twenty seconds later she returned, panting, "Leave-her-alone-just-leave-her-alone-I'm-not-going-back-over-there -*I'm-not-gonna--*"

"What *is* it with you?" asked Jessica.

"*She's not human!*" screeched Tiffany. "*She's some kind of--of THING!*"

Jessica looked at Stephanie. "Your turn."

"No." Stephanie crossed her arms decisively.

"No?"

"I'm not doing it. *You* do it. *You're* the one who gets such a big kick out of these dumb games, anyway."

"*Games?*" snapped Jessica. "You think this is a *game*, huh? This is *high school*, babe. And you can either fly with the birds or crawl with the worms." She glared at Stephanie. "I think it's about time you started deciding which you want to *do*. Or maybe I could decide it *for you*. You *know?*"

Stephanie tried, valiantly, to hold Jessica's stare. She couldn't do it. She looked at Heather, who shrugged. "Steph, just do it and get it over with, okay?" she said, not unkindly. "Bethany always liked you best, anyway."

Tiffany, who wore a companion image of Jessica's own glare, flapped a hand at her impatiently. "Go *on*."

Stephanie was not able to hide the hatred in her voice. "All right," she muttered.

"Good girl," said Jessica, in a flat voice. "You're on."

Stephanie walked over to the desk in front of Bethany and sat down. Bethany had positioned her book so that it was directly in front of her face. Stephanie could not see Bethany's features.

After a moment Stephanie sighed. "All right. I know that I was wrong to do what I did at the party. And I'm sorry. I really am."

Silence.

Stephanie stared at the book cover and said, "Look, you're not making this easy, you know."

A low and unpleasant voice came from the other side of the

book. "I don't think it should be."

"Oh, come on, Bethany," groaned Stephanie. "This is high school. You know it's all a big game--"

"I know *no game*," snarled the voice. "I don't play them. Not with people who are my friends. And you had absolutely no right to do what you did. Your little boy Bradley is an ill-mannered, preening little *bastard,* and he *attacked* one of *my* closest friends, and you *ruined* what would have been an interesting and not entirely unpleasant experience for two *very* dear, sweet, lovely girls. Grrls who would *gladly* be your friends if you would *bother* to get to know them." This last sounded as if it had been spat. "So as far as *I'm* concerned, I have nothing more to say to *any* of you. And if your friends so much as approach me or mine for any reason besides the school being on fire, I'll do something about it." The book cover lowered just enough so that Stephanie could view Bethany's eyes. They were narrowed and glowing bright red.

Stephanie gulped and said, "I guess you know the others don't think you're really a vampire."

The eyes did not change. "I'm aware of that. And considering that *they* are the center of their world, it's entirely understandable."

"What if I explain it?"

There was a low snort. "And they would believe you?"

"Jessica already thinks something weird's going on. And you've thoroughly scared Heather and Tiffany."

"The problem with that statement is that the words *Jessica* and *thinks* are in it. Your leader doesn't care for anything but herself, darling." The book returned to its former position. "Vampires are beyond her, and *way* beyond Heather. That idiot Tiffany probably would believe you, but she's not strong enough to make any moves without the other two." The voice softened only slightly. "I thought that you could until this last weekend."

Stephanie bit her lip. "Ouch," she said softly.

"Yes. Ouch." The voice was not unkind.

Stephanie was silent for a moment. "So, how long do we have until you and your monster friends attack?"

"Don't be stupid. I have no intention of attacking anyone, and neither do the others. We're here to go to *school*, not take over the world. I only told you what *will* happen if your lot decide to pull some more mischief, because I shall *not* stand by and see my friends mistreated."

Stephanie thought about this. "Okay," she said. "I guess that's fair."

There was no response.

Stephanie studied her fingernails for a moment. "So. Friends?"

There was a pause. "I think," said the voice quietly, "that you have already decided how to answer that question. I'm sorry."

Stephanie's mouth tightened. She got up and walked back to her desk, her face burning.

Over the top of the book, Bethany watched as Stephanie, her head bowed slightly, sat down with the others. Bethany sighed and returned to her book. She heard Mr. Harrington enter and direct the students to study groups; they began to move to different positions in the classroom. She did not move from her desk.

Frankie had been dreading this. She sighed as she headed toward Mrs. Parkinson's homeroom.

It had been easy for her to talk a good game last Friday, when she was trying to convince Emily and Theo of their self-worth. Somewhere between then and now, it had occurred to her that people would talk about her, *and* about what had happened with Bradley at Jessica's party.

Everyone there had seen it. She hadn't lifted a finger toward Bradley; he'd been the one showing off, and hadn't known that hitting a Creature was like ramming your fist into a brick wall. Creatures had a natural physical density; it was what made them so hard to injure. And Bradley hadn't known that, or bothered to find out, and he'd hurt himself.

But people talk.

There was no doubt in her mind that the story had been blown out of proportion and that she had been painted as the aggressor. Maybe some of them had even made her into a real monster; a snarling, baleful entity of smouldering rage, just like in that Shelley's book. Maybe they'd said she'd tottered toward him in a stiff walk, arms outstretched, just like a monster was supposed to, clutching at Bradley, her hand closing around his wrist, squeezing, *snapping...*

I saw him with his cast this morning. And that Tiffany was acting like he was some kind of conquering hero, fussing over him and everything.

She'd felt miserable at seeing that; it signified, to her, how different she was from other kids, how singular and strange. She'd wondered if it had been such a good idea to go to school with humans after all. They'd probably start being scared of her, and she'd have no friends or anything, and...

Wait a minute. I have Emily.

She thought of Emily, who'd become her best human friend. And she realized then that she had to be strong, for Emily, and Theo, and the others. It would all blow over. She was a monster, but she wasn't *that* kind of monster.

She held her head up, walking straight and tall, just as she had practiced with her father, balancing a book on her head, keeping her posture erect and proud while he watched her walk on a chalk line he'd made on the lab floor. Thank heaven her father hadn't missed her; he'd locked himself in the lab with his research, and Igor had been out on another date with Mary Mahoney. He'd come home *giggling* again, too; she *really* had to find out about that.

She walked into the room. A few people looked up, then began whispering to each other. They had gotten used to Frankie's appearance, but now there was the added titillation of fresh gossip. She steeled herself and went to her desk.

Emily was already at her desk, waiting for her. "Hi, Frankie," she whispered. "Did you guys get into trouble?"

"No, we didn't," whispered Frankie. "Dad was locked up in the lab and Igor was out. Bethany's dad was gone on business. I think Punkin had to deal with some stuff from her cousin, but her mom and Aunty were OK with it. Harriet got a small lecture from her mom. But we're all okay."

"What happened with the boogeymen?"

"Nothing. Mordecai got us back home before they knew we were missing. But we *all* got a lecture from Mr. Sabbat this morning."

She looked uncomfortably at Emily. "So... um... has anyone... you know, been saying stuff?"

"About what?"

"About... you know. The party."

"Well, I heard some things in here. Mostly, everyone seems really amazed."

Frankie stared at Emily. "Huh?"

"You've got to understand," said Emily. "No one around here challenges the Clique. They're kind of like our ruling class, almost. Everyone's in awe of you."

Frankie considered this. "But aren't they... well, frightened?"

"No."

The two felt eyes on them. Mrs. Parkinson was watching. Her eyes met Frankie's, and she beckoned to her. Frankie looked at Emily, who shrugged. Swallowing, she walked up to the desk. "Y-Yes, ma'am?"

"Morning, dear," said Mrs. Parkinson amiably. "I've heard about you and the events of the weekend. Seems to be quite a bit of talk."

Frankie hung her head. "Yes, ma'am. I'm sorry."

"You really squared off with Bradley Atkinson?"

"Ma'am, it *wasn't my fault.*" She felt terrible. Maybe the kids didn't consider her a monster, but she didn't want her favorite teacher to, either. "I was just standing there, and he came up and... well, he hit me. And he broke his hand. I didn't do anything, and I'm really sorry. I *promise* I won't cause any problems for you."

Mrs. Parkinson looked down at her notes for a moment. "Well, dear, as a teacher, I do have to say that I hope you are more careful in your choice of nocturnal activities."

Frankie looked sheepish. "Yes, ma'am."

She raised her head and fixed Frankie with a knowing look. "And as a teacher who has had the dubious pleasure of having Mr. Atkinson in her class before, I also hope that next time you don't break his *jaw,* because, as I remember, he had quite the mouth on him." She looked at Frankie kindly. "But I don't expect you to be a problem student, dear. You're made of stronger stuff than that." She raised an eyebrow. "Quite literally, I suppose. Just be careful."

"Yes, ma'am," said Frankie, relieved.

"Especially with the kid." She glanced in Emily's direction. "You're good for her, whether you know it yet or not. Back to your seat." She hefted her textbook and got up. "We've got to get class started. If you like, we can talk about all this later."

Frankie smiled gratefully. "Thank you, ma'am."

"No, thank you for being such a good student." She bent to pick up something from the floor, and as Frankie turned to go back to her seat, she heard a low mutter. "About damn *time* Atkinson got his, anyway."

Punkin eyed the cards. She looked thoughtful for a moment, and then moved one to the group lined up on the desktop. The card snapped back into the deck.

She frowned. She looked at Stuart, who shrugged. "Try another one."

She moved a different card to the group. That one snapped back into the deck as well.

Punkin sighed and moved back from the computer. They had finished the daily worksheets and were enjoying "free time," which seemed to have been established primarily for Mrs. Carson to field calls on her cell phone. "This Solitare thing don't seem like much of a fun game," she said. "You can't move no cards."

Stuart nodded. "But watch this." He tapped a few keys. The screen winked off for a moment, and Stuart typed quickly for a few minutes. He pressed the enter key and sat back. The screen returned to the Solitare game.

"Try it now," he said.

She tried moving the cards, and was surprised to find that she could place them anywhere on the desktop. "Wow! That's neat!" She looked puzzled. "How'd you do that?"

"Just talented," said Stuart, smiling.

Punkin noticed that his face turned into something almost handsome when he smiled. She returned it. "You are *very* talented, Mr. Stuart," she said. "I don't know if I'll *ever* learn as much as you about this thing."

Stuart felt a little embarrassed. She was gazing at him with rapt attention, which was something he didn't usually receive from girls. It suddenly occurred to him that Punkin was rather pretty, and he faltered a moment.

"Well, it's..." He considered making a sarcastic remark, to hide his discomfort, and found himself unable to do it. "It's not *hard.*" Inspiration hit. "I guess magic's a bit harder to do, really."

"Oh, no," said Punkin. "Well, not for me." She studied the computer for a moment. "I guess you could say we're *both* naturally talented."

Stuart considered this. "What's it like?"

"What?"

"Being able to do magic."

She sighed. "It... it's like I got a big old storm in my head all the time, and if I don't watch out, it'll get away from me. But when I'm in control of it... which I ain't, most times... then it's like I'm ridin' on a lightnin' beam. Or lettin' it ride through me."

Stuart smiled a small half-smile. "Yeah. That's how I feel when I crack a code I've been working on for hours."

"Crack a code?"

"Yeah. That's when you break into a computer file by breaking the passwords set up to protect it." He leaned back and put his hands behind his head. "Hardest one I ever broke was the one that goes into the school computer."

"What did you actually do, Stuart?" she asked. "When you broke into the computer."

"I got paid by various people around school to clean up their school records. Redo grades, wipe out discipline records, stuff like that."

She frowned. "Whose?"

He shrugged. "I don't remember half of them. The only ones I remember are Cam Johnson and Bradley Atkinson."

Punkin eyed him. "Are they football players?"

Stuart looked at her. "Yeah. Do you know them?"

"Well... no." She shivered. "And I ain't sure I want to, neither. I sort of saw them last Friday night. At--at this party that I went to. With some friends."

"That was *you?*"

She realized that he'd heard about the party, and looked sheepish. "Well, I was there, but I didn't do nothin' and Frankie didn't neither." She looked down at the table. "That Bradley boy started it. He shouldn't of hit Frankie."

"Who's Frankie? Is she that Frankenstein chick I see you with, sometimes?"

Punkin shook her finger at him. *"Don't you go callin' her that.* Frankie's the nicest, sweetest Creature in the world and she wouldn't never hurt *nobody."* She sat back and crossed her arms defensively. "An' she'd be real hurt if she knew you called her that."

He held up his hands. "Okay, okay. Sorry." He considered what to say next. "So Bradley's walking around with a cast, all because he hit... Frankie."

"Yup."

Stuart looked thoughtful. He remembered Bradley as a particularly vicious person, and could not see him getting beaten up by a girl. "She must be one tough girl."

"Yup," said Punkin. "Sometimes when she's redoin' her stitches she has trouble gettin' the needle all the way through her skin."

"Ah." He tried to imagine this, and gave up. "So anyway, what you're saying is that it wasn't true."

"Yup." She frowned at him. "Hadn't you been listenin' to me?"

"Well..." He decided to change the subject. "I was telling you about hacking into the school records. What I did was break into the files and change everything so it looked like they were passing with higher grades. Then they didn't get into trouble at home."

"Oh." She considered this. "That's kinda bad, Stuart. I mean, that don't sound right."

He snorted. "I'm getting moral lectures from a witch?"

She raised an eyebrow at him, in her best Bethany manner. "You better watch it, Stuart. I don't wanna turn you to a toad, but I will if I have to, just to teach you a lesson."

"That's what I'm talking about. Witches cast evil spells, and turn people into toads, and --"

"Okay, okay. We got a lot of bad stuff said about us by people who don't know nothin' about witches." She sighed. "And there *have been* some bad witches, too. But truth is, I wouldn't ever turn you into a toad. None of us would."

Stuart stared at her. "Why not?"

"Cause it's harder to change somethin' into somethin' else than to make somethin', or move somethin' around." She thought a moment. "See, when I do a spell, it takes energy. It takes somethin' outta *me*. And that's gotta be put back by me sleepin' or eatin' or somethin'. And it's really hard to do Transmogrification spells, 'cause you got to *change* somethin' instead of rearrangin' it. When I do some other kind of spell I'm just movin' it around or makin' it up outta my head."

"That's not exactly how the fairy tales have it."

"Well, this ain't a fairy tale." She waved a hand around the room, indicating the students, who were all engaged in animated conversations at the other tables, and Mrs. Carson, who was weaving through the students and talking with some degree of anxiety on her cell phone. "This is… I don't know. *High school*, I guess."

Stuart laughed. "Boy, that's cynical."

"Nope. Just *is*." She leaned back in her chair. "Besides, doin' harm to others is against the moral laws of witches."

"Moral laws? You mean like the Ten Commandments?"

"Yup. But we only got two, see." She looked at Stuart kindly. "The first one is, 'Do what thou wilt, but harm no one.' It means you can do whatever you want to as long as you don't hurt no one else. It's a hard law to follow."

Stuart mused over this. "Sounds like it. There's not a lot I could do that wouldn't harm someone else, somehow."

She stared at him. "You're *that* mad at everbody?"

He frowned. "I don't know if *mad* is the word." He slumped in his chair. "I… I just want everyone else to feel how I feel, for just twenty minutes."

"How do you feel?"

He looked hard at her, and she recoiled a bit. "Shut out. Like no one in the world understands me or how I feel. Like no one listens to anything I say, or even cares that I'm saying anything."

She frowned at him, not unkindly. "*I'm* listenin' to you,

Stuart."

He looked at her, and something in his face softened a bit. "I know. It's just... you don't know what it's like. Being the only one who doesn't have a car, and almost sixteen years old. Being teased because you aren't a jock or a popular kid, or because you can't go out on a date."

"I don't have no car. I don't even have no broom license."

"Well..."

"And I think I understand how you feel a lot more than you think I do."

He gave her a snide look. "Yeah? Can *you* break into a secure server in ten seconds flat?"

"Nope. But can you do *this?*" She held out her hand, palm up, and began moving her fingers one by one, in order: first, middle, ring, little. She whispered a word so low that Stuart couldn't hear. Tendrils of blue smoke began to flow from her fingers.

Stuart stared as the tendrils curled upward and merged together. They cleared, and sitting on Punkin's hand was a small sapphire-blue butterfly. It moved its wings like *this*, and a gentle glow appeared along the length of its body.

It left Punkin's hand and fluttered to Stuart, who recoiled as it flew toward his face. The butterfly landed on his nose, moved its wings like *this*, and vanished. Stuart smelled a faint odor of lilac.

He stared at Punkin, who sat looking at him with a quiet expression on her face, and he realized that he was with someone who knew *exactly* what he was talking about. "No," he said after a moment. "I guess not."

"I scare *other witches*, Stuart," she said quietly. "Witches who are older 'n me, and more experienced in the Craft than me. I *scare* them. Not because of what I can do, but because I *don't know* how I do it." She sighed. "So I have to be careful and follow the first law as well as I can, because I don't want the second law comin' back to haunt me, and I don't think you do neither. So maybe you ought to think harder about whether you want people to feel as bad as you, sometimes."

"So what's the second law?"

"'Whatever you do comes back to you, times three.'" She sat

back.

Stuart stared at her thoughtfully. "I guess you do have to be careful."

"Yup."

There was silence between them for a few minutes. Then Stuart said, "How come changing the records didn't sound right to you?"

"Cause it wasn't fair. It wasn't fair to all the other students who worked hard to pass the classes."

"So you've never cheated on a test?"

"Nope."

"*Never?*"

"Nope."

"Oh, come on--"

"*No.* I never have. And besides, if anybody had done somethin' like that at Graf Orlok, Mr. Grimm would have known about it."

"Who?"

"Our old principal."

"You have computers at Gra... at your old school?"

"Nope."

Stuart leaned back. "Well, then."

"But *even if we had,*" snapped Punkin, "he *would've.*"

"That's impossible."

"Nope, that's Mr. Grimm. And even if you were careful, Mr. Herschel's gonna figure out what happened, one of these days."

"How?" snorted Stuart. "Herschel has no idea what I did. Probably no idea that I even did anything. He calls in the computer technicians at least once a month."

"Mr. Herschel's a nice man," said Punkin defensively. She was becoming cross with Stuart. "He don't know much about us monsterkind, and he's scared to death of Harriet, but he's a nice man."

"And how do you know? Is it because of your witchy powers?"

Punkin had had enough. "No, it *ain't*. It's 'cause my mama and my aunty taught me what a good person *was*, and how to *be* one."

Her voice was developing a dangerous-sounding reverbration. Stuart felt the air take on a *tightening* effect. He swallowed and said, "Well, *I* don't think he's all that nice. I mean, he was ready to bust me for breaking into the school computers... send me to jail and stuff, and..."

"Well, gorry!" said Punkin, with a tone that was almost real sarcasm.[7] "You don't think it was 'cause it was *wrong,* do you?"

"But--" Stuart was discovering, with some irritation, that he still had a conscience. "Look, Punkin, this is the *real world.*" Her expression told him it was the wrong thing to say, but he couldn't stop himself. "Nothing's private anymore, and everything's up for sale. Even information. You know?" He shrugged lamely.

"Don't tell *me* nothin' about what's real," she whispered. "I *know* what's *real.*"

"But--I mean, that's the way it is--"

Her voice raised. "No, it *ain't.* It don't have to be that way. And if it is, then I don't want to stay here."

He snorted. "So you'd rather live in Witchy World, huh?"

She felt her Power coiling in her mind and valiantly pushed it back. "Mrs. Carson was right about you," she said. "I ain't sittin' with you no more." She shoved the chair back and gathered her things. "I just don't understand how you can be so sweet and so *mean* at the same time," she muttered. She felt tears in her eyes.

Stuart gaped. "You... "

"Don't say nothin' to me. It's true I'm a witch. I'm a *monster,* just like the others, and I was born and raised in Morlock Heights and I been there all my life. But I ain't done nothin' wrong, and I don't cheat on tests and I don't meddle around in other folks' business 'cause I'm so *bored* that I ain't got nothin' else to do." Her voice was rising. "And I *don't hurt nobody* with my Power. Least I don't try to."

"But--" Stuart stared at her, and then sighed. "Yeah, whatever," he said in a bored voice.

Punkin stared at him. Finally she threw her books on an

---

[7] For *her,* anyway.

empty table and headed for the door, pulling the bathroom pass from its hook on the wall.

Mrs. Carson, who was still on her cell phone, saw her. "Hold on a minute," she muttered into the phone. "Punkin, dear, you must ask *permission* before--"

Punkin whirled on her. Mrs. Carson gaped at her eyes, which were swollen and glowing blue. "*I gotta go, Miz Carson,*" she said.

The cell phone flew out of Mrs. Carson's hand. It smashed against the wall and exploded into a blue flame that winked out almost instantly.

Punkin fled, ignoring Mrs. Carson's shout of surprise, and raced to the bathroom. She ran to the last stall and slammed the door.

My Power got out of control. I couldn't stop it, and it's all my fault.

She plopped on the floor with her knees drawn up, and began to cry.

As the bell rang for class changes, Bethany arrived at her locker to find the Clique waiting there. She sighed. "What do you want now?"

"You aren't gonna get away with this," hissed Jessica. "Just because the teachers like you doesn't mean you're safe or anything. *And* you snubbed me. *No one* snubs *me.*"

"Yeah," said Heather and Tiffany together. Stephanie was silent.

Bethany pinched the bridge of her nose. "I really do *not* think I want to talk to any of you. Now sod off." She opened her locker and began to take out her books.

Jessica suddenly smacked Bethany's arm, and books fell to the floor. Bethany stared at the books on the floor, and felt her fangs lengthen. She advanced on Jessica, snarling, "You are the most *horrid* person I've ever known, and I would be doing the world a *favor* if I—"

A hand clamped gently but firmly on her shoulder, stopping her. "What's going on here?" said Frankie.

Jessica wore high heels as a rule of thumb, but Frankie was taller than Jessica by two feet. She swallowed as Frankie stared down at her. "You—you don't scare me," she quavered.

"Y-Yeah," added Heather. "You're just a *bully.*"

Frankie gave them a dubious look. "I'm not sure you know what scary is," she said.

"Oh, yes we do," said Tiffany. "We've spent a night in the old Pritchett House before."

"The Pritchett House?" said Bethany. "That place is not scary."

"Well, maybe not to a weird Goth chick like you," said Heather, "but I bet you'd be scared if you went there at night."

Frankie and Bethany traded a look. "They don't get it, do they?" said Bethany.

"Guess not," said Frankie.

"Get what?" asked Jessica.

"Nothing," answered Frankie. "Look, we're sorry about whatever your problem is, but we're not interested in going to some scary old house. We have plenty of scary old houses where we live."

"Oh, yeah?" shouted Jessica. "Well, I bet *our* scary old house is worse than *all* your scary old houses!"

"Yeah!" shouted Heather. "You'd think monsters wouldn't be such a bunch of *fraidy-cats!*"

There was a low growl, and the Clique jumped. Harriet had appeared with Emily, Theo, and a red-eyed, sniffling Punkin in tow. She eyed Heather and grinned. "So what was all this about cats?"

Heather, Tiffany and Stephanie all backed up behind Jessica, who snapped, "You guys are such a bunch of *losers,* coming to school every day dressed up like Halloween and crap." She raised her voice. "Bunch of *monster kids* can crash somebody's party and break somebody's hand, but can't spend the night in an old house!"

Frankie stiffened, and Harriet's grin disappeared. Students in the hall stopped and eyed the Grrls, who were all staring coldly at the Clique. Emily noticed Bradley, his arm in a cast, glaring at Frankie. She came forward and said, "That's not true and you know it! Bradley hit Frankie first and broke his own hand, and Frankie never hit him at all!"

"Yeah," mumbled Theo, uncomfortable at being stared at.

Emily noticed the crowd around her, but was too angry to

stop. She added, "And you said Bethany could invite friends anyway!"

Jessica sniffed. "Since when do little nerds have a say? I bet you couldn't stay a night in the Pritchett House either."

"Oh, yeah?" shouted Emily. "Then we accept the challenge!"

The Grrls and Theo stared. From the corner of her eye, Emily saw Harriet's face split into a huge grin, and pressed on, encouraged. "We'll stay the night in the Pritchett House this weekend," she said. "It's no big deal. It's just a house."

"But everyone knows old man Pritchett *hung himself there*," said Heather dramatically.

"That has the peculiar ring of rehearsal," said Bethany, who was warming to Emily's bravado. "What's the proof?"

"Um—"

"Never mind," said Jessica. "Just be there around eight on Friday. And make sure you bring extra diapers." She smirked and sauntered off, with the Clique in tow. The crowd around them moved on. Emily slumped.

"Are you crazy?" said Theo. "We're gonna get killed if we go there at night!"

"I know," muttered Emily. "I wasn't thinking."

"No," said Frankie. "You stood up to her, and that's the important thing. So how are we going to do this?"

"What?" Emily stared at Frankie. "But you guys can't get out at night. Or at least you aren't supposed to."

"Well, you're not supposed to stay the whole night in an old abandoned house, or get yourself into a potentially dangerous situation, *or* let your mouth run away with you," said Bethany pointedly. "Yet you've just done all three. Besides, we have rather an easier time getting out at night."

Emily hung her head. "Sorry."

"Ain't nothin to be sorry for," said Punkin. "Friends stick together, even in the rough times. And besides, ol' Jessica needs to be took down a peg."

"It'll be fun," said Harriet, grinning. "Just like going on bivouac with Pop and the army."

"Bivouac?" said Emily.

"*Army?*" said Theo.

"Sounds like a plan," said Frankie. "Okay. You guys all gather some camp supplies and we'll meet them at the Pritchett House this weekend. Besides, I'm interested in seeing more of that house."

"At least there's still furniture," sighed Bethany. "Perhaps the bedrooms will have actual beds in them."

The Grrls headed for the cafeteria, with Emily and Theo following. "So," said Theo. "I can get out of *my* house pretty easy, but you've got your mom and your little brother to deal with. What are you gonna do?"

"I don't know," sighed Emily.

Theo smiled. "You know, you were pretty cool back there."

After a moment, Emily smiled back. "Thanks. Let's go eat lunch."

They went to join the Grrls.

Eleven: The Pritchett House

Though Theo arranged for Emily to sleep over at her house on Friday night, Emily still spent most of the week stewing over her acceptance of Jessica's challenge, as she was worried about getting the Grrls in trouble at their home. This was exacerbated by the usual rumors and whispers that flew around the school, as well as Jessica's satisfied smirk whenever she saw Emily. The thing that bothered her most about the rumor mill was the idea of some gossip getting back to her mother, which would quickly squash the whole idea and make her a laughing-stock. Despite all this, she could not deny that she, as well as Theo, had been noticed by Jessica.

For their own part, the Grrls ignored all the clamor and instead preferred to view the challenge as some strange form of camping trip. Harriet in particular was quite cheerful over the prospect, and explained to Emily and Theo that the werewolf Clans of Morlock Heights served as a standing army. Due to her father being Baron of the Clans and thus commander-in-chief of said army, Harriet had quite a bit of outdoor background, and looked forward to the idea of "roughing it" in the Pritchett House.

Punkin no longer sat with Stuart in the Career Arts class, but she did not sit with another group of kids either. Instead, she took the one desk in the far corner of the room, which made her subject to dark stares from Mrs. Carson, who was still quite upset over the detruction of her cellphone. Once she glanced up from her worksheet and noticed Stuart watching her morosely. When he saw her observing him, he quickly looked away.

Friday evening came. A little before eight o'clock, two figures headed down Square Street toward the Pritchett House.

"What'd you bring?" asked Theo, shifting an old camo backpack and a bedroll. "I got some chips and snack cakes."

"I've got some drinks and water and stuff," said Emily, who also had a bedroll and a shopping bag. "But I don't think I could eat anything anyway. I'm too nervous."

"It'll be okay, Emily," said Theo. "I don't think the Grrls would ditch us."

"I'm not worried about that," muttered Emily. "I'm just worried about Mom finding out. I don't want her blaming the Grrls for this."

As they headed toward the Pritchett House, the sidewalk grew darker. The city had not gotten around to repairing streetlights yet on that part of Square Street, and because no one went around the Pritchett House much anyway, Public Works had put it off. Emily stopped near the Pritchett House's gate, which was dimly lit by an elderly, disused-looking streetlight, and got out a flashlight. "It's a good thing we're in a decent neighborhood," she sighed. "No crooks or anything to worry about."

"You won't need the flashlight to get there," said Theo. "Look."

A red sports car was waiting beside the house's front gate, its lights illuminating the sidewalk. Emily saw Heather and Stephanie in the front seat. She sighed. "Here we go."

They went to the gate and put down their loads. Heather and Stephanie got out of the car and went to meet them. Both were dressed in "party clothes," which meant short skirts, heels and anything else known to attract boys, though Stephanie's attire seemed more understated than Heather's. Heather, who held a lighted cigarette, took a deep drag and regarded them with somewhat affected hauteur.

"I didn't know you smoked," said Emily.

"She actually doesn't," said Stephanie, as Heather lost her composure and exploded into a fit of coughing. "She just thought it would be more intimidating."

"I see," said Emily, who didn't see at all. Though she did not particularly like Heather, she was not an unkind person, so she dutifully held out a bottle of water to Heather. After a bit more wheezing Heather righted herself, threw away the cigarette and swigged deeply from the bottle. "Thank you," she gurgled, handing the bottle back.

"Keep it," sighed Emily. "I've got more."

Heather eyed the bedrolls. "Nobody said you could bring all that stuff."

"Nobody said we couldn't either," answered Theo. "Where's Jessica?"

"Jessica had another engagement," said Heather, trying to regain some of her momentum.

"There was a frat mixer at Covington College this weekend," said Stephanie, ignoring Heather's mew of disappointment. "She sent us to make sure you came."

"Wow," said Emily. "When she says jump, you say how high, right?"

Heather frowned. She looked around at the dimly lit sidewalk, which was completely dark beyond the gate and the streetlight. "Where's your monster buddies?" she asked. "They too chicken to come?"

Mmm. Chicken.

They jumped. The unexpected voice was almost a whisper, and seemed to come from all around them rather than one particular direction. Emily glanced up at the streetlight and saw a dark, birdlike shape lean forward, scrutinizing them. She went cold.

It was a raven.

"They're not chicken," said Theo, trying not to shiver. "They said they'd be here--"

We are here.

The Grrls came into view, approaching them from the shadowed end of the sidewalk. They appeared to materialize from an unnervingly *solid* darkness which ebbed and flowed around them like black oil, and in those few moments they looked more monsterlike than Emily and Theo, or even Heather and Stephanie, had ever seen. Each Grrl carried her own bedroll, and also had her backpack from school. Bethany was carrying a picnic basket.

Frankie, stopping underneath the streetlight, brought out a small copper-finished device, pointed it at the light and clicked a switch. There was a loud crackle, causing the raven to caw loudly and fly away. The light flared brightly, illuminating the gate and the sidewalk around it.

"That's better," Frankie said absently, pocketing the device.

She smiled at Emily and Theo. "Did you two get out okay?"

"Uh, yeah," said Theo.

Heather, who had moved so close to Stephanie that their shoulders were almost touching, eyed the Girls' bedrolls with derision. "Man," she muttered, "this is like Girl Scouts Jamboree or something."

"I was in Wolf Cubs," offered Harriet. She looked around. "Where's Jessica?"

"Frat mixer," answered Theo.

"Oh." Harriet looked thoughtful. "What's a frat and how do you mix it?"

"Look, is there anything else?" asked Emily. "Everybody's here, so you can tell Jessica we made it."

"Just one thing," said Heather. "Jessica says you've got to stay in the house until at least midnight. That's when the ghost of old man Pritchett starts to *walk.*"

"Walk where?" said Bethany.

"Yeah, you been sayin' all week that he hung hisself," piped up Punkin. "Shouldn't he be swingin' back and forth instead?"

"Okay, *okay!*" snapped Heather. "Anyway, that's when the ghost starts moving around, so you stay in the house until then. But don't burn it down during your marshmallow roast or whatever. C'mon, Steph." She started toward the car.

"I'll be there in a minute," said Stephanie. She looked back at Bethany. "Truce? I'd like a word with you."

Bethany looked at the others and nodded. The Grrls, Emily and Theo entered the gate and started toward the house. She and Stephanie were alone on the sidewalk.

"So, truce for the moment," said Bethany. "What do you want?"

"Look," said Stephanie, "you guys don't have to do this, you know. Jessica doesn't care about them enough for it to matter. She's just mad at you."

"I know that," said Bethany. "And I don't think Emily and Theo are interested in impressing Jessica so much. They're just tired of being bullied." She put her head on one side. "Why did you lie to Jessica about Frankie? Was it because you like Bradley?"

"No!" said Stephanie. "I wasn't thinking. I--I don't know why I did it. Look, I just don't want them to get hurt, okay?"

"Well, your momentary lapse of reason has cost you, because we're all *in* this now," said Bethany. "This is the problem, Stephanie: you have a conscience, and Jessica does not. Or if she does, she doesn't listen to it. And you will not fit in with her unless you stop listening to yours. And I really don't believe you can."

Stephanie eyed her. "Do vampires have a conscience?"

"Well played," said Bethany after a moment. "Yes, I have a conscience. It's the reason I've never Turned anyone."

"Turned?"

"Made others like me. Other vampires." Her eyes went red, and her fangs extended. "After all, do you think I want *this* on *my* conscience? That I did this to someone else?"

Stephanie was silent. Then she said quietly, "I think your friends are waiting for you."

"As are yours," answered Bethany. The red in her eyes faded. "And for the record, I bear you no ill will. Have a good evening."

"Same to you. Be safe."

Stephanie got in the car, which promptly drove off. Bethany glared after them. "Don't worry about me," she muttered.

She entered the gate and joined the others on the porch. Then they went into the house.

The group entered a hallway with a disused staircase in front that led up to the second floor. To their right was a large living room with a fireplace, where Bethany and Frankie noticed the furniture they had seen, and on the left was a parlor. "Which room?" asked Bethany, glancing at the staircase. "I'm sure we shouldn't brave those stairs."

"I think the living room," said Frankie. "It's got a fireplace. We could make a fire."

"That would be a good idea," said Emily, rubbing her arms. "It's chilly in here."

"But someone might see the smoke from the chimney," said Theo. "And if the flue is closed then all the smoke will come back into the room. That happened once at my grandmother's house."

Punkin furrowed her brow in thought. "I might be able to make a magic fire," she said. "Lemme see." She closed her eyes for a moment, and Emily thought she heard her mutter, "don't burn the dang place down," then pointed at the fireplace. A blue flame flashed and sprang to life, burning brightly. There was heat from it, but no smoke, and Emily noticed that the flame did not burn away what it touched.

"Well, at least we won't need the bedrolls since we aren't sleeping here," said Emily.

"We'll sit on them," said Bethany, grimacing at the dusty floor. "There are most likely rats."

"I got that," said Harriet. She bounced to the center of the room, took a deep breath, and growled in a very low tone. The growl was so deep that it made a *thrumming* noise, and Emily felt the air vibrate. After a moment, there was a furious scuttling sound in the walls. Harriet grinned and said happily, "That's all for that, then."

"What about roaches?" asked Theo. Punkin made a face.

"No problem," answered Harriet. She growled again, but this time it was in a higher pitch. A barely audible whispering noise was present for a moment, then died away.

"Now you're just showing off," said Bethany to Harriet. To Emily and Theo she said, "Harriet has always had perfect pitch."

"It seems to work," said Frankie. She watched outside the window, where two shadowy masses headed quickly across the yard to the sidewalk. "I suppose they'll all be back in the morning, though."

"That's all right," said Punkin nervously. "We ain't gon' be here then."

"What did everybody bring?" asked Emily, spreading out her bedroll. "We can put it on here."

The group unpacked provisions. Frankie had brought a small contraption which she described as a camp stove, but neither Emily nor Theo had ever seen a camp stove that ran without a power source, or had a heating element with a green glow. Bethany had packed a full picnic kit with several cheeses, meats and crackers in addition to some bottles of blood, and Punkin had packed a neat box lunch. Harriet had brought a plastic bag filled with raw venison. "If anyone wants some, they're welcome to it," she said. "Pop went hunting this morning and killed it fresh." Emily and Theo grimaced.

"I'll take some," said Frankie. "I want to test this stove. Anyone have some salt?"

"I do," said Bethany, handing her a small crystal shaker.

"Wow," said Theo, observing the ongoing spread. "You really *do* stuff."

"I see no reason for us to stay in this horrid place without some pleasantries," said Bethany. "If *I* decide to 'rough it,' then I stay in a slightly less expensive hotel."

Emily eyed the meat, which sizzled on Frankie's stove. "Is that going to be enough for you?" she asked Harriet.

"Oh, sure," said Harriet. "We had a big supper anyway. But there's all those trees around here, so I can always catch a squirrel or two later if I need to."

"Disgusting," sniffed Bethany.

"Nutritious, delicious, and tastes just like chicken," effervesced Harriet. Emily and Theo laughed.

"I brought somethin' for us," said Punkin shyly, opening her box lunch, which contained a large section of cake. "This here's the Recipe."

They stared at it. It was a pink and brown confection of strawberry and chocolate, with strawberries along the outer edge. "My *God*," said Bethany, "that's almost too pretty to eat."

"It ain't nothin to it," said Punkin. "Great-Granny was more impressin people with the decoratin than anythin else. It's mostly just a real good fudge cake."

"Well, it sure tones down my snack cakes," muttered Theo.

"Everyone brought something, and that's what counts," said Frankie. "Let's eat."

They divided the food and ate, while the light of the fire threw shadows about the room. Bethany drank blood while the others drank the water Emily had brought, and Harriet gave Frankie more pieces of meat to roast on her camp stove, which she shared with the others. Soon everyone was full, including Harriet. "Mmm," said Emily, sitting back. "That was really good."

"Yeah, for a picnic in a haunted house," said Theo. She

turned to Punkin. "Do you think there are any real ghosts here?"

"I don't really know," answered Punkin. "I can't feel no spirits, but that don't mean nothin. Truth is, us monsterkind don't know much about ghosts."

"Really?" said Emily, surprised.

"True," added Bethany. "Monsterkind are supernatural, but as far as ghosts are concerned we know as much about them as you do. There are haunted cemeteries in the Heights, or so people say. Drafty old houses. Cold spots. All those things." She drank some more blood. "But no one has much to do with the other side, really."

"I've never seen a ghost," said Frankie. "I know there are some beings in Morlock Heights who are ectoplasmic, but I don't think they're ghosts. Not in the case of dead spirits left behind in this world."

"So no ghosts here," said Emily.

"Nah," said Harriet.

The noise came from above them; a soft thump, then creaking noises. They all looked up. After a moment Frankie said, "What was that?"

TWELVE: MAYHEM AND RESCUE

Stephanie was furious.

And the odd part of it was that she wasn't sure *why*. They'd done this before to other kids that Jessica didn't like, and no one had ever gotten *hurt* or anything. It was just a prank. But those monster kids being there made everything different. *They* would not be scared of an old house, or of what Jessica had planned.

And lately, Stephanie had found herself getting really, really *bored* with Jessica; bored with her pettiness and unscrupulous behavior and almost scientific cruelty to other people. But she couldn't bring herself to cut her dead, because she had nothing else. She had had nothing else since her father disappeared.

And now these monster kids were here, and they just seemed to make everything... *strange*.

"What is *with* you?" asked Heather, as she rubbed more makeup on Cam's face. They were in an upper room, which was accessible by an iron fire escape behind the house; the Clique had used it often for what Jessica referred to as The Initiation. They were currently making Cam and Bradley up as ghouls, which was a not very imaginative process and involved following the instructions on the back of the cheap Halloween makeup package.

"Yeah, what's up, baby?" echoed Cam. He reached for her, but Stephanie moved quickly away. "Nothing's wrong with me," she sighed, glaring out the window. "I'm just thinking maybe we shouldn't do this."

"OK," said Heather blandly. "You want to tell Jessica you chickened out, or should I?"

"No," muttered Stephanie. "I'm just--I'm thinking about what Bethany said, is all."

Heather left Cam and crossed to Stephanie. "Look, why are you letting this weird Goth chick get to you? She's not, like, a *real* vampire or anything." She paused. "Though she does a real good makeup job. It must take hours."

"Yeah," said Bradley, who was dressing himself in a black costume robe. He dabbed at his face. "Maybe she uses the good stuff instead of this drugstore crap."

"Seriously, though," continued Heather, "they're not real monsters or anything. They're just trying to get attention."

Stephanie put her head on one side. "Isn't that what *everybody* our age is doing?"

Heather frowned. "You're even starting to *sound* like her," she grumbled. She turned away and began working on Cam again. "Anyway, you can back out if you want, but Jess will make your life miserable if you do. She wants Bethany screwed over good for what happened in English class, and these other kids are just gonna be collateral damage. It'll send a message to the nerds."

"Yeah," replied Stephanie. She stared out the window at the backyard, which was mostly broken fence and overgrown grass, with a huge, ancient oak close to the house. The branches stretched close to the window.

Just go along with it, she said to herself. It'll all be done soon, and we can get back to doing something else, like joining Jessica at that frat mixer.

Of course *she would be* there *instead of* here, *darling,* said a slightly mocking voice that sounded much like Bethany's.

"Shut up," she muttered under her breath. She was about to turn away from the window, and started.

Something was moving in the branches.

"Should we go up?" whispered Theo. The group had left the living room and were now behind Frankie, who was eyeing the stairs.

"Well, we should investigate," answered Frankie.

"I'll bet anything it's Heather and Stephanie hiding up there," said Emily, but she didn't sound convinced.

"I concur," said Bethany, who did. "And most likely there are others up there as well." She hissed softly. "Frat mixer, my sodding *bum.*"

"Don't be nasty," said Punkin. She eyed the stairs and looked uncertainly at Frankie. "You think them stairs will hold all of us?"

"Hmm," said Frankie. She walked to the stairs and gently put one foot on the bottom step, then leaned forward. There was a terrible creak.

"Well, there's your answer," said Emily.

"I think *I* might do OK," said Frankie, "but I don't know about all of us. And since I'm a Creature, my body weight's pretty dense as it is." She looked sheepishly at the group. "Creatures have a natural physical density, you know."

"Well, I don't technically *need* stairs myself," replied Bethany. She closed her eyes and misted, swirling upward. In moments she had reformed at the top of the stairs and was looking down at them. "What now, MacDuff?"

"Didn't have to jump ahead," muttered Harriet.

"I agree," added Frankie, frowning.

"Well, I'm in a scrapping mood, darlings," answered Bethany. She tapped her foot on the landing. "I don't know about the stairs, but this is fairly solid. If you and Harriet come up slowly it should be all right, but do be careful. And don't bring them up," she added, pointing at Emily and Theo.

"Thanks," muttered Emily.

"No, it makes sense," said Frankie, starting carefully up the stairs. "We'll be all right, but we don't want you to get hurt. You stay down here until we see what's what."

"Wouldn't we be safer with you?" asked Theo.

There was a soft blue glow. They turned, and stared at Punkin, whose eyes flamed with blue fire. She spread her hands, which also burst into flame, and laced them together, cracking her knuckles.

"Don't guess we got to worry about that," she answered.

Stephanie stared at the man on the branch, crawling toward the window. He was dressed in some kind of dark clothing, which she guessed was meant to blend him in with the shadows.

He passed through a patch of moonlight, and Stephanie saw that the man had *no face*. There was only a black shadow where his face should have been.

He looked up, and directly into her eyes, and Stephanie saw that one of his eyes was a pure, dead white--

And then he vanished, melting away like smoke.

She felt someone shaking her shoulder. "Come on!" hissed Heather. "They're coming up the stairs!"

Stephanie, swallowing hard, stole one last glance at the window, and followed. Bradley and Cam, crouching near the door, had begun moaning and making *oooOOoo* noises. Heather took a deep breath and made a theatrical scream. She thought of what she had seen, and shivered.

"Let's just get this over with," she muttered. She never saw the black tendrils of shadow behind her, worming in around the window.

Frankie, Bethany and Harriet were halfway down the hall when the scream sounded. They stopped.

"Don't like the sound of *that*," whispered Frankie.

"Maybe they're just trying to scare us," answered Harriet.

There was another scream, and then a crash. They looked at each other. "What do we do?" said Harriet.

"Run?" said Bethany.

"No," said Frankie. "They may be in trouble." She pointed to a violently shaking door. "I think it's that door there--"

At that moment, "that door there" burst open and two badly painted ghouls rushed into the hall. *"BOO!"* they both screamed, and began jumping around. *"OOOoooOO!! Eeeee!! Ahhhhh!!"*

This was met with stony stares from the Grrls, causing the ghouls to eventually lapse into silence. After a moment, Bethany turned to Frankie and said, "Well, what do *you* think?"

"A bit shabby, on the whole," said Frankie critically. "I do acknowledge that Halloween costumes are better these days, but the makeup's not at all professional."

"Ra-*ther*," drawled Bethany. "I would say it's also a vastly over-*used* motif, and is in *much* need of an update to make it more relevant to modern times."

"I agree," said Harriet loftily. "It's perhaps the worst form of ghost makeup since the King's Ghost that appeared with John Gielgud in the second act of *Hamlet* in 1941."

"Yes, and that was *quite* shoddy, even if it was just the

understudy--*wait a minute!*" shouted Bethany. "You've never seen that!"

"Yeah, but I've heard you talk about when *you* saw it enough," groused Harriet.

"*Why* aren't they running?" whined Heather, who was watching from behind the door. "They're supposed to be *running!* Instead they're just standing there *talking!* It's like they're the judges on *Top Runway Model Project!*"

"They're obviously not scared of them," muttered Stephanie. "C'mon, let's just let it go. Jessica lost this one."

"Oh?" snapped Heather. "That's just great, then. You can tell her, because believe me, there's nothing scarier than Jessica when she gets... when she gets..."

Her voice had trailed off, and her throat was working. Stephanie turned and gaped. Black foglike shadows were pouring into the room from the window, crawling like twisted vines across the floor. They weaved upward, forming into a tall man in a long black coat with no face. Eyes gleamed from holes in the shadow-face, one ice-blue, the other dead white.

It said, "Who are you? Why are you here--"

Heather screamed, "*Ghost!*"

Down below, Emily, Theo and Punkin heard Heather's scream. "W-what was *that?*" quavered Theo.

"Dunno," said Punkin, moving toward the stairs. "Let me see--"

Behind them, the front door burst open and a figure leapt into the room. Emily and Theo screamed.

Without thinking, Punkin whirled. Magic-fire streamed from her hand and hit the figure squarely in the chest. It flew backward out the door and onto the porch with a crash.

"Oh, *gorry!*" cried Punkin. "I didn't mean to hurt him, I was tryin' to pull it--"

The three raced out the door, and stared. Beyond the porch, they saw a bicycle lying on the sidewalk. They approached the groaning figure cautiously, and winced as they saw who it was.

Punkin put her hand to her mouth in shock.

"Oh, *boy*," said Emily.

"Well, maybe the padding protected him," said Theo slowly. She pointed at the figure's chest, which was covered in an umpire's pad that now had a gaping hole with burnt edges.

Punkin stared down at the figure. After a moment she gulped, *"S-Stuart?"*

"I came to see if you were okay," mumbled Stuart, and passed out.

"I'm tired of these nerds," snarled Cam. "Let's--"

He got no further, as Heather barreled out the doorway, followed by Stephanie, and crashed into him. *"Help!"* she shouted. *"It's the ghost of old man Pritchett!!"*

"There's no--" Bradley began, and stopped, seeing the glowering mass of shadow in the doorway, blocking out the light. The Grrls stared. Cam gulped. "Uh, what's that--"

"Ghost!" shouted Bradley. He grabbed Cam and ran, pushing the Grrls aside as he went. Heather tried to follow, but wobbled and fell to the floor. There was a snap.

"My *heel!*" shouted Heather. She flung her foot upward, and the broken high heel of her pump wobbled crazily. *"How dare you!"* she screeched at the shadow-thing. "These--these are *new!*"

"Never mind that!" yelled Stephanie, pulling her up. She turned to the Grrls, shouting, "We've got to get out of here--"

"Stephanie."

Stephanie turned, her face ashen. As the shadow-thing advanced on her, Frankie moved beside her. "Friend of yours?" she asked.

"N-no," stuttered Stephanie. "H-how does that thing know my name--"

"It's a boogeyman," said Bethany in a low voice. She pulled the terrified Heather to her feet. "Harriet, get them downstairs. We'll deal with this."

Harriet threw Heather over her shoulder and, grabbing Stephanie's hand, raced for the stairway. The shadow-thing twisted, shouting, *"Stop!"* and flung tendrils toward her.

"I don't think so," said Frankie in full Voice. She stomped the floor with one foot. *"Ground,"* she growled, and her electrodes crackled. She plunged both hands into the mass of shadows, and lightning flashed through it. The shadow roiled and fell to the floor with a solid thump. Frankie and Bethany ran.

"Hurry!" shouted Frankie. "We've only got a few seconds before his morphic field restabilizes!"

"Then let's make this quick!" shouted Bethany, exploding into a huge cloud of mist. *"Brace yourself!"*

Frankie felt the mist engulf her, lifting her off the floor, then felt herself gain speed. There was a crunch. Pieces of the railing showered around her as Frankie, swathed in Bethany-mist, crashed to the floor in front of the stairway, narrowly missing Punkin, Theo and Emily, who were helping Stuart into the room. They screamed.

"Are you all right?" said Frankie. Unhurt, she picked herself up, brushing off splinters and old paint chips. The floorboards beneath her were noticeably bowed.

"Y-yeah," stuttered Emily. "What happened?"

"There seems to be a bloody boogeyman in this house," answered Bethany, reforming. She glared at Frankie. "How do you keep such a lovely figure, yet still weigh a ton?"

There was a shout, and Harriet rushed into the doorway. "Come *on!*" she yelled. "The other two are outside! Those two guys in the costumes ran off!"

"Who's that?" asked Frankie, noticing Stuart.

"It's Stuart," said Punkin, looking shamefaced. "I-I threw a spell at him. I didn't know who he was--"

"It's okay," murmured Stuart, shaking his head. The spell had worn off, and he began to right himself. "I--oh, my *God--*"

They turned. At the top of the stairs, a thick, twisting mass of shadows squirmed angrily. *"Where is she?"* it roared hollowly, and tendrils stretched down the stairway toward them.

"Run!" shouted Bethany.

The door slammed shut just as they reached it, and the house began to creak and groan around them. Outside, they could hear Heather and Stephanie pounding on the door. "Uh-oh," growled Harriet. "That doesn't sound good."

"What's *happening?*" shouted Emily.

Everything around them began to darken. The group huddled together as the shadows began to thicken, scrabbling and creeping across the walls and the floor. *"Give me what I want,"* it screeched. *"Now! Give me what I WANT!!"*

"All right," said a voice.

A blue glow suddenly flared. Punkin's eyes roiled with magic-fire, shining brightly. *"But I don't think you want it."*

The shadow-thing halted briefly, as if unsure. *"Do not try to stop me, witch,"* it growled.

"I ain't stoppin' you," said Punkin, walking toward the stairway as the shadows recoiled from her. She looked at the door, which flew open, spilling Heather and Stephanie into the room. *"What I'm doin' is banishin' you. Right now."* She raised her hands, and her entire body suddenly burst into blue flame. The group, wide-eyed, began to back toward the door, pulling Stuart, who could not stop staring at Punkin, along with them.

"No!" shouted the shadow-thing.

"RUN!" roared Frankie.

The group ran outside and from the house, dragging Heather and Stephanie as they went. Behind them, a blue glow erupted, filling the doorway, then spilling from every window of the house. It quickly turned bright white, and there was a terrible howl.

"Punkin!" shouted Stuart, trying to run back inside. Frankie and Bethany grabbed him.

"No!" yelled Frankie. "It's not her!"

The howl rose with a terrible *stretching* quality, superseded only by a loud twanging voice that echoed like a thundercrack. *"GET YOU GONE FROM HERE! GIT!"*

The white light shone brightly, then quickly faded, and the Pritchett House was still. Punkin came through the door, which closed behind her, and managed to get down the porch steps before she collapsed. The Grrls, with Stuart, ran to gather her up.

"Woo," said Punkin weakly. Frankie and Stuart helped her up.

"Are--are you all right?" asked Stuart. "I mean--"

"I--I think so," said Punkin. "I think the boogeyman is gone too. You know how they hate light."

"Well, it was quite a show," said Bethany, as they moved to where Heather and Stephanie were standing by the gate.

"Yup," said Punkin. "But I don't know how much of it was me, though. I think my magic just rared up 'cause we was all in danger."

"Whatever it was, it was pretty amazing," said Stuart. Punkin smiled at him.

They reached the gate. "So," said Emily to Heather. "How did we do?"

Heather looked at the house, and swallowed. "I-I'd rather not talk about it," she muttered. "And I'm gonna *kill* Cam and Bradley for running off and leaving us."

"W-what was that thing?" asked Stephanie. "And why did it want *me?*"

"It was a boogeyman," said Frankie. "There's still a few rogue ones around. It must have heard one of your friends say your name or something, and decided you were the one it wanted."

"For *what?*"

"Trust us," said Bethany, "you *don't* want to know. Let's just say all's well that ends well."

Heather peered down the sidewalk, where blue lights were approaching rapidly. "Um. Well, I don't know about it all *ending* well." She pointed down the street. "I think the cops are coming."

Thirteen: The Pact

"I don't think I have to tell you exactly *how* disappointed I am in all of you," sighed Joanna.

The evening's horror had ended with all teenagers (including four monsters) giving a halting and rather disjointed explanation to the Clearwater sheriff, who had captured Cam and Bradley several yards away from the Pritchett House, seen the explosion of Punkin's magic-fire and decided that illegal fireworks had been set off. He also had mentioned that Halloween would not be for another three weeks and that it was a bit early to dress up. Heather had apologized profusely shortly before going completely hysterical and attacking Cam and Bradley, which had led Stephanie to pack her into her car, explain to the sheriff that she had had too much excitement, and drive her, Cam and Bradley away. The Grrls had taken the lecture in stride, but they, Emily, Theo and Stuart had been forced to ride back to Emily's house with the sheriff. They were now all in Joanna's kitchen, except for Stuart, who was being delivered home by the sheriff.

"I know," said Emily, who upon entering had automatically begun taking one for the team. "And I'm sorry."

"We're all sorry," said Frankie. "We didn't mean to get into trouble."

"I know that," said Joanna evenly. "But I want you to understand something." She gave the Grrls a long, careful look. "Emily and Theo are human, and they aren't able to do some of the things you can do. Do you understand?"

"Yes, ma'am," said Frankie. Everyone else nodded.

"That's the reason we went with them," said Bethany. "But they were trying to stand up to Jessica."

"Ye-es," said Joanna. "I understand, and I admit to being proud of them for that, despite what happened. I'm afraid *that's* a case of daughter behaving like mother. When Charlene St. James was in high school she used to challenge people to do stunts like this." She pursed her lips. "She ev en challenged me."

Everyone stared. After a moment, Theo said, "Did you--"

"Yes," sighed Joanna. "I did. And because of that," she said, looking pointedly at Emily, "I'm not going to ground you. But I *am* going to call Charlene and tell her what went on tonight, and that if anything ever happens like this again, I will tell Sheriff Carruthers what *really* happened at the Clearwater Bowling lanes back in 1963." She smiled. "I'm sure Marlon's uncle would *love* to know."

The Grrls looked at each other. After a moment Bethany said, "So what happens now?"

"I want you to be much more careful in this world, and with my daughter and her friend," said Joanna. She eyed Punkin. "And I certainly expect you to be a *lot* more careful with Stuart. I can only hope Clarice Nelson doesn't have a fit."

"Yes, ma'am," said Punkin contritely.

"And now," said Joanna, rising from the table, "I expect you all to be in bed very soon. We'll go back for your things in the morning. You Grrls are welcome to stay here, unless you think you'll get in trouble at home." She looked at Bethany. "And you are *always* welcome in this house."

Bethany bowed solemnly. "Thank you, ma'am."

"Very well," said Joanna, heading for the stairs. "I'm going to get some aspirin."

"Oh, that's okay, Mom," said Harriet. "Nobody got hurt."

"I know that," said Joanna. "The aspirin is for *me.*"

It was Saturday night.

On Harrow Hill, the forest was thick and overgrown, almost shutting out the sunlight during the day. But deep within a small clearing was a forgotten, distended cemetery, with bent, twisted iron fencing and ancient, broken tombstones jutting from the overgrown ground like skulls' teeth. In the center of the cemetery was an old, enormous mausoleum, its gate rusted, its walls overgrown with vines.

The gate creaked open, and inside, there was a faint green glow. A figure stepped into the moonlight.

Harriet tilted her head back and stared up at the crescent

moon in the sky. Not full yet. Still safe. But she could *feel* the moonlight just the same.

"You're not supposed to be here, you know," said a voice.

Harriet turned and saw a light bobbing toward her. Bethany appeared with a lantern, its light throwing a faint glow on the mausoleum's stone steps. "Neither are you," she said.

The inside of the mausoleum glowed again, and another voice said, "None of us are, but I think we all know why we're here."

Frankie came through the gate, with Punkin behind her. Bethany placed the lantern on a nearby tombstone and sat down on top of a nearby stone tomb. "So," she said. "Show us."

Frankie reached in her pocket and placed what was there on top of the tomb. They all stared at it.

It was a dagger, with a silver crucifix attached to the hilt. In the center of the crucifix was a decorative standard: a black shield split with a lightning bolt. Stamped into the pommel were a pair of letters: *AK*.

They stared at it for some time. After a moment Harriet said, "Who's Ak?"

"Not *Ak*. A.K.," said Bethany. "And I know that standard."

"The Shadow League," said Frankie. "I found this when we went back to the Pritchett House to get our things. And I think that the boogeyman was also the man we saw in your visions at Emily's house. In fact, I'd say this confirms it." She sighed. "But I don't know why he wanted Stephanie."

"You didn't tell Emily and Theo, did you?" asked Bethany. Frankie shook her head.

"But is it really *him?*" asked Punkin. "I mean, sometimes they used to make monsterkind work for them--" She looked at the faces of the others, and sighed. "All right," she said. "What we goin' to do now?"

"We wait and watch," said Frankie. She was gazing toward the cemetery's gate, where the trees thinned out a bit to make a pathway. Through the trees, lights could be seen twinkling in the direction of Clearwater. "This world--the humans' world, from what I've seen, is a pretty cool place. And we've made some really good friends with Emily and Theo. I think it's worth it to keep an eye on them."

"I second the motion," said Bethany. Punkin nodded.

Harriet was unusually thoughtful. She looked up at the moon. "When the moon starts to go gibbous, that's the best time to make vows or pacts, as far as werewolves are concerned." She stretched out her hand. "I vote we make a pact. We stick together. We stick with Emily and Theo, and protect 'em, because friends stick together. No matter what."

The other Grrls traded a look. Frankie placed her hand on top of Harriet's. "No matter what."

"No matter what," said Punkin, clasping Frankie's hand.

"No matter what," said Bethany, taking Punkin's hand.

They looked at each other, and nodded solemnly. "And that's all for that," said Harriet. "What do we do now?"

"I vote we go back," said Bethany. "Town's still open, and we haven't seen anyone in a while. I think some of our old friends from Graf Orlok are getting curious."

"Sounds like a good idea," said Frankie. "You think The Dark Beneath's still open?"

"On Saturday night?" said Harriet, grinning. "You *know* they are."

The four friends, chatting and laughing among themselves, stepped into the mausoleum. Harriet, the last one to go in, looked up at the moon and smiled.

It's a new world. Their *world. But there's room for us, too.*

She went inside. The old gate swung shut by itself, and after a moment, there was a bright green glow, which vanished quickly.

Then there were only shadows.

--October 14, 2009

About The Author

John Rose was originally born in Meridian, MS. He now lives in Greenwood, MS, where he teaches art to middle school students, creates MonsterGrrls books, and has half ownership of a dog named Jenny Murphy and full ownership of a cat named Igor.

About The Grrls

The MonsterGrrls are Frankie Franken, Bethany Ruthven, Punkin Nightshade, and Harriet Von Lupin. Visit them on the Internet at http://www.monstergrrls.com.

Thanks for reading.

Next:
Book 2--The Shadows Lengthen
Coming Soon

www.ingramcontent.com/pod-product-compliance
Lightning Source LLC
Chambersburg PA
CBHW060138130626
46556CB00006B/2404